SHIVA'S DRUM

Chandrasekhar Kambar

Translated from the Kannada by Krishna Manavalli

SPEAKING
TIGER

SPEAKING TIGER PUBLISHING PVT. LTD
4381/4, Ansari Road, Daryaganj
New Delhi 110002

Originally published in Kannada by Ankita Pustaka in 2015
Published in English by Speaking Tiger in paperback 2017

ISBN: 978-93-86582-06-5
eISBN: 978-93-86582-05-8

10 9 8 7 6 5 4 3 2 1

Typeset in Palatino Linotype by SÜRYA, New Delhi
Printed at Gopsons Papers Ltd

Born in 1937, in Ghodgeri, northern Karnataka, **Chandrasekhar Kambar** is acclaimed for the rich mythopoeic imagination that characterizes all his writing. A stalwart playwright, Kambar is also a well-known writer of poetry, fiction, and literary and cultural criticism in Kannada. He received the Jnanpith Award in 2010. The Government of India also honoured him with the Padmashree in 2001.

Kambar's oeuvre of twenty-five plays comprises many well-known works, including *Jokumaraswami, Siri Sampige* and *Mahamayi*, among others. He has eleven poetry collections and six novels to his credit. From his earliest novel *Karimayi* to his later works like *Chakori* and *Shikharasoorya* Kambar roots himself in the folk and myth traditions of North Karnataka. His critical writing focuses majorly on folk theatre and folk literature.

A man of many interests, Kambar has made five films and several documentaries. He has also composed the music for these films.

An illustrious academic and teacher, Kambar has also held the posts of the Vice Chancellor, Kannada University (Hampi), and Chairman, National School of Drama (New Delhi).

Krishna K. Manavalli is currently Professor in the department of English at the Karnatak University, Dharwad, India. Krishna is a literary critic and translator who works in both English and Kannada languages. She has published internationally and given talks at conferences across the world. Krishna's recent publications include the translation of the well-known Kannada writer, Chandrasekhar Kambar's, novel *Karimayi* (Seagull Books, 2017).

Translator's dedication

For my Guru, Pt. Rajeev Taranathji

Introduction

Between the Modern and the Mythical

Chandrasekhar Kambar has long been flirting with the idea of connecting his opulent and rich myth world to some themes prominent in the modern mind. *Helatini Kela Gelaya* told the story of a fertility myth, so did *Rishya Shringa*. And so did his play, *Jokumaraswami*. No doubt Kambar has often distanced himself from the 'Western' modernist tradition, unlike his contemporaries in the Kannada literary world. But we cannot forget that T.S. Eliot, and many other Euro-American modernists like Eliot, had also self-consciously worked with the myth mode. This modernist appropriation of the myth had a deep impact on Kannada writing in the latter part of the twentieth century. Kambar majorly draws upon his folk, specifically 'non-Brahmin' folk, world. However, Kambar's constant effort to touch the contemporary and the global in his writing could be traced to this modernist moment in Kannada writing. It is this sensibility that manifests itself more fully in *Shivana Dangura*, a novel that he writes at a much later stage in his career. As such, the novel's experience is that of a bewildering and constant switching between the modern and the mythical.

I believe that Krishna Manavalli has undertaken a difficult task in attempting to translate the experience of Kambar's new novel into English. Why? It is obvious that

Kambar's writing deals with strong local flavours where language plays a very prominent role in invoking such culture-specific experiences that are deeply rooted in the land and its people. When Kambar moves from one time frame to another, and among characters from different time zones, he employs this language very effectively to show that diversity of experience. In this situation, what does a translator do? She cannot, of course, dip into the same local language flavours like Kambar. How then does she get around the problem of diversity, scatteredness and possible disconnections? One must remember that this translator is working with stuff which is difficult to hold together effectively and cogently. In other words, her task is that of managing the many. Kambar's world is a space that teems with this multiplicity held together by the sheer power of language. Therefore, in a translation of Kambar's work, anything but a highly controlled use of the English language would result in gibberish. In my opinion, the fact that Krishna gathers the varied and plural stuff of the novel experience together in her translation is a great achievement. She is able to hold together Kambar's 'ruritania' which includes everything—gods, myths, demons, dreams, tragic love and terrible destiny alongside tractors, co-op societies, environmental concerns, global business enterprises, and so on. Krishna brings all these together without interfering with the rich and riotous flow of experience in *Shivana Dangura*. While a less sensitive translator can end up watering down an experience in her translation, the fact that Krishna maintains the precision of experience found in the original in her English translation is something I find fascinating. I think that in the field of translation, Krishna's work, with its variety of unique situations of language use, and the manner in which she seeks to control the scatteredness of the original in the kind of English she opts for as her medium of translation, is tremendously important. For future students of translation, her work could be instructive and stimulating. This is a translation that offers the reader the same pleasures and relishes of reading a novel by Kambar in Kannada with its expansive and stimulating scope.

RAJEEV TARANATH

PART ONE

Shivapura

Earlier, Shivapura didn't have history. It only had mythology. Besides, there are two versions of this mythology. What surfaces in the songs of the jogtis, and another version you see in the shepherds' songs. According to the jogtis' song, this myth originates in the banyan tree. The tree is still there. This banyan tree, which is thousands of years old, divides the village into two parts. It has grown touching the untouchable neighbourhood on the road that goes towards the south. There is a platform under this big banyan. When you ask these people about the age of the tree, they put their hands up and count twenty times the number of their fingers. Okay, twenty times ten is two hundred years, right? You can believe that a tree is two hundred years old. But sometimes, they say hundred times ten and at other times even thousand times ten! You ask them if that's possible? Like we have historical documents, they have the jogtis' songs for their records. The story in their song goes somewhat like this:

In the beginning, God Shiva and his blessed consort Parvati created the shining heaven and all the gods in it. Below this, he made the Earth with its eighteen corners and then created the Sun and the Moon to take turns in lighting up the world. There was no air or water yet. One day, the children of the gods were playing with little stars, bouncing them up and down like a ball. When a couple of stars slipped off their hands and fell, they looked down to see where the stars had gone. Oh, there's the Earth gleaming in the light of a full moon! Immediately, the kids wanted to go there and play. But the gods warned them. Told them it was a dangerous place. Asked them to get back to heaven before sunrise. Once on Earth, the children ran on hills and valleys, skipped on mounds and knolls, played on the plains, and in all that heady excitement, forgot themselves. They didn't notice the time passing. Mother Parvati sent an old servant to Earth to bring the children back safely. Exactly at the instant this servant set foot on Earth, there was a blaze of red in the east. Children, servant and everyone stood still. The sun had risen already! The children of the gods became rooted to Earth. The anxious gods above kept calling them, but their children heard nothing! Gods who lost their children wept for them. Their tears turned into rain. And their sighs became the air that blew on Earth. Thus life began on Earth. The old servant, who had come to take the children back, became the banyan tree.

Tungavva ends her story here.

This is the beginning of creation. But there's another story that tells you how Shiva created Shivapura. Shiva created many gods and deities, including the divine architect and blacksmith, Viswakarma. He called Viswakarma, gave him a hammer, chisel and a pair of bellows, and then asked, 'What will you do now?' Viswakarma answered that he'd do any job, small or big. Shiva said, 'All right.' So, with a stroke of his chisel, Viswakarma first made the cave on the top of the hill. He turned the same chisel around, and with another stroke, created Shivalinga's shrine in the place called Chalimele. Then rose those mud-and-stone palaces. The place became peopled by the Gowdas, the Patels and the farmers. This village was called Shivapura.

Shivapura entered history only after the British arrived. History began on the hill there. Earlier, it was all dense jungle. On the hilltop, you see a cave. A holy sage did penance there and found nirvana. So it is called Nirvanappa's hill. The hill isn't very high. There are about a thousand and eight steps to go up there. If you look down from the top of the hill, you get familiar with the whole map of Shivapura. To the north of the hill, about two miles yonder, there is the Ghataprabha river. It flows from west to east. On the bank of the river sits Shivapura, as if with its feet in water. From here, you can only see half the village. The other half is hidden by the green foliage.

In the past, the British ruled the village. There were no passage routes for motor vehicles in those times. The passage roads they had were only bullock-cart ones. There is a walking path to the village. It disappears behind the shade of the trees and reappears where there is cultivated land. This path goes to the village. From the left shoulder of the hill, a small stream flows into the large basin below. This pond is Mallimadu. Water flows some two hundred feet from here, hits a large rock, breaks into two streams and forms a little rock island in the middle. Later both streams join. The little rock island is called Chalimele. There is a small stone temple on Chalimele. You see the marks of time, rain and wind on the temple. A patri tree leans against the back wall of the temple. It seems as if the temple itself has grown roots and put forth this tree. Beyond that, about twenty arms-length away, there is a bamboo grove full of very tall trees and thousands of their offspring. Since the temple is outside the village, it is called the 'Outside' temple. You can't but feel that those shepherd songs describing the hill and the temple do so very aptly. These songs imagine the hill as Nirvanappa and the temple as the little Shivalinga hanging down his chest.

Next to the temple, there is a somewhat habitable room. It has only one window and one door. On the door is the legend that says, 'Come Tomorrow.' Namahshivaya lives there. Let's get to know him later. Since the hill is close to the cemetery, and because not only Malli and Malli's mother, but two others committed suicide there of late, nobody goes there. Namahshivaya is the only soul breathing, moving and living there.

On the brink of the rock, and at the water's edge, there are jambul and fig trees. Didn't we say a stream flows down the left shoulder of the hill in the rainy season? In those deep waters, Malli, a Dalit girl, had drowned. She'd had a relationship with some Gowda. In the end, he ditched her. She tied a stone around her waist and drowned. Her mother came searching for her. She wandered calling after Malli, 'Malli, Malli, where are you Malli?'

She too fell into the lake and died. Even now, in summer, the birds circling over the lake mimic her cries:

Malli, Malli

Where are you Malli?

Whenever the river was in flood, water would rush into the pond and form a small lake. But of late, there isn't much rain. The stream on the hill doesn't flow downwards. Nor does the flood water flow into it—the pond looks like a gaping well. The land around is marshy and waterlogged. The place is a swamp. It was Baramegowda who had the bright idea of drying the place up and building an English-medium school and college on it. For this purpose, he got some nilgiri seeds that suck all the water in the soil. Even before you could say 'ha', two nilgiri trees shot up like twin giants. Their branches spread and got intertwined. The trees now looked like two scary demons standing with their arms around each other's shoulders. The villagers often gossip that they are actually the ghosts of Malli and Malli's mother. The two women have now grown into these trees and stand laughing at the Gowda. Tungavva also says that on Monday nights you hear footsteps—the sound of wooden sandals walking along with a bamboo stick. Sometimes, you also hear someone sighing deeply!

A little further away, in the middle of the pond, there is a dented female idol. You can't see it when the lake is full. When the water force abates, limpid water skips over the rocks, tickles the fish and makes them flash away. Then it flows musically towards the river. In this see-through scene, you will see that idol. Sometimes, flood water from the river throws up clean sand on the rock island. The jambul and fig trees, which form a kind of a fortress round the river, are giant fruit trees. You can see the reflections of several bunches of large fruit in the water. They look like a thousand startled eyes watching the female idol at the centre.

About half a mile from the river basin, there's a road that disappears into the forest on the south. On either side, there are six rows of small houses and huts. They have slant roofs made of dry hay or black tiles. Their stoops protect the mud walls from rain. People mix red earth with water and paint the walls with it. There are decorative pictorial motifs on these walls. It is something special to Shivapura houses. Their doors and windows are also decorated with fascinating motifs of trees, creepers, animals and birds. In the vast site on the right, there is a big homestead, a vaade of red-tiled houses. It is a very famous vaade in these parts. On the right, if you go past four houses, you see the village square.

In the stone-field there, you also see Baramegowda's private house called the 'House of Pleasure'. There is a huge rock in the corner of the acacia field. There is also a century-old kino tree. With its innumerable small and big branches spreading to the skies, the tree splits into two parts at its base. It shelters all sorts of birds, spectres and spirits. The beautiful red-tiled house is under one part of the tree. Apart from the front door, it also has a secret way out at the back. This is Baramegowda's famous House of Pleasure.

The road that runs from the river into the forest divides the village into two parts. On one side is the high-caste neighbourhood and on the other is the 'outside', the Dalit neighbourhood. This outside neighbourhood is a slum. The poor, blind and homeless live here. It's known as the worst place in the village. Usually, no officers or policemen enter this place. But once or twice the police went there looking for murderers or bandits. But over time, when everybody started believing that those who go there are worse than the worst murderers, even the cops stopped going there. If there was any cursed neighbourhood resounding with ear-piercing oaths and expletives, it was this infamous place.

The original banyan tree of the myth stands touching this neighbourhood. Opposite this are the high-caste lanes. The first lane is the farmers' lane. Then the Gowda lane. Here you see the famous Gowda homestead, the vaade. The Kulkarni's house is on the same lane. At the end of the lane, you see the village square. Beyond this, the little lane of those who get the aaya. Right next to this, you have the co-operative bank, post office and the Boys' school.

No one living now has seen how this village was during the British times. Nobody knows how life was then. They say that they can only imagine it a bit by what they have heard from their elders. All farmers in those times cultivated land. Even the cattle were seen as part of the household. People of different castes followed the trades of their caste.

The poor and the oppressed didn't have any irrigated land. They threw some grains like millet and baraga in the open fields and grew something for themselves. Those who had no other form of livelihood worked for others or were servants. Shivapura farmers are those who work and sweat until their bodies melt with fatigue. They only grew food crops like corn, sajje, navane, paddy, saave and baraga. This was enough for their livelihood. People feared gods and ghosts. There was something called contentment in everybody's life. In those times, people thought of Earth as their mother. Even in the face of danger, they continued to cherish life-giving values.

But of late, it looks like the rhythm of Shivapura life is upset. Even the seasons don't keep time. The river looks wasted. The waves no longer run with a youthful vigour. The rocks under water are like bones jutting out of an old face. People cannot see their faces in the water-mirror anymore. Unable to drink the muddy water of this river, the high-castes have already dug a well with a six-wheel pulley attached to it. There is also a new village panchayat. These days, Shivapura gods have stopped prophesying about rain and crops. They predict election results now. The neighbouring village, Yamakanamaradi, even has a police station.

Here I invoke the holy feet of Savalagi Shivalingaswami. With Sangayyaswami of Bhoosunoormath and Kambara Basappa as my witnesses, I will tell you the whole story of Shivapura. Do listen to it.

Baramegowda

Baramegowda heads Shivapura. Didn't I say that Shivapura, which only had mythology, entered history with the coming of the British? The first historical figure of Shivapura was Dyamegowda. He was born in the Gownda clan, whose folk had seen small-time glory as subsidiary rulers under the Muslim king of Pashchapura. Gowda's people had always got their ancestral lands, thousands of acres of it, cultivated by other farmers. Sixth in this line, Shivagonda, had two sons—Baramegowda and Esuragowda.

Let's move to our Baramegowda's story: Baramegowda is neither tall nor short. He is corpulent. Though he is still young, half his head has gone bald. So he grew the hair above his ears very long and combed it right across the bald patch at the centre. He was under the illusion that this hair would hide the patch. But unfortunately, this hair didn't sit well on the bald scalp. Instead, it created the effect of hairy stripes drawn over the bald pate. Add to this, his left eye was smaller than the right. Therefore, even when he looked at a person straight, his gaze seemed crooked. As a result, whatever he said, people thought it was something mischievous. Etched beneath the straight nose was a sharp and polished moustache. The tight lips reminded one of a sharp axe. Only when he laughed did those flashing rows of teeth appear, and he beamed a smile that mesmerized everyone. He used this charming attribute to maximum effect.

Every morning, he polished his moustache till the ends were pointy-sharp. He kept massaging it on and off to keep it trim. He always wore a rustling white dhotra and a colourful kurta. Four out of his ten fingers were adorned with rings. Around eightish in the morning, he ate a nice breakfast. Then holding a pack of cigarettes and matches in his left hand, and holding up the end of his dhotra in the right, he emerged from the house in great style. He sat on the platform near the wooden gate of the house, caressing the curves of women's bodies with his lewd gaze as they went back and forth fetching water from the stream. He cursed all the husbands of lovely women who were alive. Many of his caste came forward to get their girls married to this lech. Finally, he married a relation, Paroti, who was the daughter of a doctor called Kotresha.

Wife Paroti hadn't learnt any of the female arts that could attract the husband. On the first night, Baramegowda was upset that he'd married such a woman. But moved by Paroti's innocence, deep affection and lack of wiles, he experienced domestic happiness for a few days. He remained under control until Paroti got pregnant. But when she went to her mother's house to give birth and returned with a precious little girl-child, the lustre in Baramegowda's eyes and his smile vanished altogether. He was disappointed that his wife hadn't borne a male child.

Anyway, he didn't simply sit there feeling dejected. He performed many religious rites and rituals. He got his and his wife's horoscopes checked. They all prophesied a male child. In fact, there is a story about Gowda's ancestors in the Helava mendicant's books. In the beginning, this household wasn't that of the Gowda headmen. They were only poor farmers. Doddegowda and Doddavva were husband and wife. They grew something on the two acres of land they had. Doddavva was the mother of six children! All she possessed was the one sari she wore. At night, she draped it around her to the extent that decency demanded. The rest she spread on the floor for the six children to sleep on—in a row. It seems, once, after all the kids lay down, there was still some place for an extra child! Doddavva sighed saying, 'God, if only I had another child'—because she had always dreamt of being the mother of seven children. Surprisingly enough, she had another child! It was this child who made the family prosperous. Soon they also had the headship of the village. Inspired by this story of their ancestor, the Baramegowda couple tried very hard to have a male child. The result, they got a female child who died in a month. This was followed by a still-born child. Finally, they had to give up when the doctors warned about Paroti's health.

After this, Baramegowda neglected Paroti completely. He believed that she had let him down by not having a male child. Overwhelmed by easily got pleasures, he strayed very quickly into this world of lust. He renovated the house in his fields nicely, turned it into the House of Pleasure, and filled it with tales of his erotic exploits. His courage, strength and willpower in the matter of women were not something he needed to learn. He was born with these virtues. Every cell in his body oozed these qualities. He decided to make full use of such talents. But first, he had a duty to perform. He must get his brother married. Although Esuragowda was reluctant to get married, he got him married off to a girl from Suladhala. This Shivakka was Rajappa's sister. The Gowda was free of a big responsibility now.

Both brothers were married now. Still there was great affection between them. They all lived in the same house for a while. The older one, Baramegowda, looked after the land and property. The younger brother, Esuragowda, pushed all the household responsibility onto the brother and became active in the Gandhian freedom struggle. Though the brothers had a strong bond, their wives didn't. Village elders intervened and got the land divided equally between them. They also stipulated that the brothers should take turns and manage the village administration for five years each. Despite this division of authority over the house and the land, Baramegowda still had all control. That's because Esuragowda never desired it.

Baramegowda once went alone on horseback to the goddess Savadatti Ellamma's festival. There he saw this dark devadasi and stood spellbound. If a woman is dark and has teeth like white jasmine flowers, which man wouldn't get disturbed by her intoxicating moon-light smile? Who knows what happened to the Gowda, he suddenly held her right hand and made this proposal, 'You become my woman in life. Or kill me now and leave.'

He went on his knees in front of the entire festival crowd and begged her. The lissom, dark-eyed girl opened the doors of her heart gently and took him in. Full of zest and pride over this fortunate possession, he put her on the horse and flew from there.

They sped on and on until late into the night. They soon realized they'd lost their way. They suddenly saw a ruined temple in front of them, right in the middle of the deep woods! It was inky dark. He decided it made no difference where you had your first night of love— whether it's a palace or a ruined temple, it doesn't matter. He took her inside the temple and embraced her. He was greatly aroused, she opened up to him like a flower. They gave themselves to each other bit by bit, and then fully. Love sprang up like the fountain of life. Love rushed like the roaring river Ghataprabha in flood! Intoxicated by the

waves of pleasure that swept over them, the young lovers
slowly fell asleep. At midnight, Gowda woke up when he
heard the jingling of bangles and anklets. The temple looked
like a magnificent palace! It was dazzling. The lovers were
sleeping in front of the inner sanctum. Even as the Gowda
watched in amazement, the goddess, who had gone for a
walk outside, returned to the temple. She wore a red sari
with a green seragu. She spread the rows of pleats of the
sari artistically over the altar and seated herself. She wore
a huge red vermilion dot on her forehead and a diamond
nose ornament. The goddess's face looked burnished with
the glow of meditation. Gowda stood up in consternation.
Mother looked at them with a smile on her face—the nose
ornament flashed brilliantly, and some vermilion powder
fell from her forehead to the forefinger of her right hand.
Mother threw this at them as a blessing. It fell directly on
the forehead of the sleeping devadasi. The flustered Gowda
called quickly, 'Tungi' (her name was Tungavva) and tried
to wake her up. Tungi sat up looking like an auspicious
married woman with that vermilion dot on her forehead.
She prostrated in front of the Mother and saluted her.
Mother vanished.

Baramegowda made Tungavva sit on his horse like
a bride, and they came back to Shivapura. Outside the
village, he built her a small house. When needed, Tungavva
went to Gowda's House of Pleasure. Her native place was
Suladhala, which was also the village of Esuragowda's
wife Shivakka. They had known each other. Now they met
again sometimes and became great friends. Both became
pregnant more or less at the same time. And both went to
their maternal village Suladhala almost at the same time.

On another note, Esuragowda had turned into an
unbearable headache for the British soldiers from Hudali to
Yaragatti and also in the northern regions like Athani and

Nippani. He was the leader of a small group of freedom fighters. The British army had often backed out because they had no clue to his war tactics or from where he struck. They announced a reward of five thousand rupees to anyone who helped them catch him and also offered hundred acres of land to that person. When they found out that Esuragowda's wife had come to Suladhala to deliver the child, they intensified the watch in that area.

In these unfortunate circumstances, Shivakka gave birth to a male child. She developed some postnatal problems and died. How do we take care of the infant in this situation? This became a real challenge for the Gowda household. As luck would have it, Tungavva, Baramegowda's concubine, who was also in Suladhala at the time, had delivered a baby two days earlier. Not bothering about whether she was an 'insider' or an 'outsider' to the family, they put the baby on her lap. Tungavva breastfed both this child of her dead friend and her own. She took care of him. But Shivakka's brother Rajappa suffered from an imaginary fear that the British government might try to grab the child too. He thought that instead of being caught unawares when danger struck, it was better to take preventive action. He sent the child off to Savalagi Swami to be brought up there. Tungavva rushed to the Savalagi matha (the ashram of the Swami) that same night, gathering both babies to her bosom. She flung the babies on the Swami's feet, narrated everything that had happened, spread the end of her seragu in a gesture of supplication and begged for shelter. The Swami assured them of it and gave them his blessing.

Meanwhile, a lot of water had flowed under that bridge called 'history'. When they were convinced that Esuragowda had died in the shooting at Belagavi, the British army receded from the area of Kundaranaadu. Now

Suladhala breathed in relief. Until now, the fact that the Savalagi matha was sheltering Tungavva and the children was kept a secret. Baramegowda, who heard the news, rushed to the matha. The Swamiji blessed him, wishing him happiness and prosperity in life. He said, 'Gowda, you yearned for a male child until now—look he is here. This is your son Lakshmana. The other one you see there? He is Esuragowda's son, Chambasava. Your concubine Tungavva breastfed them and brought them up. Now you must take their responsibility.' He pointed in the direction of two kids playing far away. Tungavva stood with them, looking at Gowda with longing eyes. She bent down and saluted the Gowda from where she was.

Baramegowda was happy to see both his sons. But Tungavva, who in the meanwhile had breastfed two kids, had lost all her former charm. Her face was gaunt, and her cheeks were no longer rounded. But Gowda didn't disregard the Swami's words. He brought all three to Shivapura. He arranged for Tungavva to live in the same house she had lived in earlier. He also gave her five acres of land. He called Esuragowda's brother-in-law Rajappa and put him in charge of his brother's land. He asked Tungavva to take care of Esuragowda's son and his own. He gave them a herd of cattle. The names that the Swami had given the boys, Chambasava and Lakshmana (Lasuma), continued here too. Tungavva brought her brother Nagappa and his wife Yamunavva from Suladhala to oversee work on the land she had got. She got them a house there. With them came their daughter, Sharavva.

But Gowda's disappointment didn't end. True, he had a male child from Tungavva. But that doesn't really count. You know why—can the son born to a warrior-class kshatriya like the Gowda from a devadasi become an heir to his social position, house, property and land? It wasn't possible, and people would simply laugh at something like that. So he kept her at a distance. But since he didn't want any trouble from her, he also gave her those five acres of land and washed his hands off her. But Tungavva decided, whatever Baramegowda's attitude towards her, she would remain true to him and the auspicious vermilion that the goddess put on her forehead. She lived like a loyal wife. Tungavva's heart was like a limpid river, like fresh green woods, and at the same time, also like the hard boulder on a hill. True, she didn't have her former youth. But even now, her eyes shone like twin blue lotuses floating in a calm forest lake. Only, the Gowda didn't have the eyes to see them.

Now God alone should hear Paroti's woes! She lay on the bed along with her daughter in the house and soaked her pillow with tears. On the other hand, the Gowda lived happily in his House of Pleasure, oblivious of her plight. Paroti cried and tried to make him pity her. She shed many tears. She begged him. She got angry. She fought with him. Whatever she did, Gowda wasn't on the mend. Her smile never returned. Soon she lost her youth. Her blouse hung loose on her bosom. Paroti became a woman who wallows in self-pity. She repeatedly told her neighbours what a lovely and good woman she was. She said her vile husband neglected her and was having fun with other cheap women. They had to listen to this again and again. When she couldn't find anyone to tell this to, she told it to herself. Then, she grew hypochondriac, assuming a series of ailments—headache today, chest pain in the morning, cramps in her limbs in the evening, and so on. She blamed the Gowda for all her misery. When he came home feeling concerned about her, she complained, 'Did you come to check if I'm dead or not?' She pretended to be deeply hurt and wailed, 'Don't you have a heart, Gowda?'

But Baramegowda didn't curtail his pleasures. A bed that gave warmth in winter and felt soft and cool in summer, some young girl to share his bed, and nicely done meat and whiskey—these were enough. Since his wife was sick, he assumed that it was his right as the headman of the village to enjoy his pleasures. So he drank, ate well, hugged some woman and slept on his bed snoring loudly. The village ladies called him a lech, a completely shameless man in matters related to women. They cursed him. They said that his house must be barred with a fence, and that there should no births or deaths in that house. He knew nothing of this.

Paroti became alarmed when she heard that Tungavva had arrived with her son. A savage expression settled on her face. She became agitated like a trapped bird. But she tried to hide her fear and anxiety with great effort when the Gowda came to see her. She pretended to smile. There were no feelings of intimacy or desire between them. She thought that he only saw her as a flower shorn of its petals (and that he was the one who had done this to her). She thought, 'This Barama is a dirty liar. The only thing left in him is animal lust. If he had at least an iota of honesty in him, he would have killed me. But he can't kill me. Because he is happy to see me suffer endlessly. Will this dirty man love my daughter when this jogti's son is here...'

She heard Bagirti call her, 'Yavva.' Her eyes shone in a face clouded by anxiety and sorrow. She called, 'My little one, I was thinking of you and you came here like a God. Come child, come.' She embraced the daughter. She caressed the child's back and head, and tried to forget her sorrow in the warmth of this touch. She felt something electrifying, warm and powerful in her daughter's looks and talk. She cracked her knuckles to ward off the evil eye on her precious daughter. Her daughter was growing up. She looked at her as if she was seeing her for the first time. She was struck by wonder. The chin, the curve of the lip, the smile winding in and out of those lips, shining eyes, the grace and charm in her movements, that melody in her voice—Bagirti was beautiful. She regretted, 'I have this goddess for a daughter. Why did I ever crave for a male child?' She thanked Shiva, 'What a goddess you put into my womb, Lord!' She hugged her daughter repeatedly.

Then she remembered Chambasa. Everybody loves this boy. What is it that makes him so adorable? She wondered.

Even when Bagirti came close and patted her on her chest, she remained looking at her. She didn't even respond when the daughter asked, 'What are you thinking of, Mother?' She took her daughter's hand lovingly and made her sit next to her. Caressing the girl's head, she inquired, 'Child, has Chambasa ever spoken to you?'

'I will tell you only if you promise you won't tell Father.'

'No, I won't. Tell me child.'

'He gave me some jambul.'

'Who? Chambasa? When?'

'The day before yesterday. Father found out and slapped my cheek.'

'Why did you tell your father?'

'I didn't. Slimy Ramesha did. Appa called and asked, "Who gave you the jambul?" I was silent.'

'He said, "You shouldn't eat anything anybody at all gives you," and beat me.'

'Let a scorpion sting his hand! Were you hurt, child?' She sympathized and tried to take her daughter into her confidence. She asked again, 'Do you talk to him sometimes? What does he call you?'

'He calls me "sister". I call him "brother". He even asks after you.' Love surged into Paroti's face, and even that gaunt face was flushed with happiness. With a new sense of joy, she hugged her daughter, and patting her on the back, added, 'Did your brother ask after me too?'

This was more unexpected joy. Chambasa giving the fruit to Bagirti sometimes, both of them meeting when they could dodge Ramesha's eye—Paroti was happy when she heard all this. It was the welcome news she was awaiting for a long time. She thought her daughter safe now. Pleased, she encouraged her daughter to bond with her brother:

'If he gives you the fruit, shouldn't you also give him that sweet unde we made for the Panchami festival?'

'You are brother and sister. Why should you bother about your elders' enmity? It makes me happy to see you both happy. Bring Chambasa home some day when your father goes out of the village.' She began to think of Chambasa.

Chambasava

Tungavva brought up Chambasa not like a son of her own, but better than her own. Along with her milk, she also fed him with immense love and affection. She was a god-like mother to Chambasa. From the day they put him on her lap to the day he grew his wisdom tooth, she told him stories, nourished his imagination and created in his mind a marvellous dream world. The stories she told him even before he went to school were a treasure trove. When he was sick or ailing, she became both father and mother to him and looked after him. She always guarded him like watchful hawk.

Tungavva was now middle-aged. Her feet had grown coarse with walking in the forest. Her complexion had tanned because of constant exposure to the sun. Pendulous breasts on a broad chest. Her nose was long and sharp. Under this nose, there bloomed a lovely smile on her lovely lips. She had large eyes. Although her speech was a little rough, she was a soft-hearted woman. Her bold speech and manner were complemented by a ripe and tranquil mind. Overall, she looked like a folk goddess. If anyone as much as suggested that there was some danger to Chambasa, she turned into a hungry tigress and her eyes became disturbed lakes. At those times, even Chambasa would be upset. To bring her back to normalcy, he teased, 'Tungavva, when I was a child suckling your breasts, what sort of noises did

I make?' She calmed down, and with an out-of-the-world smile on her face, tweaked his ears playfully and told him, 'Like a chirping sparrow.'

Chambasa didn't just listen to Tungavva's stories by filling them with life. He saw them happen in front of his eyes. Especially the story of the originary banyan tree. It was something he never forgot all his life. In Tungavva's stories, people didn't have castes, or any other genealogical identities. There were only poor or rich, gods or demons, good or evil people, and saints or villains. There were animals—fox, tiger, bear, lion, rabbit, and so on. All these creatures lived in another world beyond the forest. But they visited here when Tungavva told her stories.

Meanwhile, Rajappa Gowda enrolled Chambasa in the Kannada Boys (KB) School. The same year, Rameshi too had joined the school. Rameshi was involved in all kinds of slimy things. He was the son of a farmer close to Baramegowda. After registering his name, the schoolmaster asked Chambasa to sit in the same row as Rameshi. When he did, Rameshi got up cursing—'Che, che, how can I sit with someone born in the untouchable neighbourhood?' He walked away to the other end of the row to sit. Everyone looked at Chambasa. Meanwhile, the boy who was sitting next to Chambasa also got up and went and sat next to Rameshi. The others too moved away from him. The master stood watching all this in silence. Chambasa later came to know that he was seen as an untouchable because he grew up on Tungavva's milk. From that day, a strand of sadness got woven into his awareness of the world. He felt bad whenever he remembered this incident. He had no friends. Although he was acquainted with boys from upper-caste families, he realized that their attitude towards him was different.

There was nobody to equal Chambasa in learning. He learnt everything the master taught. Still, nobody would let him touch them. One day, when he went to the village, a street cur saw Rameshi trying to attack him. He too tried to attack Chambasa. And whenever the dog saw Chambasa, he would try to attack him. Rameshi rewarded the dog by making him his pet.

Chambasa also learnt that the place where Tungavva lived was the untouchable neighbourhood outside the village. Everybody there is an untouchable. They have no right to mix, talk or eat with the villagers on an equal basis. They are like talking animals. What is more, even though the villagers touch dumb animals, they do not touch the untouchables. He first thought that the people in the untouchable neighbourhood were not aware of it. Later he came to know that although these dark men knew everything, they acted as if they didn't. The result, Chambasa grew lonely.

The characters in Tungavva's stories sang melodiously. They were also great talkers! They spoke, and when they sang and danced, they conjured up musical instruments by merely clapping their hands. As they slowly built up the rhythm, they turned the whole story into a ritual performance. Even gods like Shiva and Parvati appeared in Tungavva's hut. They wore no shiny clothes or flashy ornaments. They looked like poor people. Sometimes, when Tungavva pointed to Chambasa and Lasuma and begged the gods to protect them, they assured her sweetly that they would. Tungavva then became enthralled and saluted them with fear and reverence. When the story ended, only Tungavva, Chambasa and Lasuma would be present there with Shiva and Parvati.

When the monsoon winds blew and rains began, you

could see men, women and cattle in the fields. The farmers acted as if they now found some pretext for chewing areca nut and betel leaves. They walked around with a mouthful, wearing turbans on their heads and poising a walking stick over their shoulders. They yoked the bullocks with festive zeal and started planting the seeds. They remembered the names of their bullocks now and called them loudly, giving them instructions on how to walk. The whole village seemed rapt in this planting ritual, what with all the excited talk, the colourful saris of women and herds of well-fed bullocks around.

Tungavva's brother, Naga, was not only cultivating the fields gifted to them, but also the sixty acres of Chambasa's land. That fortnight, he'd prepared the earth with the help of many farmers. The rains were timely. For the sowing, Chambasa was also present with Tungavva. Lasuma had gone to graze the cattle. Ten workers, who were sowing peanuts, were far away. Apart from the Pandavas, Tungavva and Naga invoked all the gods of all the clans in the region, without forgetting even one of them! They turned in every direction, saluted, smeared the earth on their foreheads and began sowing. A worker was making sure that the bulls were walking in line. Naga held the seed drill and was planting corn. Tungavva strew akkadi grains over the earth. Chambasa sat on the barrier between his land and Baramegowda's.

The sky was overcast. Clouds strayed like cattle in all directions when the western breeze blew. In all the fields, excited voices of men, which sounded like singing, mingled with the lilting laughter of women. The whole region was celebrating the planting season. Nobody wanted to make their hearts bitter. People just focused on planting and enjoyed the atmosphere. It is easy to make a farmer happy.

When the cool breeze blows from the fields, pleasures his body, and plants moist green dreams in his mind, there is none happier than him. Even nature knows this secret. At this time, the farmer community in Shivapura forgets all its bitterness and discontents and simply feels happy. Mother Nature blesses them with a smile—a joy that emanates from the rich scent of the earth and the blooming green of the forest. The planting was going on even in Baramegowda's neighbouring field. Rameshi was overseeing this. God knows why, suddenly he walked towards Chambasa and the others, looking like he was about to pay a neighbourly visit. He came there, stretched his arms to stop Naga's bullocks, and spat out, 'You son of a bitch, Nagya! There are furrows made by your levelling instrument in Gowda's fields. Have you added his fields to your son's?'

'Son' here meant Chambasa, implying that Chambasa was fathered by Naga. Naga was scared. Tungavva trembled within.

'Sorry, there was a mistake. The wandering cattle must have made those furrows when they ran into Gowda's fields. We have not touched that line. We only planted on our side of the lands.'

'Oh, yes. Didn't you see the barrier stone when you made that furrow? Or did you shit in this Nagya's eyes?'

Saying this, he hit Nagya on the head with his stick. Chambasa's patience was at an end. He got up, went to Rameshi, and stood facing him, 'Why, Ramya? Have your arms grown longer that you've begun to hit my people?'

Rameshi was a little scared. But without showing it, he said, 'Yes, what are you going to do about it?'

'What do we look like in your eyes?'

'Like human beings.'

'Then talk to us like human beings talk to other human

beings. If you talk to us like you talk to cattle, what do you think we will do? We too will speak to you in the same language. Shall I show it now? You bastard, Ramya, the furrow was made in my uncle's fields. He should have come here and asked us about it. Are you a bastard of my uncle or what? I can't recognize you.'

Rameshi hadn't expected this. His face turned pale like that of a corpse about to be buried. Tungavva felt weak in the legs.

She collapsed, saying, 'Rameshi, son, I will fall at your feet…'

By then, Chambasa had snatched away Rameshi's stick. Rameshi lost his balance and fell. While falling, he muttered, 'You son born to a jogti…' Before he could even finish, Chambasa had already hit him four times. He was squirming and screaming, 'He is going to kill me.' Naga ran to Chambasa, held him tight, and took him away from Rameshi. Nobody had expected such an act from Chambasa. Meanwhile, those working in the neighbouring fields also came. Rameshi's voice stopped. Shamed thus, he tried to support himself on his knees and get up. He was inching away from the scene. Still unable to shut up, he was cursing under his breath. Chambasa came up to him again and demanded, 'What did you say?'

'I was cursing myself, not you.'

Chambasa threw the stick at him and returned. The farmers standing there gave him the stick to support himself. Without making any noise, but mumbling some curses, Rameshi left.

Whenever Chambasa had time off from school, he would attach himself to Lasuma. Chambasa didn't have to go to the forest. But Lasuma, who was his age, didn't go to school. 'Why does he need to go to school? It is enough if he learns farming', Baramegowda, Tungavva and Naga had decided. Chambasa had no companions except Lasuma. Therefore, defying Tungavva, he too went to the forest with Lasuma. Once you cross the village, the main road which leads to the forest swerves off to the right—that is, towards Chalimele. Chalimele is the little jambul island at the centre of the stream. Children get scared at the very mention of Chalimele. There is a white swami in the Chalimele temple. There are stories that this swami turns people who go there into eagles and makes them fly away. Tungavva had told Chambasa this story. Chambasa had opened his eyes wide in fear and shivered. This swami is called Namahshivaya Swami.

Namahshivaya Swami

The only human being who lives in Chalimele is Namahshivaya Swami. Old man. His wrinkled face told the story of a life spent in hardships. But his was a story written in an undecipherable hand. The old man was wiser than his years. His eyesight had grown dim because he read too many books, and he read holding them close to his eyes. But if this old man decided to read someone's soul, the same dim eyes would acquire a penetrating power. Some strange restlessness and apprehension appeared on his face when he did this. Only for a second, though. With his tremendous willpower, he controlled his agitation and became calm again. But there was also a mellowness, proper to his age, in him. Clear and white arching brows. Large and extremely sensitive eyes which shone with great moral strength. They suggested control. Although he was born with many sterling qualities, and then acquired all the other scholarly equipment, because of his age and the responsibilities he had, he didn't want to live among the villagers. He was happier alone.

Every day, he read the holy book, *Shoonyasampadane*, as if he had taken a vow to do this. His method of reading was all his own. He read every word in a clear and loud voice. He stopped after he read a sentence, questioned that sentence and then answered it himself. If the answer didn't seem right, he kept this question-answer routine going on and on—some days his reading would stop at some sentence. If people heard him from outside, they'd think that the Swami was 'fighting' with someone!

He read the *Shoonyasampadane* and discussed it with himself until he felt tired. This made his mind grow sharp. In the spiritual world he had created in his mind, he was in contact with saints like Allama. People believed that he had a flaming tongue, and that what he spoke serenely turned into a boon, and what he said in anger turned around and bit them like a curse.

When Namahshivaya first entered the village, he came to know that it was called Shivapura. He felt as if he had known this village all his life. Then he remembered: Shivapura is a name that often appears in the newspapers— it is famous for murders. When illiterate people from this village go to other villages to ask for brides, they boast that their village is very famous and pull out some newspaper cuttings to prove it. What you find in them is something like this: 'A Terrible Murder in Shivapura' or 'Horrible Double Murder in Shivapura' or 'Three Ghastly Murders on the Same Day', and so on!

The prospective bride's people read it, laugh to their hearts' content, and say, 'Yes, of course, your village is super-famous. How can we of this little obscure village give our daughter to someone as big as you are?' This might have happened a couple of times. But the joke was popular in all the villages around.

This much is true. Woman and land are vulnerable spots for Shivapura men who want to assert their masculinity. If a man loses either of them, there's bound to be a murder. That too during the rainy season. When the river is in flood, it is a certain thing. The reason is simple. During the rainy season, if you murder someone and throw the corpse into the flooded river, in a couple of seconds, the fish feed on it and make it impossible for anybody to recognize the body. Then there will be a trial in the place where the unrecognizable body is found. This is a simple trick that people here have found to dodge the law.

But God knows what sense of guilt haunts these murderers! There was a strange custom in the village. Like any corpse that dies a natural death, even murdered corpses have to be given a proper funeral before they are thrown into the river! The only man who had the right to perform it was the priest. The former village priest was dead. They hadn't found a new one yet. Although Baramegowda begged many from other villages, nobody came forward to do this. Reasons are obvious. You know that little hut next to the temple in Chalimele? The one on which you find the legend, 'Come Tomorrow'? The one who comes as a priest must live there. The temple has no property. Who would come to live there on alms? And those who come as priests would mainly do that wonderful job—giving funerals to murdered bodies. Does this act even happen in any civilized fashion? Those who arrange the funeral are the murderers themselves! They don't trust the priest. So they come to the priest in the dead of the night on the day of the murder. Their faces are blackened with soot. They cover their whole face, except the eyes, with a cloth so that even the priest cannot recognize them. Two, three or more—depending on how many murderers there are— they all arrive at the 'Come Tomorrow' house and knock on the door. The moment the priest opens the door, they blindfold him and take him to the place where the corpse is. At this point, they do the kindly act of removing the priest's blindfold, and if he is still alive and hasn't become another corpse already, they make him perform the funeral.

After this, they yank the priest's foot and forcibly place it on the corpse's forehead. It's all over now. They blindfold the priest again, bring him to the 'Come Tomorrow' house, throw him and a gift of seventy-two rupees inside, and run away. Which priest would want to come to Shivapura for this pleasure?

Baramegowda was upset because of this. According to him, the reason he couldn't have a male child was because they had thrown so many corpses into the river without proper funerals. He thought he was cursed. He blamed this on the absence of a village priest. It was happenstance that Namahshivaya came to the village. Gowda promptly got hold of him.

Nobody knew what caste or clan Namahashivaya belonged to. Was he a priest at all? Nobody even asked that. Since nobody asked, he didn't tell them either. It was also by accident that he came to the Come Tomorrow house. It had been raining like mad at the time. While he was looking for some shelter, he found a ruined temple there. He got up in the morning and saw that there was also a little hut next to the temple with the legend 'Come Tomorrow' written on the door. He opened the door and went in. There was nobody. He became its occupant. In the morning, he went into the village to find out where he was. Strangely enough, not a single dog—and Shivapura dogs are famous for barking—barked at Namahshivaya. He wandered around for a bit and returned to the Come Tomorrow house!

The house became everything to him—living room, kitchen, dining room and bedroom. Except a small hole in the wall that worked as a window, he blocked all other holes and cracks. He waited for two days. Nobody came. Then Baramegowda came, saluted him, and begged, 'Please be kind to us, stay on here, and take care of the God in the temple.' He promised to supply grocery for a whole year. Our man said okay. Nobody in the village even knew his name. Since he kept muttering 'Namahshivaya' all the time, they called him Namahshivaya Swami. He was like a guru to the whole village. He read big, bulky books. He kept fasts and vows, and meditated. Even the schoolmaster began to fold his hands and salute the swami.

Sometime later, Baramegowda came and told him of the priest's duties. Namahshivaya didn't worry too much about that. He thought of it as some necessary karma he had to endure if he wanted to live in the village. The murderers came in the middle of the night after the world slept. When they knocked on his door, he was ready for them. He had decided that instead of surrendering his face to the touch of their rough hands, he would help himself. He blindfolded himself and opened the door to them. Over time, both Namahshivaya and these people began to accept this as some sort of a secret ritual they performed jointly.

Whatever others thought of him, Namahshivaya was oblivious of it. He was happy with his *Shoonyasampadane*. Because of the disinterest he showed in worldly affairs, the villagers' respect and fear of him doubled. Some thought him naïve. But he actually knew of the murk in their minds. He prayed to the Shivalinga to make them better. He didn't form any attachments. He didn't depend on anybody. He didn't let anybody enter his life. He believed that only wind, water and the forest green were really pure. Shivalinga had given him those. He remembered the God, morning and evening, 'Shivalinga, I salute you for your kindness of giving me pure air, water and all this green.'

Still he hadn't lost faith in human beings. Every Monday, he picked the leaves from the patri tree, filled his bag with them, slung the bag on his shoulder, and went to every house in the village, including those of the Dalits, to distribute the leaves. In return, they gave him some grain or flour. He put those into another bag, got back home, cooked and ate his meal. Until now, no high-caste man had ever gone to the Dalit neighbourhood so coolly and openly. When he went there and gave them the patri leaf, they didn't take it at first. He too didn't leave. He stood there in front of their houses muttering 'Namahshivaya' until they mustered some courage and took the leaf. Later, when he started coming there every Monday, the Dalits placed a small Shivalinga-like stone on their attics, put the patri leaf in front of it, and saluted the God with reverence. In a sense, Namahshivaya Swami gave the oppressed a God to worship, and thus, became Namahshivaya Swami.

When you come to think of it, nobody knows the Swami's caste or antecedents. Nobody even bothered to find out. Why do we need to know the antecedents of a saint? They decided to remain quiet about it.

Jambul Fruit

Namahshivaya was a loner with a wooden face. His face was covered with grey hair that had grown matted in places. In the two deep wells of his eyes, there shone a brilliant light like that of newly lit candles. Because of his thick moustache and white beard, he looked like a scary ghost. Forget people, he was not even fond of children. But how can kids, who had tasted the jambul there, forget the little rock island? They sat at a distance and waited for the old man to disappear. If he as much as disappeared for a minute, they immediately climbed the tree and shook the branches till the fruit fell on the ground. They gathered the fruit quickly without the old man's knowledge and ran away. Lasuma, Chambasa and many other children were experts at this business.

The temple where the old man lived was a ruined one, without paint or colour. Who wants the God who's in that temple? Even the small house next to it was singularly uninviting—the mud walls, door like a little cavity, and add to that, the legend 'Come Tomorrow' written on it! Chambasa had sketched a palace, which figured in one of Tungavva's stories, on the model of this house. But the house of his imagination was a tall house with colourful glass windows and doors. It was owned by a demon. The demon's face and body were covered with coarse dark hair. Small eyes. Long, sharp canines jutting out of the corners of his mouth. This creature kidnaps an unparallely beautiful princess, turns her into a parrot, and imprisons her in that house. Parrots, which came there for the jambul, sang of her and tried to talk to her. She tried to make a song of her sadness and sing it. Chambasa had heard the song many times in his dreams!

One time, the inspector of schools came to Shivapura like he did every year. When the inspector comes, it's like the schoolmaster is on trial. The master led the inspector only towards kids who were known to be smart. The inspector came up to Rameshi and asked, 'In which direction does your river flow?'

Rameshi answered confidently, 'Towards the east.'

'If water gathers here, where does it flow?'

With greater self-confidence, Rameshi replied, 'To the east.' Inspector asked two more students. They too said the same thing. At last, he asked Chambasa. Chambasa replied, 'Towards the slope.'

'What is non-violence?'

Rameshi shut up. It was Chambasa's turn.

'Not hurting others either physically or mentally.' The inspector was pleased with these answers. He asked again:

'What is untouchability?'

'Not touching or allowing to be touched by others.'

'Who are the untouchables among you?'

'None.'

Happy with Chambasa's answers, the inspector patted him on the shoulder and also complimented the master, 'You have trained your students well.' After he left, the master ordered Chambasa to hold the nose of those other students and slap them on the cheek. He slapped two of them, and when it was Rameshi's turn, he slapped hard until his hand smarted. All five of his fingers were imprinted on Rameshi's cheeks.

On that day, Chambasa felt content that he had taken revenge for all the insults he was subjected to. He went to the untouchable neighbourhood feeling elated and looking for Lasuma. Lasuma wasn't there. He went to the forest searching for him. On the way, he came to Chalimele. Lasuma had told him that the white devil wouldn't be in the temple. He thought this was a nice opportunity and went to the ruined temple. It was noon. Scorching sun. The ground burned like an over-heated pan.

The little rock island looked deserted. The region was so silent that you could even hear the noises insects were making. The old man's Come Tomorrow house was locked. The door of the temple was open. He went in slowly. It felt cool and pleasant inside. He sighed and sat down. There was a stone like a Shivalinga. Some said a smooth stone was placed there in memory of Malli who had died in the pond. Others believed that it was a Shivalinga. A black stone, about two-feet tall, stood there. On this black stone, some dried patri leaves had fallen. He remembered seeing a linga like this in Savalagi when he was a child. But that was in the inner shrine. Except the priest, nobody could touch it. On a hot and sunny afternoon, when he had seen that black stone, he had imagined running his hand over it and experiencing the cool touch. But this one was within his hand's reach. So look! He put his hand on God Shivalinga! Ah, how cool it is! He put his other hand on the stone and felt it. Lost in the beauty of the sensation, he embraced it. He forgot where he was. He closed his eyes, experiencing every bit of this serene moment. He said contentedly, 'Shivalinga.' He said, 'Ha!' Even before this exclamation was out of his mouth, he heard someone shouting, 'Come, come, this bastard is touching the Shivalinga and polluting it.' Even as these words fell on his ears, four or five hulks pulled him out of the temple, cursed and called him a son of a bitch, and beat him up without giving him a chance to escape or scream. They kicked him on his mouth. Even when blood oozed out of his mouth, they didn't let go. He tore his shirt, escaped somehow, ran, and collapsed under a rock. Although he could see the men searching for him, they couldn't see him. Rameshi was among them. Seepya from his class was there. Basya and another boy from school. There were two kids who were sons of Baramegowda's farmers. He lay there, naked, until dark. Then he came out.

This was an insult to Chambasa's valour, courage and masculinity. The very state of his mind and thinking had altered now. His body was sore with all the kicking and beating he had taken. He didn't tell either Tungavva or Naga. He didn't even mention it to his aunt. He told Lasuma about it at night. Lasuma too ground his teeth in anger. That night, both didn't sleep for a long time. They decided to keep the secret between themselves. They began to think of plans of revenge. First they had to disengage Rameshi from his group and get him alone. Then, how to thrash him and where—these were Lasuma's thoughts. Chambasa sat up on his bed in the middle of the night, screaming, 'Shiva, how can I bear this humiliation?' He thumped on his chest in agony. That Chalimele, that God Shivalinga. He spat out thrice in pain. He got up and started pacing up and down. Lasuma too got up and consoled him, 'Wait until the morning, Brother. You will see what Rameshi's fate is going to be. Come, sleep now.' He held his hand and made him sit on the bed. Chambasa struggled with anger and shame like a worm caught in the fire.

Early morning. The cockerel hadn't crowed yet. Chambasa got up. Lasuma was still sleeping. He took his underpants and went to Chalimele. He dived off the rock into the lake. He swam six or seven times across it. He was deliberately noisy, hoping that the old man would hear him and come out. He was ready to face him. He leapt in and out of the water. He was about to wear his underpants, when his gaze fell on the temple. The sun had risen. The temple door was open. Inside, the dark stone shone as if mocking him. He picked up a big stone, the size of his fist, aimed it at the dark linga, and threw it. A spark flew from where the stone touched the linga. He was happy, as well as scared, when he heard the sound and saw the spark fly. He ran away. When he returned home, Lasuma had already gone out. He sat on a three-legged sack-stand and closed his eyes. He felt as if he had performed some great feat and was now fatigued. He closed his eyes.

Even on the next day, his heart burnt with the feelings of insult. Rameshi couldn't be traced. A trustworthy boy whom they sent to spy on Rameshi returned and informed them that he wasn't in the village. They searched for Seepya who was with Rameshi. He too couldn't be found. Then they looked for the other two who had beaten Chambasa along with Rameshi. They too had vanished. Chambasa spent some time cursing his fate. He went to the fields late in the evening. He could neither sit nor stand anywhere. On the way back, Chalimele drew him to itself. He went there.

Chalimele was deserted. The temple door was open. But the door of the Come Tomorrow house was also open. He turned back thinking that the white devil was there. Then thought again, 'What's the point of going home?' He climbed up a tall jambul tree and hid there. Time wouldn't pass. Was Baramegowda behind Rameshi's act? No idea. Whatever. This much is true: Rameshi had given him an unforgettable beating and taken revenge on him. By then, it was growing dark. A heavy wind screeched through the trees and the plants. The branches over his head swayed. The wind blew into the hollow of the old and dignified tree. This created a wailing sound, as if it was telling the tragic tale of Chambasa's insult to the world.

He climbed down the tree. The door of the Come Tomorrow house was closed. The stone in the temple seemed to sneer and mock at him. Yes, all this started here, he remembered, got angry, clenched his teeth, picked up two big stones again and threw them at the linga one after the other. They hit their mark, two sparks flew, and seeing this, Chambasa ran away.

Who Is the Miscreant?

That morning, Namahshivaya went to the river to bathe earlier than usual. He swam until his limbs felt loose, then he swam again until they felt tense. Finally, he came out of the water. But the sun hadn't risen yet. He came to the temple, put his dhotra to dry, and spreading a mat under the patri tree, sat to meditate. Usually, when he sat for meditation, the image of the Kashi Vishwanatha linga, which he had seen earlier, appeared before his closed eyes. He would fix this image in his mind like fixing something on a wall, and then chant the panchakshari mantra. But on that day, this linga didn't appear at all. Okay, if not this linga, let me try some other, he thought. He tried to bring up the images of Savalagi Shivalinga and Ghodageri Gajalinga. None of them appeared in his mind. What's more, there was only darkness there. He thought he must have committed some error and begged forgiveness. Uttering, 'Shiva, Shiva', he said again, 'My Father, Shiva, Shivalinga.' Whatever he did, the darkness inside him couldn't be dispelled. He closed his eyes forcefully, and saying, 'Shivalinga', tried to remember the linga again. He sat like this for a while, he saw a light flash from the corner of his eye. A Shivalinga appeared! Soon he realized that it was the same Shivalinga that he worshipped every day in the temple. Although the linga was the same, the temple wasn't the same. There was an inner sanctum built in Sangamavari stone. There was a ghee-lamp in front of the linga. A flame burned in it. The scent of dhoopa and sandalwood spread everywhere. Namahshivaya was overjoyed and began meditating.

Namahshivaya's happiness was simply boundless. Moreover, this experience was new. As he stood worshipping, feeling grateful to Shiva and shedding tears of joy, a single flame of devotion burned within him. Suddenly, he heard a sound like somebody pelting a stone at something. He opened his eyes. He hadn't been hit by the stone. He was sitting under the patri tree. The sun had already risen, and a golden sunlight fell on everything around. The pelting sound came from the temple. When he realized this, he went in. Nothing there! Next to the wall was a stone the size of his fist. The Shivalinga had a dent like it was hit by a stone. He picked up the stone and checked it. As not a lot of time had elapsed since the stone pelting, he thought the culprit must be somewhere close by. He came out of the temple and looked around. He didn't see anybody. He searched everywhere—temple, house, and all around the place. Still he didn't see anybody.

He was agitated the whole day. He thought some enemy of his had thrown the stone at the God in order to take revenge on him. But to his knowledge, he hadn't hurt anybody. There was one possibility, though. Did some murderer suspect him of revealing the secret to others and do this out of vengeance? Although he hadn't said anything to anybody, somebody could have harboured such doubts, right? But these aren't the days of murder. Whatever. He wandered among the trees aimlessly. 'I worshipped the linga because there was nobody to care for it. Now what did this Shiva, who submitted to my worship, get in the end? Getting stones thrown at him?' He wept. That night, he couldn't sleep for a long time. His ears were alert to any sound coming from the temple.

He got up the next morning, bathed, cleaned the Shivalinga, rubbed it with a wet cloth, smeared ash on it, adorned the head with a couple of patri leaves, and sat in front of the stone to meditate. He couldn't concentrate. His mind was full of stones, and sounds of stones being pelted. He sat waiting. If someone throws a stone, I will catch the sinner immediately, he thought. The result: no pelting of stones. But he couldn't meditate either. He got up saying, 'Well, today I can only manage this much devotion.' He went to the Come Tomorrow house. The sound of a stone being pelted hit his ears like a clap of thunder. He ran instantly and looked. He searched everywhere. There was nobody! When he came to the temple and checked, he found that the linga had been hit by a stone. To the left of the linga lay a fist-sized stone. There was a mark where the new stone hit the linga. The patri leaves on it had faded already. He almost thought that the Shivalinga bled from where it was hit. He wanted to weep.

The next day, before Namahshivaya bathed in the river and got back, somebody had thrown two stones already. 'Why do you hurt yourself to test me, Shivalinga?' he screamed in frustration. The Shivalinga didn't reply. The great man who threw stones wasn't to be found either. On the fifth day, five or six stones fell there. He gathered all the stones, put them in a basket and kept the basket in a corner of the temple. For a minute, he thought someone had planned all this to get him out of that place. But it was highly improbable. 'I wait for the stone with my eyes peeled day and night to catch this miscreant. By now, with all this intense surveillance, he should have been caught already. So this must be God's plan to throw me out of here,' he decided. The moment he had such thoughts, Namahshivaya felt like crying.

'Throw me out if you don't want me. Instead, why do you hurt yourself like this, my Father, my God, Shivalinga?' He kept wailing. After his heart became a little lighter with crying, he made up his mind, 'Fine, I'll leave the place right now,' and got up. He looked at the Shivalinga again. Feeling that he shouldn't leave in this careless fashion in spite of seeing the mark the stone had made on the linga, he took a pure wet cloth and wiped it. He saluted the idol and came out. He also thought of embracing Shivalinga once before leaving. But he decided against it. 'God is actually pushing me away, so why hurt him more by embracing him?' He came out again and went to the Come Tomorrow house. He didn't have many possessions. A couple of dhotras, one towel, a water-pot and a copy of *Shoonyasampadane*— he put everything into one bag and came out. A boy with a profoundly sorrowful face stood there with his head bent. Tears had collected in the corners of his eyes. You couldn't see, either in his stance or on his face, any trace of deviousness, mischief or hate.

'How long have you been here?' Namahshivaya asked.

'Must be two hours,' said the boy without raising his head.

So he had heard everything—my crying and screaming. Namahshivaya felt a bit embarrassed. He asked again, 'What do you want?'

'I came to say something.'

'What?'

'I am the one who throws stones at the Shivalinga every day.'

'What did you say?'

'Yes, me,' he confessed, fell prostrate at Namahshivaya's feet, and clutched them fast, washing them with his tears. Namahshivaya felt the warm tears on his feet, and perhaps because he had found the thief, or because he had realized that this wasn't Shivalinga's trick to send him away, he pressed his hands on the boy's head and sat weeping.

Later he slowly raised the boy up and looked at him. The boy was tall for his age. He had grown big like a pongamia tree in spring. He had washed away all of Namahshivaya's anger with his tears.

'It wasn't me you threw stones at. You did that to Shivalinga. Go and ask His forgiveness,' Namahshivaya told the boy. Chambasa nodded and went into the temple. When he saluted the idol and looked back, he saw Namahshivaya standing at the temple door. The boy touched his feet, folded his hands respectfully, and begged him, 'Please don't go away.' Namahshivaya's eyes became moist. It had been years since he had seen such compassion. Chambasa evoked a new surge of tenderness within him.

'What's your name?'

'Chambasa.'

'All right, Chambasava! Come tomorrow,' he said this with a heavy heart and looked at the Shivalinga through a film of tears. Those hazy eyes couldn't see the dents made by the stones on the Shivalinga anymore.

Love

The annual exams were over. Schools were on vacation. The forest bloomed with the onset of spring. It was thick with many fragrances. Chambasa now attached himself to Lasuma who went to herd the cattle. Plucking kari and bari fruit, eating unripe mangoes and gooseberries, and wandering in the forest gave great joy to Chambasa. They'd pack some food and eat together, like brothers, in the forest, all the while happily chatting about something or the other. Moreover, Lasuma knew many things about the forest that Chambasa didn't. Lasuma knew what tree or creeper was safe to touch and what was not. He also knew much about what was poisonous and what was medicinal. There was no snake, bird or animal he didn't know. He could tell a bird by its sound. He knew the nature, vulnerabilities, and habits of all these birds. Once, Chambasa tore a leaf without heeding Lasuma's warning. He ended up scratching and rubbing his arm through the day. As a result, the arm was swollen by the evening. Later Lasuma told him that it was the 'itchy' leaf. You mustn't touch it. If you do, you get this terrible itch. Lasuma never made such mistakes.

One day, Lasuma filled his pockets with kari fruit, and when it was time for the cattle to go home, he called Chambasa, 'Come, let's go home.'

Lasuma had plucked the rare kari with so much zeal, but why? Chambasa began to wonder, kari is a small fruit that you find in a bush full of hard and sharp thorns. He is taking them home without as much as offering me one. To whom is he taking these?

'Whom are you taking them for?' he asked.

'For Shari.'

'Who is Shari? What's she to you?'

'You know Naganna of the house with the cattle shed, don't you? My maternal uncle? Shari is his daughter. She is so fond of kari fruit. I promised her I'd get some in the evening. She'll be waiting.'

Chambasa teased Lasuma, 'So will you marry her?'

'No, Brother! She is already goddess Ellamma's devotee. Look, there's her house. I'll go and give her the fruit.'

Meanwhile, a buffalo had strayed away from the herd. 'You go and bring it back,' even as Chambasa said this, he saw at a distance a girl coming up to them, herding that buffalo. Chambasa was stunned by her beauty, her stature and gait. He stood as if he had touched a live electric wire. He knew Yamunakka of the house with the cattle shed. Once, when he happened to run into her, she moved and made way for him to pass. He had passed her as if he hadn't even seen her. Looking at this beautiful daughter of hers now, Chambasa frowned.

Sharavva, who stood there, was also surprised. She found it funny that Chambasa stood as if he hadn't even recognized her. She is Tungavva's niece. Although she hadn't talked to Chambasa in person, she had always referred to him with pride as 'mava' when she talked about him to others. Now when he looked at her in this manner, she looked back at him mischievously. He seemed to be smiling at her. When he smiled under the newly grown moustache, his teeth flashed. An array of emotions spread over her like a rainbow, and she turned away looking shy. Walking mechanically behind the cattle, Chambasa thought, 'I have seen this girl somewhere earlier. But where?' Chambasa tried to remember. 'Yes, it must have been a week or two ago.' At that time, Namahshivaya was still a devil in his mind.

One Friday, the day of the village fair, at noon. He had school only half day. After school, he went to the forest to look for Lasuma. He suddenly wanted some jambul. Softly, so that the white devil wouldn't get a wind of it, he watched every side and came to the rock island. He wasn't sure if the old man was there or not. But he imagined the man slouching about. He remembered the story Tungavva had told him when he was young. Namahshivaya Swami was the white devil. She'd told him he caught children who went there, turned them into eagles, and made them fly away. Chambasa believed it.

That day, Chambasa had managed to escape Namahshivaya's eye and climb the tree. Since there were many fruits at hand's reach, he didn't have to shake the branch. He filled his pockets and was about to climb down when he saw a girl standing under the tree, blinking. Apparently, she too had sneaked into the place for the fruit. Large beautiful eyes, round rosy face, rounded arms, thick, dark and unruly hair which she had tried to gather at the back (but now it was flying all over her back), and half-open red mouth—she was looking at him longingly. He didn't know there was such a lovely girl in his village. He was lost, gazing at her. She signalled to him, asking him to shake some fruit off the branch for her. She laughed a floral laugh—a flash of white teeth inside the lovely mouth. Of course, he would get some fruit for her. But they suddenly heard the white devil shout, 'Who is it?' Instantly, like the goddess in Tungavva's stories, the girl vanished. When the devil came there, he too jumped into some bush and hid. The old man looked around for a bit and went back. He emerged from the bush and searched for her. With an animal-cunning, the girl hid somewhere—where, how, when—he didn't know. But the form of the fair and lovely girl with half-open lips was imprinted on his mind. The girl had wounded the boy's heart with that knife-like flash of her smile. Now finding out that she was Yamunakka's daughter made him happy.

Another evening, both Lasuma and Chambasa were returning home with their cattle. Lasuma took the milch cows to the village. Chambasa began to herd the bulls towards their house in the fields outside the village. By this time, clouds started gathering in the sky. And the rain-breeze blew. It was going to rain. He hurried the bulls and tethered them in the shed of the house in the fields. He put some fodder in front of them. Large raindrops fell. He thought Lasuma might not come and lit the lamp. He heard something fall outside. He came out and saw the same Shari. She had thrown a bundle of firewood on the porch and stood wringing water out of her seragu. The lower part of her sari was also wet and clung to her knees. Dark clouds clamoured in the sky, dashed against each other and somersaulted. Lightning sprang up. Add to that, claps of thunder like drumbeats.

The girl looked at him helplessly and brought out a smile on her drenched face. Chambasa went in, picked up the blanket hanging on the peg, and brought it to her saying, 'Leave the firewood bundle there. Go back to the village before it gets dark.' The girl tried to make a cloak out of the blanket. She was struggling. He realized she didn't know how to do this. He plucked the blanket from her hands, made a cloak and covered her with it. Sharavva found it difficult to take her eyes off him. She stood looking at him. 'Hold it here,' he said, taking her left hand and attaching it to the blanket. He thought, 'Ah, how beautiful she has grown!' and took his hand back. He caressed the hand that had touched her with his other hand and looked at her in a state of bliss. She too stood holding the end of the blanket with her fair, long fingers, and obviously she was in no mood to leave. She looked agitated, uncertain and scared. Chambasa hurried her, 'Run now, you can return the blanket tomorrow.' She left the bundle there and ran.

Chambasa now knew that she was Tungavva's niece. The rain stopped, and it was dark. He thanked God for the rain, picked up her bundle and walked towards the village. He went straight to the cattle shed of her house, put the bundle on the porch, and returned home. In fact, when she was only ten, Sharavva had already grown up like a fourteen-year-old. Yamunakka became alert and placed some control on her daughter. She was growing up under the careful eye of aunt Tungavva and the protection of Naga and Lasuma's strong arms.

That night, when he slept, Chambasa again conjured up images of that beauty before and after rain. He thought of her drenched body. Complexion of a tender mango shoot, slender waist, but nicely rounded body, an expression of fear mixed with wonder in her large lamp-like eyes. Lovely nose, cheeks red like the flame of the forest, dishevelled hair—someone about to be a young woman! Why shouldn't I love her? Yes! What's wrong with loving her? Nothing. But she is of a different caste and clan. People ostracized me just because I grew up drinking Tungavva's milk. Will they be quiet if I marry Shari? No. But what of it? Who cares whether they chastise me for it or not? I will love her at any cost, he decided. But then, she too must love me, right? If she accepts me only because of my social status or because I am the son of the village Gowda, can we call it love? No. Can't I keep loving her in my mind? Nobody would know if I did that. He bore her image like she bore her bundle earlier. Now, he furtively drew that image out of his mind, fondled it, turned over and slept.

The next morning, Yamunakka got up to sweep the front yard. She called her sleeping daughter, 'Sharavva, Sharavva, it's morning already. Wake up.' Looking at Shari, she said loudly to herself, 'Look at the evil thing, she has pushed her blanket away and wrapped herself with her mava's blanket!' When she came out, she saw the bundle of firewood on the porch. She said again, 'Evil thing, you said you didn't bring the bundle. Look, it is here. She's forgotten that.' Yamunakka started sweeping the yard. Sharavva, who heard this, came out instantly. She saw the bundle and was sure that Chambasa had brought it there. She felt shy, bit her lip, and without the mother's knowledge, ran back and slept like before. Stealthily, she brought up the image of Chambasa, who had looked at her with hungry eyes, and fixed it in front of her eyes. 'How dare you look at me like that! If it was once or twice, I'd have passed it. I remained silent because, after all, he is the village Gowda, rich guy, aunt Tungavva's grandson, mava—but did he have to stare at me without even blinking his eyes? What does he think of me? He must have thought, she is a cheap woman, she'll come to me the moment I call her! No, no, it can't be that. He made a cloak for me out of the blanket, covered my head with it with such care, and told me to run home quickly—charmed me, really! When I was leaving, he smiled at me so sweetly. All the village girls wait for him to look at them and talk to them, as if their whole life depended on it. But he doesn't so much as look at them. If he smiled so nicely at me…whatever, I must at least kiss this mava,' she told herself and drew Chambasa's image closer, embraced him, kissed him, turned over and went back to sleep.

Meanwhile, a girl in Tungavva's neighbourhood was getting married to a bridegroom from Suladhala. The marriage party set off from Shivapura. When Chambasa came to know that Tungavva's niece Shari was also in that party, he said, 'Avva, I too will come with the marriage party.' Can a Gowda accompany an untouchable marriage party? But since Suladhala was his mother's village and all his relatives lived there, she thought, 'Let him spend a couple of days with his grandmother, aunt and uncle,' and said yes. Chambasa hadn't thought that his wish would be granted so quickly. With great enthusiasm, he gathered his shirt, shorts and towel, put them in a bag and got ready. His aunt (Rajappa Gowda's wife) packed a sticky sweet called antinunde and also a good meal for the journey. There were two bullock carts ready for the marriage party. In the cart for men, old men and Chambasa sat. In the other were women. Since Sharavva was in the cart for women, Chambasa was a bit disappointed. They crossed Pashchapura and stopped their carts near the Tamraparni river to have their meal. Chambasa and Shari were the only young ones in the party. He unwrapped the lunch his aunt had packed for him. He remembered Shari. He took two antinundes to her. She looked at Tungavva's face. Tungavva said, 'Take it.' Both ate the antinundes.

By the time their carts reached Suladhala, it was already dark. They waited in the temple outside Suladhala for the bridegroom's people to come and receive them. It is a part of their tradition to receive guests and take them in a grand procession into their village. Meanwhile, the Shivapura party got some scary news. In a marriage ceremony, it is customary for both the bride's and the bridegroom's parties to engage in playful taunting and a lot of mischief. Throwing colour at each other, adding hot peppers instead of sweet jaggery to the pongal, mocking each other, and so on. All this is customary fun during any wedding. But the scary news that the Shivapura party heard was that the Suladhala people planned to throw tar on them instead of colour when they arrived in the procession. Shivapura party was totally confused when this news spread. As it is, they are poor. They only have one set of good clothes—shirt, dhotra and turban—to wear on festivals or holidays. They wear these on those rare occasions, and then wrap them up in some cloth to keep them safe. They open these bundles only when the next festival or holiday comes. If those Suladhala people throw tar on these precious clothes, could they ever use them again? Besides, could you even wear these tar-smeared clothes to the wedding? The men already looked dejected, like defeated wrestlers. They complained. But the bridegroom's party that came to receive them didn't pay any attention. Some said they knew nothing about this business and laughed. Finally, a Shivapura elder suggested, let no man join the procession. But then, won't everybody think of the bride's party as a set of cowards? So said a young man with a sharp and trimmed moustache. In the end, they decided that every man in the bride's party would take off his shirt and turban, bunch them up, stick them safely under his armpit and participate.

What followed was simply hilarious! The procession didn't go through the main streets of the village. Only the untouchable neighbourhood, and that too, just a couple of lanes. But a huge number of people had gathered to watch this procession on those small lanes. The lanes got impossibly crowded. You know why? Because the men in the bride's party have taken off all their clothes—shirt, dhotra and turban—stuck them under their armpits, and are now walking in double file with just the loin cloth on them. Behind them, the women are walking, covering their faces with their seragus. The drummers danced and jumped around in glee. Not only the untouchables from the nearby neighbourhoods, even high-caste people are rushing to watch this singular spectacle. The whole gathering is laughing. Children point fingers at the procession and laugh. Let me tell you the truth, so many people had never gathered to watch a bridal procession in any locality around the village. People who came to watch roared with laughter. The bride's people were mad at their in-laws and ashamed of themselves.

The next morning, Chambasa, who had slept in his uncle's house the night before, suspected that there would be a fight because of the previous day's incident. He decided to go and check. He left his uncle's place and came to the marriage hall. Instantly, Shari appeared and asked, 'Shall I call aunt Tungavva?'

'Where are the men? Have they gone to bathe?' he asked. Shari laughed aloud and hastily covered her mouth. There was nobody around. A fine opportunity to talk!

'Okay, isn't it time for the main ritual, the muhurta?'

'All the men are sitting on the train tracks. You must go and bring them here, Mava.'

'Why, what happened?'

After all, the two marriage parties are bound to have some friction and sparks flying between them.

'Ayyo, walk a couple of steps and see what's happening, Mava,' said Sharavva with mock anger. When he turned to go, she covered her mouth and laughed. The women were busy with wedding arrangements. But they too were laughing.

When he went towards the train tracks, he saw all the men sitting there in a row. For some reason, it looked as if they were all embarrassed to see him. There was a look of defeat on every face. From time to time, every man there is furiously rubbing his arse on the tracks! When he went to an elder and asked what happened, the latter told him:

'Sir, what can I say about our in-laws? They had put some itchy leaf into the water cauldron. In the morning, we took a pot of water and sat to shit in the fields. We have been scratching our arses since then. The morning sun has warmed the train tracks nicely. Sitting on them gives some comfort. Thank God we sent a message to the women asking them not to use that water.'

The Suladhala in-laws had won again. Our Shivapura village bumpkins were defeated again and again. By the time all the rituals got over, and everybody threw the grains of rice on the couple's head to bless them, it was already late afternoon.

Chambasa's great gain from going to the wedding was this. On the wedding evening, it is customary these days to make the new husband and wife say each other's names. Then they smear turmeric on each other's faces. Making this a pretext, all the young girls and boys who gather there also smear turmeric on each other's faces. This gives them an opportunity to indulge in a bit of lust, a bit of love and a bit of dreaming without, of course, getting into any excess. Chambasa smeared his hands with turmeric and went searching for Shari in the wedding hall. She too was searching for him. The moment she saw him, she made as if to run saying, 'No, Mava!' But at the same time, she got into his arms as if asking him to smear that turmeric on her face. Her slender waist shook. She half-opened those doe eyes, looked at him, and promptly thrust her soft cheeks into his hands. Then, pushing her soft round breasts against his chest, she enjoyed sharing the warmth of his body and the intoxication of youth. When he loosened his embrace so that she too could smear turmeric on him, he found her exhausted. She just stood at his hand's reach as if saying, 'Smear all you like.' Suddenly, they heard Tungavva's voice and moved away from each other. Both were sweating. What the mouths couldn't say, their eyes did in a language of their own. What the eyes couldn't see, their youthful bodies were aware of already. The fruit of love was ripe. Both dreamed colourful dreams through the night. The cool morning breeze and the chirping of birds revived the memories of the day before.

Kuntirapa

These days, Paroti always lay in bed. Baramegowda sometimes came and inquired after her health. But Paroti knew that his visits were only pretence, play-acting. She was convinced that he couldn't care for her ever again. She also knew that she could not fulfil his desires. Even then, when he came into her room, she'd melt like butter in front of fire and listen to his empty words. She'd wait for his visits and feel bad. Baramegowda, on the other hand, was sick of her face. He tried, as much as possible, to stay away from her. Some days, he didn't want anybody or anything. He'd even think of Tungavva and turn into a salivating old bull. Be that as it may, we'll now move to Kuntirapa and get to know something about him.

Paroti had started feeling alone despite her daughter being there. If she had at least talked to Tungavva casually, Tungavva would perhaps have become a friend. But Paroti listened to stories the servants told her and became more and more paranoid about Tungavva. Some stories were about how Tungavva went to the House of Pleasure every other day and pestered Baramegowda to write his property in her son's name. Others were about Tungavva threatening to bring the Dalits from Belagavi to help her. Moreover, Lasuma was growing up. He worked like other grown men. This irked her. She believed that all this was a conspiracy to throw her out and establish Tungavva in the House of

Pleasure. She was scared that Baramegowda would get
Bagirti married off and give all his property to Lasuma.
Now she remembered Kuntirapa's name like a drowning
man clutches at a straw.

The same day, she wrote a letter to her brother Erapa,
describing her predicament and asking him to come to
Shivapura post-haste. Get her daughter Bagirti married to
Kuntirapa right away, keep him in the house, and then
make sure that he gets all the property—this was Paroti's
plan. Kuntirapa read the letter, and in just about three days
after that, he descended on Shivapura from Belagavi—like a
snake moving into a crumbling nest of white ants!

Paroti's father Kotrappa was the only doctor in all the
four villages around. He wasn't trained in any medical
institution, nor had he learnt his trade from any other senior
practitioner. Since his father was a doctor, he too ground
some herb or root and practised as a medicine man. What
is more, he used his cunning and experience in dealing
with people to get all the symptoms of the disease from
the patients themselves. Then he'd pretend that he had
gleaned all this by checking the patient's pulse. He'd made
some herbal lambative for increasing virility by mixing
different medicinal lambatives made by other doctors. He
marketed this virility drug well and made good money out
of it. He was more famous because of this lambative rather
than his medical acumen. Although it was labelled virility
lambative, people called it Kotra's lambative.

Paroti was born to Kotra's first wife. After only two
years of her birth, her mother had died. The great Dr Kotra
didn't even speak to the second wife he married, Kashibai,
for ten years because she hadn't brought any dowry with
her. When he wanted a meal, he would go and sit in
the kitchen. She served him. Somehow, after the bloody

first night, the couple managed to have two children and attained the blessed state of parenthood. Kashibai's first son was Erapa, the second Ganapa. But in the sixth year after all this, Dr Kotra, who was overjoyed by the super-sales of his virility lambative, bought a sari for his wife and said, 'Wear it today.' The moment he said this, wife Kashibai died! She was so overwhelmed by happiness when her husband spoke to her that she died with the folded sari still in her hands!

Kashibai's first son Erapa limped on his left leg because he'd had a polio attack. His peers called him Kuntirapa. As time went by, even people at home began calling him that. Fair and lean man. Small eyes, long nose, angular face with high cheek bones. He covered the buck teeth in front by forcefully closing his lips over them. Such facial features apart, he leant somewhat to the left side when he stood because his legs were of unequal length. You can't call him handsome, but certainly he wasn't ugly either. Moreover, what gave him confidence was also his belief that youth was more than enough to attract the opposite sex, you didn't also need to be beautiful.

Father Kotra hadn't left any money for the sons. Two old shirts, one dhotra and the turban which the first wife brought him at the time of the wedding—that's all. Forget wearing these, they weren't even fit to be given to charity. Since the children were orphans, they grew up learning nothing but obedience. But before dying, Kashibai had whispered a wish in her stepdaughter, Paroti's, ear. If Paroti gives birth to a daughter, she should get her married to Kuntirapa. Kashibai held Paroti's hand and made her promise. The penniless orphans had grown up hearing everything others said as either commands or curses.

Kuntirapa had dreamt of becoming the Chief Swami of

a matha and also having an illicit relationship with a minx who fetched two pots of water—bearing one on her head, and the other on her waist. He prayed to God to make his dream come true. But when he told his peers about his dream, they had laughed like crazy. So he didn't tell anyone again.

Although he maintained that medicine was his family profession, his main talent lay in marketing that virility lambative. We could almost say that this was his side profession. With what he got out of it, he not only took care of his brother, but graduated in law himself. This was really an achievement. But he was a man of many interests. He knew everything about every young boy and girl in the village—love, whoring, property, fights, friendships—he had detailed information about everything. Besides, he not only knew everything about the people in his village, but even knew some secret information about big people in the neighbouring villages, particularly all their shady secrets. Matchmakers always checked with him about girls and boys before proceeding any further. Kuntirapa's information was that trustworthy. Therefore he was known to, and wanted by, everybody.

The moment Kuntirapa came to Shivapura and entered the Gowda's house on the day of Vijayadashami, even as he began inquiring after sister Paroti's health, he found out a lot about Gowda's, as well as his family's, sickness. While finding out about Baramegowda's sickness, he also found out the village's sickness. Let's talk about the village's sickness later. As he pondered on some personal matters, Kuntirapa became certain about two things: if he wants the Gowda's property, he should marry Bagirti. If the dream of marrying Bagirti should come true, both sister Paroti and Baramegowda should remain living. Of the two,

Baramegowda's life was more important, Kuntirapa's smart mind decided. He set to work immediately. At the same time, he also made up his mind to break the pride of Chambasa who had gone to college, studied law and had a lot of influence on the villagers. This Chambasa might also have an eye on Baramegowda's property because the Gowda had no sons!

The same evening of his arrival, he went to see his mava Baramegowda who was in the House of Pleasure. The man who stood watch outside informed him that Baramegowda was discussing something confidential inside. Kuntirapa came to know that this man was Rameshi. Some time elapsed, and even as both of them stood outside, Gowda shouted from inside, 'You cunt!' Ramesha pushed the door saying, 'Master.' He entered the room. Kuntirapa stood outside and peeped in. He was shocked to see Baramegowda's state! It was a nauseating sight. Baramegowda was drooling copiously from the mouth. There were spit-marks all over the coloured walls. Inside, some woman was draping her sari back on. Kuntirapa now knew all the secrets his mava was sharing inside.

'Give that bitch some money and send her away, you cunt!' Gowda screamed and threw a ten-rupee note at Rameshi. The woman left without a word the moment she got the money. Her face was full of contempt.

After a long time, Gowda looked up. Kuntirapa stood in Rameshi's place.

'When did you come, Kuntirapa?'

'At noon.'

'How's everyone at your place?'

'Everybody's fine, with your blessings.'

Gowda thought Kuntirapa would leave after this phatic exchange. But Kuntirapa stood on.

'Did you want to say something to me?'

'Mava, Sir! I am not fit to talk in front of someone of your stature. But I still want to say a word…'

'What? Tell me.'

'I will say this because I too know a little bit about medicine. Have you seen the strings of a veena? When you pluck the string, you should know how much tension it can stand. Instead, if you think that because the veena is yours you can pluck it all you like, you know what happens? I needn't expand on that theme to someone like you.'

'What will happen?'

'It'll snap.'

Saying this, he bit his tongue as if he repented saying it.

'Mava, you've been managing everything—village headmanship, land, property and administration. Naturally, your body is very tired now. If you allow me, I'll give you a special medicine. Please take it for about a week. That's enough. Further, you will know what…'

Baramegowda was amazed by his brother-in-law's cleverness. 'His mother's…! How well he talks!' he thought and replied, 'I've heard of it. People talk about some lambative your father made. Are you talking about that?'

'Yes, many have found it effective.'

'Okay, I'll take it. Give it today.'

The moment he heard this, Kuntirapa thought that on this day of Vijayadashami, a festival of victory, he had crossed the border of his village to find a new kingdom. That day, his one-and-a-half leg didn't touch the ground. He seemed to be flying in the air. He got into such a state of devilish ecstasy that his whole body was striving to express this joy. He ran into the cattle shed. Thinking that there was no one there except the cows, he lifted both his arms up to the sky, kicked away in the air, jumped, danced and performed a series of other excessive acts. The cows stood with their ears perked up, and there was Rameshi in the corner behind the door, watching it all with his mouth wide open.

He gave the virility lambative to Baramegowda the same day. In a totally unexpected manner, Baramegowda's cheap lust increased and Kuntirapa's luck turned for the better— every second, every minute and each day.

Time was unkind to Paroti. Her health worsened day after day. The nearness to death was evident in the wrinkles on her face, the shivering hands, stammering speech and difficulty in walking. The husband and wife had taunted and wounded each other's souls. Her body was a ruined house, a fossil of lost youth, the relic of a bygone spring. It lay there stubbornly. Her sole concern was her daughter's future.

When Baramegowda came there, Paroti's body lay on a filthy bed. He noticed the long arm with a pronounced elbow lying next to her. Sparse and dry hair stuck to her forehead. Her corpse-like body was still alive. When she recognized Baramegowda, her eyes suddenly shone like the light of a lamp about to be extinguished. Some energy passed through her body. She tried to get up, lost her balance, and fell at the Gowda's feet. She held those feet, 'Gowda, I beg you. Please, I want to see my daughter married before I die. Get her married soon'

She clutched his feet. Gowda helped her up and slowly made her sit on the bed. He said, 'Okay, we will do it this year.'

'Now, now! We should do this now. If you want my blessing, get her married right now.'

'Okay...'

'Put your hand on mine and promise.'

When Baramegowda put his hand on hers and gently pressed it, Paroti leant on his chest and cried.

Devadasi's Love

Chambasa did his BA in Belagavi and returned to Shivapura. One day, Lasuma had gone to the forest, herding cattle as usual. Sharavva went with him. She made arrangements for Chambasa to know of it. Chambasa got her message, and he too went to the forest a little later. The cattle grazed near Nirvanappa's cave. Sharavva sat alone under the kino tree on the top of the hill. He went where she was sitting. Sharavva became animated. Her eyes shone. After exchanging a smile, he asked, 'Where is Lasuma?' 'The dark calf is lost. He went looking for it,' she replied. He sat next to her.

Memories of Suladhala, of smearing and getting smeared with turmeric, all those games they played—everything was still fresh in their minds. It was a while since they last met. Sharavva expected a lot from this meeting. She was surprised that he sat so quiet now. He hasn't even cast a sneaking look at me. Or is it that he is rough-mannered? A man of little speech? Not one who can laugh easily? After all, he is college-educated, always frowning, someone who doesn't care about other people's business, a lone tusker—this is his image in the minds of village girls. No girl in the untouchable neighbourhood has any other feelings for him except fear. Girls gossip that it is only with that old woman Tungavva and sister Bagirti that he speaks gently and like a human being. His physique too contributes to such ideas about him. He has grown rough and anyhow like a big kino tree. When he walked on the road with his long strides, he seemed to fill the roads. When he stood waiting, he looked like a leopard on the prowl. When he returned from Belagavi, he seemed to be attracted to my beauty. But today, when I am here at arm's length, he doesn't even cast a sidelong glance at me. Look at him sitting like a scorched stone in the sun! Or perhaps he thinks—compared to the girls in Belagavi college, what is she, this village bumpkin? Then why do I long for him to speak to me? What draws me to him?—she wondered. She was scared that if she went out of the way and initiated a conversation, he would think of her as a forward and cheap woman. On the other hand, if she didn't talk, he might think that she is haughty. Except for this one, no man in the village can sit next to me and neglect me like this, she decided.

Since they were on the hilltop, they could see nothing but the river Ghataprabha flowing faraway and the expanse of green beyond that. The jambul that Lasuma had promised her grew on the tree in Chalimele under the hill. But Chambasa wasn't even looking at any of these. Something was bothering him. He is a high-caste man, no doubt. But he grew up drinking Tungavva's milk. Sharavva had believed that he looked at all of them as his people. She had a soft spot for him because of this. Finally, she ventured, 'What are you looking at, Mava?' For a while, he didn't speak. Didn't even turn to look at her. Then he said, 'Look at the strange thing about men. And look at the stream. It doesn't think these are high-caste people and those others are untouchables. I should give water only to these people and not the others. It gives water to all alike. Look at the wind. Doesn't discriminate between anyone. It blows on everything the same way. Only men make these distinctions of high and low, and keep fighting with each other!' Sharavva didn't understand why he said this. Before the puzzled girl could even frown, he continued, 'Shari, I came to tell you something. I'll tell you that only if you promise you won't be angry.'

Ah, even the high-caste girls in the village are scared of him as if he were a tiger or something! He's such a tough guy. What could he want to say to me? Moreover, it seems he'll tell me whatever only if I promise not to get angry! Why should he worry about my anger? She felt a thrill inside her. She could hardly speak, but got highly curious. She hid all these feelings inside her, moved closer to him in an intimate manner, and then asked, 'Why should I be angry with you, Mava? Tell me that.' Chambasa turned to her and looked into her eyes. Even he could have heard the wild beating of her heart.

'Shari, there's no one as beautiful as you in this world. You look like a goddess, you evil woman!'

He said this and sat looking at her with singular concentration. His words brought a glow to her face. Dark curls played on her forehead, making her face look lovelier than ever. Time stood still, the forest seemed to be filled with a strange silence. Intoxicated by this joy, unaware of what she was doing, shaking her sweet face and curly hair, she said shyly, 'Go away, Mava! You say all sorts of things.' She hid her face in her hands. Chambasa felt her excitement. Hesitantly and softly, he put his left hand on her back. She didn't resist. Slowly, he pressed his chest to her back. The scent of her hair filled his nostrils. He felt a joy that was beyond the senses, out of this world, 'I'll ask you something. You shouldn't refuse me. Shall I ask?' She thought, 'God Shiva! Why does he struggle so much to ask what he wants to ask?' She asked again, 'What is it? Ask me, Mava.'

'If you say no?'

'I don't know what you want to ask. How can I say no to it?'

'Shari.'

He lifted her chin and asked, 'Will you marry me?'

Shari had a pleasant shock. No man until now had had the guts to ask her this question. Now this high-caste man had asked it! She realized that although he spoke calmly and slowly, his mind was filled with intense anxiety, agitation and confusion. Since she hadn't replied yet, he asked again, 'Tell me, Shari.' Shari moved away, and crying loudly, 'Mava, Mava,' hid her face in her hands and began to sob. He thought she was hesitating because of the caste business. He was uncertain about how to broach the matter now, but also curious about how she'd reply. Finally, taking courage into his hands, he called, 'Shari.' He couldn't speak. He cursed himself, and looking straight at the river, uttered the following words:

'Shari, I am telling you the truth. Until I saw you, I didn't know I was a human being. I became human only after I saw you. I felt pride in my humanness. Then I saw other human beings. I saw the bonds between them. There, in front of my eyes, was the green, the river, the sun and the moon. You are the goddess who showed all this to me. It is the fortune of many births! Please say yes, Shari,' he begged.

Unaware of what she was doing, she took his hand and striking her forehead with it, wailed, 'Mava, I am a devadasi.'

'I know that. Did you wish to be a devadasi?'

'No.'

'Then why did you let them tie the pearl around your neck?'

'My mother had taken a vow. I didn't see a way out.'

'Do you want to tear that pearl away and marry me now?'

For an instant, she weighed everything—the pain of responsibility, her love and the tragic consequences. She realized that although he hadn't talked with her much he was the only one in the world who understood her. The meaningful look in his eyes made her feel certain that he knew what was going on in her mind. She declared boldly, 'I will, if you marry me.'

Chambasa's eyes caught fire and shone. An uncontrollable joy made his voice sound awkward, like singing out of tune. But he didn't lose his courage. He shouted shrilly, 'Lord Nirvani, Shivalinga of the temple outside the village, you are too kind.'

Shedding happy tears, he lifted Shari like a child, held her arm and whispered: 'Shari, Shari.' Spring came into the forest and made it bloom instantly. It filled the forest with a thousand scents. Shari's happiness equalled his. She absorbed that spring into her body. She became that laugh, that love, and all those words of ecstasy. She gave a sidelong glance and observed him looking at her. She luxuriated in his love.

The next day, Chambasa came home and sat waiting for Lasuma. People who were in the cattle shed didn't know he was there. Inside, Tungavva was speaking to someone. He didn't know who that was. Tungavva was saying, 'You sly woman! What charm have you used on my son, you wench!'

Chambasa became alert. Her 'son' meant him of course! The one who was with Tungavva was Shari then.

'Why should I use any charm on your son, Mother! Who am I after all to think of big shots like him?'

'You minx! You had him smear turmeric on your chin on

that day at the wedding. You smeared turmeric on him too. Did you think I hadn't noticed?'

'Oh come on Aayi, everybody did that at the wedding. Why do you blow this up into something big?'

'Oh really? What about the day he brought your firewood bundle and left it in your front yard?'

'Avva! When, Aayi? You talk as if you were an eyewitness to this event! Don't lie like this,' she protested. Then, with a sense of thrill, added, 'Did mother tell you this?' she laughed like a flower, sprang up and ran away feeling shy. Chambasa was watching all this through the window. His excitement rose to a fever pitch now. His mind registered everything accurately—Shari's laugh, her shyness, the way she sprinted with a sidelong glance!

Shari came back suddenly, and pretending to be angry, warned Tungavva, 'Don't tell anyone such things, Aayi! There are many people in the village who don't like us.' She gave Tungavva a seemingly disapproving look and ran away again.

Shari and Chambasa's innocent love blossomed like a creeper of flowers. Time was young too. It soothed their burning daydreams. It filled those dreams with moonlight. It calmed their minds with cool breezes and made sure that it was always spring for them.

Before you could say 'ha', the news of their love spread all over the village. Nobody was surprised. 'He is the village Gowda. She is a devadasi. Who else can handle such a relationship except a rich man like Chambasa?' So said the high-caste people. He isn't an outsider to us. When Yamunavva herself thinks of him as a brother, and is thrilled about the whole thing, why should anybody else object? But everyone thought of it only as a relationship between a devadasi and her lover. Nobody even suspected that they would marry. Some who knew how fickle Baramegowda's mind was, felt a bit apprehensive about how he would react to this. But those who knew Chambasa's character, his aims and self-esteem, felt no fear of that sort. Even if he wasn't the village headman, Chambasa had all the dignity and pride of one. He was a responsible person. He grew up drinking Tungavva's milk. Yamunavva is like a daughter to Tungavva. They must have arranged it all among themselves, said others. But Kuntirapa became sleepless.

The moment he heard the news, he yearned to see Shari. Rameshi knew that she fetched water from the stream every morning. The very next morning, both sat waiting for Shari to come. Soon Rameshi patted Kuntirapa's back and signalled with his eyes that Shari was coming. God, God, look at this! One on the head and another on her waist— poising two water pots, really, poising two water pots—she comes! She comes to turn his childhood dream of a minx fetching two water pots into reality! Without blinking his eyes, wide-eyed, gaping, crazed, he watched her, the way she bore those pots, the manner in which she walked with her eyes fixed on the ground in front of her—he drank in the image. Kept looking at her until she disappeared. The moment she disappeared, he hugged Rameshi and declared, 'I found her Ramya, I found her!'

He hugged Rameshi again in the style of Sangya hugging his friend Balya in the popular folk-play *Sangya-Balya*.

'Whom did you find?'

'I found my dream!' He got up. Both walked home silently.

'The rest is your job,' said Kuntirapa.

'Okay,' said Rameshi.

Chambasa, Rameshi, Basya and Kuntirapa are all of the same age. Rameshi and Basya are Chambasa's schoolmates.

Their fathers are farmers who work for Baramegowda. So these boys had the same attitude towards Chambasa that their fathers had. Naturally, they now became Kuntirapa's followers. It is true that there were two factions among the farmers—Baramegowda's farmers and Chambasa's farmers. But even among farmers, you can't say that everybody accepted Baramegowda's ways. Even if they didn't talk about these things openly, they knew all the mischief he was up to. Although Baramegowda knew this about the farmers, he acted as if he didn't care. But Rameshi and Basya weren't like that. Basya's father had committed suicide because of debts. The son survived on some meagre government allowance. Rameshi, however, was totally loyal to Baramegowda and Kuntirapa and did what they asked him to do.

Rameshi is a lout. Flabby man with a bloated body. His small eyes looked lost in the abundant flesh of his face. He had no rules or morals to live by. God and religion didn't matter to him much either. He drank a whole vat of liquor. He never lost his senses however much he drank. Kuntirapa trusted only this man in the whole of Shivapura. Reason is clear. Rameshi is also a lech like him. Whether it is love, deceit, or some other matter of self-interest, their minds worked alike. Kuntirapa whored secretly. But he wasn't scared about people finding out either. Finally, Rameshi did get some happy news for Kuntirapa. Shari had come of age!

She Came of Age

Early in the morning, even as Chambasa was in bed, Yamunakka came and met his aunt. When she was leaving, she met Chambasa who was up by then. She looked at him with a broad smile on her face and said, 'Look how my brother's face is bursting with joy!' She snapped her knuckles to ward off the evil eye on Chambasa. Chambasa was puzzled. In a little while, his aunt called him, 'Chambasa, come in.' He went. She asked him to get a sari and a piece of cloth for making a blouse. Then she told him to bathe quickly. It was then that he came to know—Shari had come of age!

However personal the matter was, since this had to do with the age-old relationship between a devadasi and village headmanship, there was of course some disturbance in Baramegowda's vaade. Paroti didn't know the news. But Bagirti did, and she anxiously instructed the servants not to breathe a word to her mother. Her mind was a little relieved by hearing people gossip about Chambasa and Shari. She wanted to make sure. If they loved each other, she'd be proud of her brother after all! Since Baramegowda hadn't seen Shari, he didn't develop any interest in this matter. But Kuntirapa had seen her and salivated for her. He knew that if Baramegowda had seen her, he too would have acted like a bull with a flea biting his thigh. If Baramegowda gets enamoured of Shari, isn't it like taking revenge on

Chambasa? Can you find a better opportunity in life for my revenge? So he told the news to Baramegowda with great gusto.

But Baramegowda no longer had the same zeal for getting new girls. He couldn't find any pleasure in taming those struggling wenches under him, watching their animal-fear turn into pleasure, and feeling the thrill of a hunter. It's no wonder that he preferred the ripe pleasure he could get from compliant bodies. But this would be an overt affront to Chambasa's masculinity! He can never hold his head up again! To lose such an opportunity! Kuntirapa sorrowed over this. He tried hard. Gowda didn't get interested. In the end, he thought he should inflame the man's pride in his headmanship. 'Master, if devadasis strut about without showing respect to the Gowda's position, who will fear us anymore?' he asked.

Baramegowda scolded him: 'Hey cripple, times have changed, you idiot! District panchayat, taluk panchayat, reservation policy—such things have already loosened the older structure of village life! What golden age of the Vijayanagara Empire are you still living in? Where's your brain? Shut up and sit quiet.'

'At least let her touch your feet and get your blessing. Is this too much to ask?'

'Why? Do you have any extra stock of saris and blouses in the house? If you have to act the Gowda today, it is very different. It's not enough to shout at the watchman and the accountant. What you need is money, real money.'

But Kuntirapa didn't keep quiet. He told Gowda that the watchman had come to inform him about something and went out to fetch him.

Bagirti eavesdropped on all this. But she didn't want to tell her mother any of this. It would only make her more anxious. And Kuntirapa never learns a lesson. It's better to talk to Chambasa. In the meanwhile, Kuntirapa brought the watchman to Baramegowda.

A disinterested Baramegowda tried to act otherwise and asked, 'What man? It seems Yamunakka's daughter has come of age.'

'I don't know. If she had, wouldn't she have come here to get your blessings? She hasn't done that.'

'They may not come.'

'Che, che, how can you give up old customs?'

'Why don't you walk to the place and find out?' Kuntirapa ordered the watchman.

'Che, che, they should come with the child and ask her to fall at the master's feet. She will become pure only if she wears the clothes he gives.'

'Yes, but now reservation, village panchayat and things like that have come and changed our times completely, right? You cannot call a Dalit a Dalit these days,' said Kuntirapa. Kuntirapa's tone of pity and disappointment when he talked about the headmanship, and the way he was acting as if he was its champion, irked the Gowda.

'Hey cripple, will you be quiet? Or shall I kick your arse?' he shouted. Kuntirapa realized his error and signalled to the watchman to go. He left the place.

But Bagirti knew vaguely that according to the custom, a low-caste devadasi who comes of age should come to the Gowda. He should touch her on the first night. She hadn't known the disgusting facts hidden behind this custom until now. Now, she realized quickly that it was her father who had kept up this vile custom, that it was this that made him stray and made her mother upset. Then the charge that her brother 'kept' Shari must be false because it is only now that Shari has come of age. She was relieved that this gossip, which was spreading, was baseless. 'Whatever happens, my father shouldn't see Shari or give her that disgusting customary gift of sari and blouse.' She decided to prevent it. She also decided that since Kuntirapa was involved in all this with some selfish or evil motive, she must prevent him from becoming interested in it further. She made up her mind to go to Chambasa's house in answer to the invitation she got. In addition, she was also confident that if things got out of her control, her brother would support her. She told her mother that she was going to see her brother, and if possible bring him home, and left.

Chambasa's aunt was surprised and excited to see Bagirti come to her house. The old woman knew that the brother and sister had forgotten the enmity between the elders and were talking to each other. Bagirti looked around. Chambasa sat with a frowning face. The old woman asked Bagirti to sit and went in. Bagirti asked, 'Hasn't Tungavva come?' Chambasa pointed to the cattle shed and went out. When she went into the cattle shed, she found Tungavva's face swollen with crying. As Bagirti entered, she said, 'Please come in,' and stood up. Bagirti went to the place where she stood and sat on the hay stacks near the grazing platform.

'What Tungavva Aayi? Why is the whole house so glum?' she asked confidentially.

In answer to that Tungavva tapped on her forehead twice, sighed and said, 'What should I say, my child? I cut down on the milk I gave my own son and gave it to him. Now he has turned into my enemy.'

'What? Explain all this. You have taken care of him more than a mother can. You squeezed the milk out of your breasts for him and brought him up. How can he become your enemy? Tell me what's happening,' she scolded, and showing great generosity, moved closer to Tungavva.

Tungavva turned to Bagirti, 'My child, how can I say

this? Wasn't I like a sister to his dead mother? My niece Shari has come of age. Her mother has tied the jogti's pearl around her neck. So when the devadasi comes of age, who should present her with a sari? The village Gowda, your father, right? But your brother comes in the way, and tells me to tear the pearl off her neck and get her married.'

'Hasn't he said something that is only proper? Who makes their daughters devadasis in this day and age?'

'Yamunakka has made her that, right? Look, daughter, Yamunakka made a vow to the goddess and tied the pearl around her daughter's neck. All this is done already. It seems the Gowda is waiting for Shari. Let her go. If not, your father...well why talk of all that now?' Bagirti exploded with anger.

'Why, Aayi? Is there nobody responsible or respectable in this village? My father may be the village Gowda. But is he bigger than the elders?' Tungavva was astonished to hear Bagirti speak against her own father. But since she didn't want any contradiction, she consoled herself and spoke again.

'Daughter, if we tear the pearl away from Shari's neck, isn't it disrespectful to the goddess? I have brought him up like a son. Now can I sit quiet and see him do such things? You tell me.'

In the meantime, Namahshivaya and Chambasa came there. The moment Tungavva saw Namahshivaya, she frowned.

'What, Tungavva? I know the whole story. Even the devotees of Shiva, the sharanas, themselves say...'

'The words of the sharanas and the word of the goddess are two different things. Swami, please don't interfere in this matter.'

She said this firmly, saluted him and went out. Bagirti realized that she left because she was unable to face the

Swami. Bagirti noticed that Yamunakka and her daughter
had come some time back and were standing in the corner
with the cows. She felt bad. Immediately, she stretched her
arms and stood in the way of Tungavva saying, 'You want
to leave? Just listen to my final words before you do that.
Your niece has tied the pearl around her neck, right? She
has come of age too, okay? The Gowda should gift her with
the sari and the blouse? It is the same thing if my brother
does it or my father does it. Both are gowdas. Shari needn't
come to the Gowda's house. And let not my father's glad
eye fall on her. Let her wear the sari my brother gives her
and salute the God. What do you say to that?'

Right from Tungavva, everyone just shut their mouths,
heard what Bagirti had to say and felt highly relieved.
Namahshivaya perked up now. He admired her words, and
his eyes shone, 'Wonderful, my daughter! You untied this
problematic knot so easily! Tungavva, no one else can say
anything better than this. The goddess herself has made this
child speak. Accept it and be a good woman.'

Tungavva looked at Bagirti's face anxiously and became
mute. Chambasa looked at his sister Bagirti. His eyes shone
with admiration at how she had solved this problem. It was
like she'd used her finger nail to break open something that
couldn't be broken with an axe! The aunt went in, brought
the sari bundle which Chambasa had brought, put it in front
of him, went to Bagirti and told her, 'What a brilliant thing
you said!' She cracked her knuckles to ward off the evil
eye. Chambasa gifted a sari and blouse each to Tungavva,
Yamunakka and Shari. He saluted Tungavva, his aunt and
Namahshivaya. He took a couple more saris and went to
the Gowda's vaade. When he heard all this, Baramegowda
felt a sense of relief. But Kuntirapa was the one who became
restless. His heart was on fire.

Village Concerns

These days, there wasn't much strength left in Tungavva's body. She had an ache in the legs. She had exposed herself to the bitter cold this winter and now had knee pain too. This pain travelled all over her body and rose to her chest. When she felt this heaviness in her chest, she began moaning. She couldn't breathe properly. But she didn't talk of it. She thought, maybe Chambasa doesn't know. If he did, he would come back to her. But he had stopped talking to her. Lasuma too was heartless, she thought.

Meanwhile, an old woman in the neighbourhood died. Tungavva insisted on going there to have the last sight of the body. She walked there with the support of a stick. When she entered, the others made way and let her see the dead woman's face. Although her legs ached, she stood there and cried, 'Why didn't you take me along with you, mother who bore me?' She shed tears and returned. On her way back, she felt a sharp pain in her knees. Seeing her in this state, Lasuma came to hold her hand. She pushed him away. She rested all her weight on the stick, and taking small steps, tried to walk back. She almost collapsed when she reached home. Her daughter-in-law came out, held her hand, helped her to the kitchen stove, and made her sit near it. The burning cinders gave some warmth to her feet. She felt a little better. Then the daughter-in-law dipped a cloth in warm water with salt in it. She gave this warm compress to Tungavva's feet for a while. Tungavva felt some relief and cursed herself, 'Why didn't you die, Tungi?' Then she slowly crawled to the plate. She ate a couple of morsels of porridge made of navane rice along with the lentil soup her daughter-in-law gave her. She washed her hands, wiped her mouth and lay down right there. She slept soundly.

Tungavva dreamt that someone had hanged her upside down on the swaying nilgiri tree. She woke up screaming, 'Ayyo!' Then she complained, 'What sin have I committed, God? Shouldn't you at least hang me on a banyan tree? Why did you hang me on the nilgiri tree?' she wailed, and went back to bed. In the morning, when the cockerel crowed, she sat up suddenly asking, 'Is Chambasa calling me?' She had stopped talking to him. Why did she remember my brother again?—thought Lasuma, and went to Chambasa's house.

Sleepless birds had already begun making noises and rending the silence of the banyan tree and the sky. Tungavva's eyes were still full of sleep. But she sat up disturbed by her dream. Tungavva could hear Yamunakka singing as she milled something a little far away:

> He called her a rose, he said she's like the champak shoot
> Then that lucky lad went and held her! Chambasava—
> He got my daughter Shari

As usual Chambasa had a whole pot of tea made and brought it to her. Before she started to speak, he poured tea into a steel saucer and gave it to her. After she sipped the tea noisily and wiped her mouth with her seragu, he asked quietly, 'Why did you send for me, Mother?' Being angry with her, or not speaking to her for a while—these things didn't come in the way of his concern for her now.

'I saw a terrible dream, son! I felt like telling it to you. So I called you. Listen:

'A bare field of about two-and-a-half miles. Two-and-a-half miles in length, and two-and-a-half miles in breadth.

There was moonlight. In this moonlight, the smooth sand spread like a white carpet on the ground. Right there, flowed our stream. On the bank, there was a rock which looked a sleeping elephant. Even as I looked on, our stream filled with white smoke. Out of that smoke, look, there came a beautiful woman! Have you seen that face? Like the essence of moonlight. Silky hair fell on her shoulders. She turned aside and sat looking at her reflection in the water!

'Who is this spirit, this yakshi?

'Then there came this eunuch. When devadasis danced bearing a water pot, this eunuch danced bearing two water pots, my son! "Who is he? Tell me." "Her devotee." She smiled at him. He fell at her feet. The moment he did that, she hugged him tight, put her mouth to his throat, and sucked all the blood in him! This eunuch became empty, he went hugging anybody at all and sucking their blood in turn. She'd then come and suck all his blood again. This went on.

'You were standing there. He came to you to suck your blood. You ran and ran and ran…did you run forward? Or did you run backward?—can't say, but you ran and ran. I kept watching. Then I blacked out. When I opened my eyes again, I saw that somebody had hanged me upside down on the nilgiri tree! I had worn the talisman on my arm, so I was saved! You're sitting here. Otherwise, you'd be gone… and I'd be gone too...'

Chambasa was concerned. This certainly wasn't a good dream. He had realized that many of her dreams about village matters had some meaning. He asked, 'What is the meaning, Mother?'

'What else, son? You'll keep running forward and backward. I will keep hanging on the nilgiri tree. And the eunuch will keep sucking blood!'

Bagirti's Wedding

From the moment that prowling beast, Kuntirapa, saw the minx bearing two water pots, he had been melting like butter in front of fire. He cursed his luck because Shari's father was a farmer who worked for Chambasa. On top of it, Chambasa had come and given the ceremonial gift to Paroti and Bagirti. Then he had saluted Baramegowda. Gowda, according to the news Kuntirapa got, had embraced Chambasa and shed tears. Kuntirapa's nasty face blanched like paper. His lower jaw and cheeks twitched. He had never shivered like this before. He interpreted all these signs as predicting something terrible for him. He stood where he saw the minx with two pots and waited for that sight again. Sharavva didn't come to fetch water the whole week. He boiled with frustration. He sent word with Rameshi to Naga—Shari's father—to start working for Baramegowda and promised him some land. That just wasn't possible. Because Nagappa is Tungavva's brother. He and his wife Yamunakka are from Suladhala. Esuragowda's wife was also from Suladhala. They came here with Tungavva because of that relationship, and they bore that same loyalty towards Chambasa too.

However, the longing that Kuntirapa felt for Shari, the minx of his dreams who bore two water pots, didn't diminish. He began to see her everywhere. One day, when Shari went to fetch water, he sat all by himself on the platform there and watched her. His eyes filled with light, and his face became ecstatic. He looked at her feeling fascinated, joyful and also humble. Her body was not swaying. She walked upright and with a measured step. This time, she carried only one water pot. But he added another pot in his imagination. She was different from the other women, way more attractive than all of them. When she saw him, she bent her head. Her politeness, gentleness and beauty of form captured his heart. Those shy eyes and that magical smile! For once in his life, he felt vulnerable and moved by something higher than himself. He couldn't remember any other youthful experience like this. He got up, determined to get her.

Rameshi spied on Shari for three days to know her movements. He got information about when she would be alone. Finally, he told Kuntirapa, 'It'll work today!' Everybody knew that Kuntirapa would go to any shameless length in matters related to women. He fixed his evil gaze on Chambasa's house in the fields and went there.

In the scorching noon, the whole village, including the fields and forest, were calm. It is the time when man and beast try to find a cool corner and doze off. 'Shari is beautiful, but she is also a sturdy woman. She makes the mouths of connoisseurs like me water. She may be rough and hardy. So what, can she try to be rough with Erapanagowda? Not one, but if I throw a couple of notes at her, won't she come dancing to me, calling me 'mava'? These were his conjectures as he walked into the front yard of Chambasa's house. At the same instant, Shari came to the door. He looked at her breasts. They seemed to pierce his eyes like pointed arrows. Kuntirapa stood smiling at her.

He had come at an unusual moment. Like Rameshi had told him, Lasuma had gone to the forest. Nagappa was in another field. There was nobody around. Aware of this, he walked up stealthily to Shari and asked, 'Who's this? Shari?' Shari was surprised.

'Erapanagowda, who hardly visits here, has come today. Please come in. Lasuma isn't in.'

'You are here. That'll do.'

Saying this, and smiling as attractively as possible, he sat on the platform near the door. Sharavva's shyness was replaced by anxiety. Like all the girls in the village, Sharavva too had some fear of Kuntirapa. She felt an inward shiver. As a precaution—that is, to prevent him from coming inside, and if he did, to be able to run out of the house herself—she stood a little away from the door and talked. Kuntirapa isn't so dumb that he can't understand this. Seeing the anxiety on her face, he moved towards the door and asked:

'Won't it be better if I sit inside?'

'Inside smells of cow dung. It's very hot too. Sit comfortably here.'

'Nothing really. But if I sit here what if someone sees me and talks about it?'

'We aren't doing anything for people to talk about, are we?'

'No, but still these village people are always waiting to badmouth someone.'

'Why? Would you do anything foul for people to badmouth?' She said this to bring out some goodness in him.

'Ah, a clever woman! If I can't even take her in with my words, can I take her physically? All right, this devadasi doesn't know Erapanagowda's strength yet,' he thought. He pulled two hundred-rupee notes out of his pocket and held them before her, saying: 'I heard you came of age. Buy a sari or something.'

Shari was sweating with fear. Everything around her seemed to spin. Unprotected and despairing, she folded her trembling hands and told him, 'No, I don't want it.' She moved further away from him. Her face shone in the yellow sun. She turned round and wondered loudly, 'Why hasn't my father come back yet?'

Immediately, Kuntirapa knelt in front of her. With folded hands, and in a humble manner, he opened up every corner of his soul to her: 'Shari, a man should fear either death or God. I'm not scared of death, but I fear God. Because God created all of us. I will swear on his name. I love you. If I can get your love, I will give up all my evil ways. I will do whatever you ask me to do. Come with me. Both of us will leave this village and go wherever. These words are hundred percent true.'

'What do I care about your truth or lies? I am a jogti. Whatever I had, I gave all that to my mava already. My body is a pot he has drunk out of. Honestly, I don't know what is there in this pot called my body now. But my soul sits like a parrot at the centre of his palm. Why do you want such a pot that he has drunk the milk from?' She started to go towards the corn fields. Kuntirapa held her suddenly and tried to bite her cheek. She freed herself from his hands and shouted, 'Appa, where are you?' Then she turned back and stood in front of him like an unsheathed sword and screamed, 'Useless pimp!' Kuntirapa stepped back like a beaten leopard. In another half-second, he was on her. He pounced without giving her another chance to scream, and gathering all his strength together, closed her mouth with one of his hands and with the other held her around the waist so that she couldn't move. Mad with fury, Sharavva tried to bite his hand which was over her mouth. She tried to kick him. She tried to scream with all the hatred and hurt pride inside her. He closed her mouth again. It seemed like her heart was going to burst. He too had blanched and was a little disturbed by her unexpected strength. He tried to hold her more forcefully and control her. God knows where she got more strength from! The moment his grip on her left hand loosened a bit, she pushed Kuntirapa, who was holding her and standing behind, with her elbow. His front teeth broke, and he began to bleed profusely from the mouth. His shirt was soaked with blood. He let her go shouting, 'You bitch!' Immediately, Shari screamed, 'Lasimya,' and kicked him. When Kuntirapa lost his balance and fell on the stony ground, she ran into the house and bolted the door from inside.

Kuntirapa was trembling with helplessness, hatred and fury. He blacked out for a bit. His face went green, bloody and ghastly. Soon, he became aware of flowing blood, of defeat, shame and disappointment. He got up in a hurry and limped away into the corn field. Rameshi, who stood watching all this secretly, came out quietly, picked up both the hundred-rupee notes and vanished.

Tungavva was the first to know about Kuntirapa's taunting of Sharavva. Instantly, she ordered both Sharavva and Yamunakka not to tell anyone, including son Lasuma, about this. But she indicated something about this to Bagirti. As Bagirti could guess, Tungavva's fear was only natural. If all this comes out, there's bound to be some disaster or the other. What if Baramegowda, who had got many people killed, listened to Kuntirapa's tales and got Chambasa also killed? When it is bad enough dealing with Kuntirapa, how can you manage two violent people like Kuntirapa and Baramegowda together? In addition, Tungavva also feared something else. If Chambasa came to know of this, he would break Kuntirapa's other leg too. She wished

Chambasa didn't have anything to do with Shari because Kuntirapa had cast his eyes on her. Shari was of a lower caste. But Bagirti appreciated Shari's pure friendship. She certainly didn't have the heart to separate the lovers. She couldn't even imagine something like that.

The same night, Shari's father Naga went to Baramegowda and complained about Kuntirapa. Gowda consoled him, asked him not to tell anyone about this, and sent him back. He went home, and making sure that neither Paroti nor Bagirti knew of the matter, told them that the auspicious time for marriage had come. Paroti was happy. She got up from bed and thanked God: 'Shivalinga, you gave my husband some wisdom at last!' She took her husband's hand and touched it to her forehead respectfully.

After all, they didn't have to go looking for a bridegroom. No elaborate preparations were needed. Besides, there was the fear that Paroti might die anytime. So, within a week, they found some auspicious time for this and got the wedding done.

Mr Baramegowda and Mrs Paroti's daughter Ms Bagirti was married to Mr Erappanna (BA, LLB) in a grand ceremony.

Mallimadu Is Polluted

True, Kuntirapa wasn't born rich. But once the marriage got him into Baramegowda's fold, his dreams of wealth began to soar high. He thought people would also fear and respect him for his wealth someday and started imitating Baramegowda in everything he did. He hid his real feelings and pretended love on the outside. But Bagirti's doubts about and mistrust in Kuntirapa only kept increasing. If he was at home, she always kept an eye on him. Kuntirapa began to feel that she even slept with one eye open. Going into his room suddenly, opening any cabinet of his she liked and examining it thoroughly, watching his movements, eavesdropping on his talk—all these had become habitual to Bagirti. She also suspected that this man, who took her father to the House of Pleasure, pimped for him.

If Chambasa talked to Bagirti, or gave her some fruit, Kuntirapa's eyes would fill with deep contempt. He would listen to their conversation on the sly. He would look at them as if Chambasa was his enemy. Bagirti suspected Kuntirapa of telling tales on Chambasa to her father. She wanted to give the right information about Chambasa to her father. But he only met with, and relied on, Kuntirapa all the time.

There was another problem. Although Bagirti was not the minx fetching two water pots, her financial prospects were unparalleled by that of any other woman in the village. But Kuntirapa could never understand her mind. Was she angry? In a laughing mood? Anxious, agitated? And what pleases her? Or annoys her? He didn't know anything. On the other hand, Bagirti too was confused. Whispering things in her father's ears, moving away when he saw her, or speaking in hushed tones—the young girl didn't like all these. Kuntirapa was someone who had found success by spying on people. If it was only this, it wouldn't have been so bad. He was eavesdropping on Bagirti's every conversation. Her doubts about him became stronger.

Paroti, on the other hand, trusted Kuntirapa beyond words. He was a sibling, and there was a blood-bond between them. 'My brother is like a field rabbit, very mild and gentle. Husband Baramegowda is a fickle-minded fellow. All he wants is a bellyful of food and some woman in bed. He forgets everything else. Then, let alone a daughter, he even forgets my existence.' Paroti became worried about her daughter's future again. She believed that her daughter needed Kuntirapa's protection evermore.

One evening, the Gowda sent for Kuntirapa. Kuntirapa went to the House of Pleasure and stood there. He didn't know why he was called there. Gowda's sight had already become blurry with drink. He stood in a corner and said, 'I salute you, Mava.' Gowda looked up kindly. When he realized it was Erapa, he smiled. His eyes became a little brighter, 'Hey, cripple!'

'Mava? Sir?'

'What do you think of Talati?'

Kuntirapa was surprised, shocked and scared. The friendship between Gowda and Talati is known to all. Nobody could complain or tell on one to the other. In this context—if Gowda asks him this question! Or is it some test for me? He asked again, 'Mava? Sir?' and stood on. After a while, Gowda raised his eyes with difficulty and ordered, 'Tomorrow, you too go with Talati to Belagavi.'

'Okay, Mava.'

He said this, folded his hands and stood there. Meanwhile, there was someone outside. A woman who stepped inside saw Kuntirapa and pulled her foot back instantly. When Gowda signalled to him to leave, he got ready to descend the steps and vanish. Then he noticed Talati standing outside the House of Pleasure. He saluted Talati and disappeared into the dark. But he didn't go away. He hid somewhere close by and watched Talati. Talati wasn't aware of this.

As Baramegowda had instructed him, Kuntirapa went with Talati to Belagavi and returned. With his great business acumen and shrewdness, he collected a lot of information from the revenue officer himself without Talati's knowledge and stored it in his mind. Later without the knowledge of the revenue officer, he went and met the district collector and found out that man's weak spot. The DC's name was Bhimesh. Poor man. Also greedy. Someone from a village near Bangalore. He had come here. Has wife and children. He secretly nourished the dream of becoming a rich man. He strongly believed that he could fulfill this desire only through conniving, being pretentious and cheating others. He hid these evil tendencies with an effort. He boasted that the chief minister was his buddy, and they addressed each other in familiar terms. In order to show what a harsh and uncompromising officer he was, he scolded the officials under him, addressed them in disrespectful singular terms, and shouted at them frequently. Kuntirapa talked to the DC personally, in his own language, and as if he had read the man's mind in his left palm. He found out a few useful secrets from the DC.

The day after returning from Belagavi, he took Talati to Mallimadu and inspected the place thoroughly. Now there weren't much rains. Water didn't flow down the hill. Nor was the flood water there. So Mallimadu was not full like it used to be earlier. Except the large dip in the middle, most of it was dry. He found out that this was Balavanta's land, and that he was a farmer working for the Gowda.

He gave a generous tip to Talati and went to the House of Pleasure, brimming with self-confidence!

The Gowda sat leaning back on a large chair and enjoying a cigarette. There was nobody around. Kuntirapa realized that Gowda was absorbed in something and looked happy. He went in. He took out the whiskey bottle from his bag and put it in front of the Gowda. Gowda took the bottle quickly, checked the label, found that it was 'foreign' and beamed at Kuntirapa.

'What is this, cripple?' he asked with a mix of familiarity, affection and pride in his son-in-law.

'Friends gave it,' Kuntirapa grinned and added, 'please open it yourself.' He put the bottle in Gowda's hand. By this, he indicated that he actually had friends who visited America and got him this stuff from there. Gowda opened the lid and smelled it deeply and noisily. Kuntirapa brought a glass, and pouring the whiskey, told him, 'It seems even the President of America drinks the same brand of whiskey.'

He gave it to Gowda. Tasting it, Gowda said, 'I am sure the President drinks this. It is really strong stuff.' He felt blissful and looked at his son-in-law with a sense of gratitude and pride in him. He closed his eyes.

'Mava, you should stand for the elections this time.' Hearing this, the Gowda got up like he had seen a nightmare, and looking at Kuntirapa wide-eyed, demanded, 'What?' Kuntirapa stood looming over him. He advised the

Gowda: there's nobody as popular as you are in these parts. Important party members will be here soon to make you stand for the elections. Wealthy people are waiting to come and meet you. They will make you win. You won't get a chance like this again. You shouldn't refuse. He said all this, and without giving an opportunity to the Gowda to say anything, he vanished dramatically. Still with his eyes and mouth wide open, Baramegowda sat there looking stunned.

First Night

But Bagirti was restless like a child lost in a forest. After the wedding, when all relatives and friends had left, she came to her room alone and shut the door. She sighed as if she had escaped from a noisy village fair and entered a serene place at last. It had seemed like what ought to have happened in two years' time was all packed into these two weeks. She was shocked. She was a victim, but couldn't protest. She had accepted everything. Now she held her head in her hands and sat feeling desperate. True, I remained silent whenever Mother broached the subject of my marriage. Of course, I pitied my mother a lot. It is also true that my father's devilish nature and his neglect of Mother were responsible for all this. Despite all these truths, what is the specific reason for my accepting this marriage? She found no reasonable answer to this question. She realized that she was to blame for it all. She had embraced the victimhood voluntarily. She felt ashamed of herself and struck her head. She lost her willpower and self-confidence. Didn't I always feel that Kuntirapa wasn't a fit bridegroom for me in any way? Why didn't I tell this to Mother?

He came and told me that he'd give me everything he had. What arrogance! Did I ask him to give me anything? When this beggar told me this as if he was going to offer me a kingdom, didn't I remain silent? She remembered that and felt mortified. She choked with pain and a sense of shame.

He came on his own to talk to her. He'd keep moving around Mother's bed always. He said, 'I'll give her the medicine I brought for her.' When I thrust the tablets into his hands and went into the kitchen, or when I looked at Mother's face feeling confused, she always told her brother, 'The child is shy, brother Erapa.' Did he conveniently think that it was a form of 'yes' from my side and revel in it? My agitation increased. But I had nobody to share this with. Father alienated Chambasa. Chambasa came to the wedding without an invitation. Father insulted him and didn't even bother to talk to him then. He is forever busy with his debaucheries. Always restless like an old bull infested with fleas. If I try to tell him something, he doesn't listen. He is lost in some calculation of his own, some dialogue with himself. It is always the soliloquy mode with him.

A childhood photograph of hers was hanging next to the mirror. She felt a constriction in her throat. Mother used to say that I am restless like the wind. Those days I dreamt beautiful dreams. In those dreams, a handsome prince from Bangalore came, presented her with a bouquet, and took her away in his car! Where is he? What a difference between him and this cripple!

Two wedding invites lay on the table. When she took them and flung them into the still burning stove, they burned like straw. Two bunches of flowers and their two names on the invitations got burnt, charred, and the black ash blew away. Now she sat facing the wall and cursing herself for the injustice that had happened to her.

On the evening of the first night, Kuntirapa had gone to the House of Pleasure. She stealthily went to his cabinet and searched inside. There was a bag of personal belongings. She poured the contents on the table. A shirt, shorts, comb and a notebook—just as she thought there was nothing else, she noticed two bones at the bottom of the bag! If she tried to ask him, he'd know that she had checked his personal belongings. She decided to ask in an indirect manner, and put the bones carefully back into the bag. She opened the notebook to see what it contained—with a small hope that he might have written a love letter to her. It was full of sketches—of bones! She turned the pages. More pictures of bones. For about twenty pages there were pictures of bones, bones of a variety of sizes and shapes. Arm bones, leg bones, and on one page, there was a picture of a skull too! Alarmed, she shut the book quickly, stuffed everything that she had taken out of the bag, put the bag back in the cabinet like it was before and came out.

She sat musing, supporting her chin with her hand. It was impossible to get the images of bones off her mind! She tried to look at other things around the place to forget the bones. Didn't work. She got up and came out. Although she didn't want to talk to him, she was determined to ask him about this. She called the servant Lagimi and started asking all sorts of irrelevant questions like, have you milked the cow, did the calf get the udder, and so on. A surprised, and totally confused, Lagimi stood there. She screwed her eyes and answered all of Bagirti's questions with one word, 'Avva, Avva.' Bagirti felt weary of her own questions. She came in. When the bones didn't go away from her mind, she thought: 'Is he a black magic guy? There's that thing they use to enthral someone? Some spell? Is he into that business? I must ask him today.' She was determined.

Paroti had been waiting for this moment in her daughter's life, and she was dying. Bagirti couldn't disappoint her. She waited in the room that was arranged for the first-night ritual. Although everything was neat and tidy, she upset the clothes and things. Then she began to rearrange them. But her attention was on the door. It wasn't fully shut. Hearing the footsteps of her husband and master, she glared at the door. She was scared of him. She was trying to hide it. When it seemed like she was done with arranging things, she pulled out everything again and began rearranging them. But even that got over too soon. She set everything aside. Suddenly, she realized that he had come in. She sat with her back to the door. She, too, was scared about the first night. Anxious. Finally, not knowing what to do, she stood up. In her transparent, black Chandrakali sari, Bagirti looked adorable, like the moon amidst dark clouds. Her tender arms, decorated with many bangles, looked very attractive. It seemed like love, joy and élan oozed out of her body.

She thought he would come to her humbly, with a trembling voice, and try to win her over with sweet words. She turned a little and saw him standing there. He was trying to hide his excitement and eagerness. He looked anxious too. She said to herself, 'Oh God, he is standing like nothing has happened, and this is like any other day. Am I out of my mind?' She pitied herself and sat with her back to him.

Kuntirapa was watching the subtle changes in her body language. He was trying to understand her shyness and hesitation. She wasn't the minx with two water pots. But she was an extraordinarily attractive girl. He understood her new behaviour. This one is smart, beautiful and fetching... above all, someone who is frank. She knows no deception. Of course she has a little pride because she is rich. A little intoxicated with her youth. Also some vanity about her looks, he thought as he inched towards her. Gently and breezily, he put his hand on her shoulder. Bagirti shivered, bent her head, and turned a little. In her profile that was visible, there was a special kind of beauty, not found in any other woman he had seen. With a tremor in his voice, he pressed his lips to her shoulder. Her warm sweat had a sharp, but endearing, fragrance about it. He found it heady. Wanting to show off his knowledge of women, he brought in some drama and a lot of excitement into his behaviour. Calling her, 'Bagirti, my love', he began to play. As he played, he lost his balance and fell. The kind of accident he was desperately hoping wouldn't happen on his first night had actually happened. If he fell, he would have to put in a lot of effort to get up. Even if he attempted to use both hands and one leg to raise himself up, he still needed the help of his left leg. Kuntirapa himself knew how ridiculous he looked when he tried to raise himself in this manner. He felt embarrassed. In order to find some balance, he tried to hold her left leg. In the process, he pulled the pleats of her sari, and it came off. This unexpected thing scared Bagirti. She kicked — to defend herself. She had actually kicked his face. The moment Kuntirapa saw her bare leg, he felt a raging lust. His body was aflame. Then he tried to hold her other foot, she kicked him with that too. Reading the gamut of emotions on her face, he pulled her leg so that she too fell on him. When she fell, he embraced her hard and kissed all over her face. He knew that her body was like a musical instrument that couldn't be tuned at once. He became a hungry animal. He conquered her with the cunning and the alacrity of a leopard. At every turn and toss, he rolled and whined like a dog, uttered disconnected words, muttered and exclaimed. Finally, at the climax when he screamed, her body vibrated like the shrill and aching string of a sarod. He collapsed on her like a tree felled at the base.

Paroti heard this, and smilingly addressed God, 'Your compassion is great, Shivalinga, Father, Lord.' She filled her eyes with dreams of seven grandsons, and then closed them.

She didn't open her eyes again. After performing her final rites, both father-in-law and son-in-law went to Bangalore.

PART TWO

Village Concerns Again

Meanwhile, new water had flowed into Ghataprabha and it didn't remain the same river anymore. Chambasa, who came from the city, and Baramegowda, who had been in the village, had both observed this. The law, 'Land for the Tiller', came into force. Chambasa and his uncle, Rajappa Gowda, got together, and excluding Chambasa's sixty acres of land, gave away the rest of the land to those who were tilling them. They duly registered the land in the names of those farmers. On that day, Chambasa also gave a short speech. He thanked all those who had tilled his land with great loyalty until then, and said: 'You too have become land-owners now. Please don't sell this land to anyone from outside the village.' The farmers became very emotional and promised that they wouldn't. They vowed in the name of God that their friendship and bonds would always remain the same.

But Baramegowda didn't show the same generosity. Besides, he gossiped with others that Chambasa distributing the land without even informing him was like betraying his clan. Since it was no go, he said he too would follow the law. He pretended to give some barren land full of stone and rocks to two farmers who were on his side. He had the documents altered to show that the other farmers were only his labourers. When both Baramegowda and Kuntirapa had gone out of the village, some discontented farmers gathered together and thought of going to court. When they were planning this, they came to know that there wasn't a single document which said the land was in their names!

Of these farmers, six were those who had murdered people at the Gowda's behest. They kept quiet because they were scared that a murder case might be filed against them. Although they paid taxes every year, the papers were all in Gowda's name. They squirmed like worms in a fire when they heard all this.

Among the farmers who were murderers, four were Dalits and two high castes. They argued that at least they should get the land. The Gowda had given them land when he wanted them to kill other farmers who opposed him. Now he was taking those lands away. When they wailed that this was injustice, he promised, 'I will give the land after the elections.' When they showed some distrust in his words, he warned: 'Many murder cases are still not over. If they get re-opened who knows what will happen!' These foolish farmers realized now that they had been cheated. They struck their foreheads with their hands, regretted what they'd done and then kept quiet.

But now the Dalit neighbourhood had acquired a new identity. If someone asked, 'What happens to our values in these bad days?' there were brave Dalit boys who'd come forward and say: 'Why? Aren't we here to take care of them?' They had become aware of their rights. They asserted the power the law gave them. Not only getting reservations, but shaping their lives and moving towards a better future, were all a part of their agenda.

These days, Chambasa and Namahshivaya arranged some event or the other under the banyan tree every evening. All through the sravana month, Namahshivaya read the *Basavapurana*. Chambasa supplied the Petromax light. People who worked in the fields until evening came there to rest and listen to these holy books. When there were no readings, they'd just gather there and talk. This became the routine especially for the Dalit men. Scenes of drinking and drunken fights decreased considerably. Addicts went to the liquor shop, drank a bit, and went back to their nests.

But the village was rather disturbed. The high-caste set of Baramegowda seemed to own everything—village panchayat, village eldership, much of the land and also a lot of wealth! Then there was the group of farmers who worked for Chambasa. They were disinterested in politics and power. Chambasa himself didn't bother about such things. God knows how many years had passed since the five-year term of Baramegowda's headmanship had ended. Anytime he wanted, Chambasa could have gone and asked for the headmanship. He didn't crave for it. In fact, he had written to the government that he didn't want it. As a result, Baramegowda turned into an autocrat. At the same time, he also shed his hatred of Chambasa and felt particularly happy when Chambasa talked to Bagirti. Apart from these two factions, there is a new mind that has surfaced in the village. This is the third set. The set of the murderers.

They remained labourers. There was nobody to listen to their discontents. Baramegowda neglected them now. As the proverb goes, 'Once you cross the stream, you shrug off the boatman like you shrug off an old paramour!' All these days, he had silenced them by threats of murder cases. The four Dalits in this set went to seek the help of the Ambedkar Association in Belagavi.

One day, when Namahshivaya was reading the holy books under the banyan tree, these four farmers, along with three from Belagavi, came, put a chair there, placed Ambedkar's photo on it, garlanded and saluted it. People sat quietly. Namahshivaya and Chambasa also sat quietly. In the still assembly, the Belagavi man folded his hands and saluted all. Then he began: 'Today is Ambedkar Jayanti. I want to say a couple of words about his achievements. Please give me the opportunity to do so.' Namahshivaya Swami agreed happily. Not only did he let the Belagavi man speak, he too gave a short and wonderful speech about Ambedkar. The Dalits were extremely happy that day. Chambasa too participated in their joy and also gave a brief speech on what he knew about Ambedkar. The Ambedkar Association people talked in a very effective manner about the condition of the Dalits in the country and the oppression they were subjected to. They also mentioned how, even in Shivapura, Dalits were not allowed to fetch water from the big well with the six-wheel pulley. People looked at each other.

The news spread like an epidemic even before you could say 'ha'. It made the cold breath of people grow warm. From that day, the villagers began to see these four men differently. The villagers kind of kept a watch over their activities. Even when they talked to these four, they did it with a kind of self-consciousness. But Rameshi turned this news into many stories and told them to Kuntirapa.

Marriage

After his BA exams, Chambasa decided that he had enough education and settled down in the village. Rajappa Gowda, his maternal uncle from Suladhala, gave him advice and information on how to manage his property, house and lands. He gave him the keys of responsibility and instructed: 'If anything goes wrong, send word for me.'

'Look Chambasava, you are grown up now. You did your BA. But you don't need to do a job. All you need to do is take care of your land. I have kept the papers of your property and land in the cabinet. I have given you the key. If we get you married, your aunt and I will feel like we're free of all our responsibilities. We will go to Davanagere and look for a bride. Let's talk more after we return.'

He set off. Chambasa told him, 'Uncle, what's the urgency about my marriage? Give me some time. I'll let you know when I want to marry. Then we can look for a bride. What do you say, Aunt?'

'Why? Have you found someone?'

'No. But why this hurry? I have just come here after my exams. The results are not out yet. Let me get the exam results first. Let's see about marriage later.'

Rajappa thought for a while and said, 'I think you are right.'

'Ayyo, do people who want to marry come skipping and ask for it? He probably feels shy about it. You go, look for the bride now,' said his wife, Akku Taayi. Rajappa left, laughing.

Tungavva was going to get her son married this year. She had even looked for a bride in Suladhala, her maternal village, and come back after deciding on things. But there was some disquiet in her mind. Chambasa and Lasuma had grown up together like Rama and Lakshmana of Ramayana. It would be so nice if they could also get married on the same day. This was Tungavva's desire. But Chambasa wasn't ready for marriage. She knew that his uncle Rajappa Gowda was searching a bride for his nephew. She also knew he'd told his uncle that he wouldn't get married that year. She decided to discuss the matter with Chambasa's aunt, Akku Taayi. She came to Chambasa's house one day at a late hour. She had also sent word for Bagirti to come.

Tungavva sat at the main door on the porch, Akku Taayi sat on a wooden three-seater there. They began with routine conversation about household matters. Bagirti too came and joined them. She immediately asked: 'What, Aayi? Why are you sitting on the floor? Can't you sit on the gunny sack?'

Tungavva didn't move. She answered, 'I am comfortable on the floor.'

In the course of the conversation, Akku Taayi asked Tungavva: 'I heard you're getting your son married this year?'

'Yes, Avva. That's exactly what I came here to talk about. Why don't you get Chambasa too married this year?'

'He said not this year.'

'Look, we should always manure the plants at the right time. If that time is past, what's the use of doing it?'

Bagirti piped in, 'You are his mother. Why don't you tell him?' Even as she was saying this, Chambasa came out of his room. He was trying to wear a shirt.

'Some meeting is going on here. What's it, Sister?'

'Tungavva is getting her son married this year. I asked, "Won't you get your other son married too, Aayi?"' She said you had refused. Tell me why.'

Bagirti asked him directly.

'Look, Sister, you don't like the girl I like. I don't like the girl you like. In these circumstances, how can marriage happen?'

Now Akku Taayi didn't keep quiet.

'Ayya, what's this you are saying? When your uncle asked you if you had some girl in mind, you kept quiet.'

'Okay. Now aunt is asking you. Tell me which Belagavi beauty have you fallen in love with? I will get you married to her,' Bagirti said, as if she was going to take charge of the whole thing.

'I'll tell you. Will you make my aunt and Tungavva agree to it?' asked Chambasa.

'Oh, did you think they are your enemies? They'll agree with joy. Tell me who she is, Brother.'

'Later if you say you can't?'

'I am going to keep my word, right!'

'Okay, listen,' he looked at Tungavva and Akku Taayi's faces. Akku Taayi seemed curious, but Tungavva had gone pale with fear. 'Look, she has blanched like a sheet of white paper.'

'Ayya, I asked you to tell me the girl's name. Why are you talking about something else?' asked Bagirti, feeling weary.

'Then listen. I'm telling you because you asked. The one who must give me the bride and bless us is this Tungavva. The girl I like is Shari. Ask her if she will get her niece married to me.'

He stood looking at Tungavva. All three were shocked.

They looked at each other in consternation. They all knew one thing: it is useless to try to change his mind. He won't give up. He won't change his mind. Tungavva knew this. Tears welled up in her eyes. Chambasa pounced on her, 'Look, look! See how her face looks like the face of a new corpse.'

'Should I laugh when I hear such things?' she asked, hid her face with her hands, and started weeping hard.

'What's it you're saying, Brother? Who will accept your marrying someone not your caste? Will they let you remain in their caste after that? They will throw you out of the village. You wait and watch.'

'Then listen. Sister Bagirti, you too listen…if you want to get me married, get me married to Shari. If not, I shan't marry ever. I will become a monk. This is my last word. Please don't talk with me about anything else.'

He said this and was about to leave. Tungavva taunted: 'If it was only a matter of marrying outside caste, maybe I'd have agreed. But this is like standing against the goddess, son. Shari has tied a pearl around her neck.'

'Why do you bring up the name of the goddess after every word? Are you trying to scare me with that? Does your goddess tell you, "Don't get your daughter married. Make her a whore"? Sister, does any goddess say such a thing? You are Shari's aunt. You should come forward to get her married. Instead, you say that you'll send her to the whorehouse. Are you really an aunt? A mother? You're a monster! You made a mistake by tying that pearl around her neck. Will you set it right now or not? What do you say, Sister?'

Bagirti too remained silent and sat looking at the faces of Tungavva and Akku Taayi. A weary Chambasa went out saying, 'You aren't a mother. A monster. Monster!' Tungavva hid her face with her hands and sat still.

When Chambasa told Bagirti of his intention of marrying Shari, Bagirti was very confused. You know why? She'd heard the story of Kuntirapa taunting Shari and getting his teeth broken. But looks like Chambasa hasn't heard this story. After the episode, Shari had come crying to her mother Yamunakka and told her everything. Then Yamunakka took Tungavva home and informed her about this. The first thing Tungavva did was to make sure that this matter didn't go out to others. She instructed them not to tell even her son Laguma. Bagirti understood Tungavva's fear. Baramegowda had got many people murdered. Kuntirapa was a worse sort. He might get Chambasa killed if Chambasa married the woman he was eyeing. Bagirti was also afraid of something else...if Chambasa came to know that Kuntirapa had tried to mess with Shari, he'd break Kuntirapa's other leg too. Yet she didn't want injustice to happen to her close friend Shari. Yamunakka loved, and was proud of, Chambasa whom she looked on as her brother. She wanted her daughter to be his lover. But she too wouldn't agree to this marriage. Bagirti couldn't imagine Chambasa and Shari moving apart. She valued Sharavva's pure friendship. At the time of her marriage, she had sent baagina saris and blouses to Tungavva, Yamunakka and Shari without her father's knowledge. Chambasa too had gone to Bagirti's marriage and given a baagina to Paroti and Bagirti. As anyone could guess, Kuntirapa hadn't liked it. He was scared that at some point Chambasa would win Baramegowda's heart and take away all the property.

Without taking things to heart, Chambasa took care of Lasuma's marriage celebration. He made sure that all the rituals of the Dalit caste were performed correctly. He got two sheep for the special meal they give to the bride's people. They had splendid meat fare. He gave generous gifts to the bride's people and other relations. Such a grand marriage had never taken place among the Dalits in the past, and perhaps wouldn't take place in the future. He brought the bride and bridegroom together, then went home and slept peacefully. But he had not even looked at, or talked to, Tungavva the whole time. Tungavva had tried to attract Chambasa's attention. She called him, asked him something, tried to give him something—whatever, he hadn't responded. He spent money, got his brother married, and without telling even Shari, went home. The so-called father of Lasuma, Baramegowda, didn't even appear on the scene of marriage.

Panchami

Then came Panchami. Chambasa was still not talking to Tungavva. Yesterday, they'd seen each other. Before they could make eye contact, Chambasa had carefully looked away. Tungavva was very hurt. She kept getting up and crying the whole night, saying, 'My son has shunned me.' In the morning, she had fever. Her body was burning and had turned red. Lasuma had gone and told Chambasa everything. Since Chambasa was coming home, her daughter-in-law hadn't made any tea. Chambasa brought a potful of tea, and also a doctor, with him.

When he touched Tungavva's body, it was hot like a rotti pan. All his anger melted. He relented, and calling her 'mother', put his arm around her, helped her up and propped up a pillow against the wall for her to lean on as she sat. Lasuma said, 'Mother, see who has come.' She opened her eyes slowly. When she recognized Chambasa, she asked, 'Have you come to find out whether I'm alive or not?' She shed hot tears on his hand. Chambasa looked at the doctor and let him examine her pulse. The doctor gave her a tablet and asked her to swallow that. Then he gave some more tablets, asking her to take them afternoon, night and morning. He told them to give her a light meal of gruel and rice and left. Chambasa held a tablet to her lips. Like an obstinate child, she shook her head and refused to take the medicine. Chambasa asked, 'Won't you take it?'

She replied, 'I'll die.'

'How will you die?'

'I'll jump into the stream.'

'There's no water in the stream. How will you jump?'

'I'll jump into the well.'

'The high-caste people will prevent you. There's only one well. Did Tungi pollute it? They'll curse you.'

'Tell me how I should die.'

'Swallow this tablet. You'll die.'

'I don't want your tablet. I don't want to see your face,' she turned away towards the wall.

'Fine! You do what you want. I don't want to see your face either. Lasuma, you take care of her.' The moment he got up, she turned and looked at him. Seeing that Chambasa had really stood up to go, she pulled at his shirt saying: 'You bury my corpse and then leave.'

She began crying. Chambasa sat down, wiped away her tears and consoled her: 'You have a high temperature. Don't get upset.' He talked to her as if he was talking to a child. He told her, 'Don't be obstinate. Take it,' and put the tablet into her mouth. Meanwhile, Sharavva came and stood on the other side of Tungavva. Tungavva held her hand and made her sit next to her. Pouring tea into a steel saucer, they held it to her lips. She swallowed the tablet and started drinking the tea slowly. Chambasa looked at Sharavva unemotionally. She looked tired. She had been hurt by unexpected shocks. For a long time, I haven't shown any concern for her. Haven't seen her. She must have thought that I am trying to forget her. She had a weepy face. How should she know that I keep stoking her memory every day like a beast worrying its raw wound? He sat looking guilty. He got up, took Shari's hand which was on Tungavva's lap and pressed it. This little thing made Shari happy. She shed mixed tears of joy and pain. She stood looking at him longingly. Chambasa gave the Panchami undi to Lasuma. He gave Tungavva a sari. The tea had seeped into her system, filling it with some warmth. Tungavva hugged the sari for a while, felt consoled and pointing to Shari, asked: 'No sari for her?' The other bundle was the sister's. 'It's here. Take it,' he gave it to Shari. 'I'll take it if you come home and give it to me. Otherwise, I don't want it,' she said and strode away in anger. Appreciating the style in which her niece showed her anger, Tungavva said,'Sharavva is yours. Keep her well.'

'I will marry her and keep her in my house. Say, "Yes".'

Suddenly, she remembered everything and felt a constriction in her throat. There was fear and anxiety on her face.

'Evil eyes will fall on you, son. How can I say yes?' She shed tears profusely and wiping them away, said: 'When your mother put you on my lap, you were only a two-day -old baby. You were so little. Your mother, that good soul, went to heaven soon after. I put you on my left. Lasumya was on my right. When I put my breast to your mouth, I slept. Your mother came in my dream. Your mother loved me very much. She had looked after me like a sister. She came in the dream, put her hand on your head and said: "Tungi, from today, he is your son. Look after him well." She stretched her hand asking me to promise. I said, "Don't worry, Sister. I'll take better care of him than of my son," and put my hand in hers to promise. She laughed with a sense of relief and vanished. When I got up, I saw you at my breast. Did you go to the hill with this whore Shari? Some devadasi told me that these are bad times. If you marry Shari, you'll be destroyed! If you are harmed, how can I keep my promise to your mother?' She began to sob.

'Don't tell me about some superstitious cowrie prophecy. I'll marry Shari. Will keep her in my house. This is my last word.' He said this and left for Shari's house.

It was Yamunakka who noticed Chambasa walking towards the house at a distance. 'My daughter, look who is coming home,' she said in wonder, placing her hand on her mouth. Since she had walked away in anger from him just a few minutes ago, Shari hadn't expected him to come. She hurriedly and excitedly spread a blanket on the floor. Then she moved all the unnecessary things from there into the room and cattle shed. Even as she was trying to tidy the house as much as possible, Chambasa came in. Yamunakka folded her hands and said, 'Come, Sir.' Chambasa came and stretched his hand to give the sweet undi and the sari bundle. Worried that he'd leave now, she said again: 'Ayya, please sit.'

Chambasa sat and told Yamunakka: 'Please take the Panchami undi and a sari.'

Yamunakka replied laughing mischievously, 'Which one is mine now? Give me that. You give Shari's sari to her.' When he also gave one to Shari, she took it feeling shy and happy.

He said, 'I'll leave,' and got up.

Yamunakka told him, 'Ayya, she keeps crying "Mava, Mava" day and night. Sit for a minute, talk to her and console her. I will go to the fields and get back later.'

She left laughing. 'Give your mava a glass of milk,' she instructed her daughter. She was feeling happy—as if she was receiving a son-in-law. Chambasa said, 'Sister, wait.'

Yamunakka melted the moment he called her 'sister'.

'What, son?'

'I came to ask you something.'

'Ask.'

'You should come to Belagavi with me.'

'Who? Me?'

'Yes.'

'Will your mother come too?'

'No, only you.'

Yamunakka was confused. She couldn't figure out why he was asking this. Go to Belagavi with him? What do I say? Chambasa's voice turned harsh, 'I am asking you. Will you come or not?'

She stood silently. Shari was scared too.

'Ask me why.'

He said again in harsher tones. Yamunakka asked in fear, 'Why, Appa?'

'Shari and I are getting married at the registrar's office. Lasuma, Naga and Swami will go with us. You too should come and sign as a witness.'

For a minute, Yamunakka looked at Chambasa's face. She was sure that he was determined to do this. She asked her daughter, 'Did you hear Mava's words?'

'I heard.'

'Will you come to Belagavi too?'

'I'll come.'

Instantly, Yamunakka said in a robust voice, as if to assure them that she was with them in all this, 'We'll come, Brother.'

Chambasa touched Yamunakka's feet. Sharavva saluted her mother and Chambasa.

'Brother, please drink some milk.'

She went to the kitchen. Before you could say 'ha', she brought some warm milk, gave it to Chambasa and said, 'Talk to each other for a bit. I'll be back.' She left laughing to herself. Chambasa drank half of it and put the glass to Shari's mouth. When she turned her face away saying 'no', he held her tight and made her drink. Before she finished drinking it, he gave her a long kiss and left.

Tara Came

That day Chambasa and Namahshivaya had gone up the hill. When they stood on the top, they couldn't see the road they had taken. It was hidden by trees and plants. At a little distance from Mallimadu, the twin nilgiri trees stood swaying. As the wind was getting stronger, they felt that they shouldn't have come. The two trees bent in unexpected directions, embraced each other as if they were whispering into each other's ears. Then they seemed to move apart, whistle, call out to each other and laugh. As the wind got more and more forceful, they dashed against each other. They were very scary. Without proper light, you couldn't even see the water in Mallimadu. The water in the depression at the middle resembled a well more than a stream. The place where water fell from the hill had dried up. It looked more like an empty road now. Chambasa and Namahshivaya were astonished. There were marks of car or truck tires on that path!

The ashy clouds turned black. They darted all over the sky. Both men didn't realize that the sun had set. The white light they saw at the edges of the clouds before the sun set must have been a trick of those clouds. They seemed to be mocking the men! The wind grew violent. It swept away all the clouds and piled them up in one corner of the sky. Chambasa and Namahshivaya came leaping and bounding down the hill. By the time they got down, the horizon between the sky and the Earth had disappeared. The wind blew furiously over the trees and the plants. The dusty haze of the open fields rose to the sky. Thunder roared amidst the clouds. The wind moaned and blew like it was going to blow away the whole village. Leaves rustled as if they were sighing. It began to rain. The hailstorm pelted against the Earth. It was already dark. Both were fully drenched. They ran until they reached Yamunkka's house and knocked on her door.

The one who opened the door was Yamunakka. She felt happy to see these unexpected guests. Not knowing where to make them sit, she spread her blanket on the floor and told them, 'Please sit.' They were looking at the pouring rain outside the door. They said, 'Don't worry, we'll stand here, Avva.' Sharavva, who also came out, quickly tried to tidy the place where they stood. She looked upset that she was unable to clean it adequately.

There was a sudden flash of lightning across the horizon. It rent the sky and a comet fell. The brilliant light lit up every little detail of the sky, the dense dark clouds, and the streets and the huts below, as if it was daylight. This extraordinary light evoked fear and wonder. The row of huts, the trees which hugged them, the houses faraway, their steps, the beaten bullock-cart path—all of them shone with a strange glow as if revealing a new metaphor for creation. Yamunakka, Sharavva, Namahshivaya, who stood open-eyed after the comet fell, the buffalo who stood two yards away, Chambasa who saw each little detail vividly— all stood wonderstruck.

Namahshivaya, who believed that such phenomena of Nature were manifestations of a divine Truth, declared, 'Brother, these are not any common occurrences. It is through such events that God prophecies the future of the village. I don't think anything good will happen to the village.' He looked up at the sky, folded his hands and cried, 'Shivalinga', and saluted. God knows what Sharavva saw. She suddenly touched Namahshivaya's feet, saluted Chambasa too, and patted both her cheeks to atone for some unknown sins. Namahshivaya, who was disturbed by the meteor, saw Sharavva and came back to his senses. His face relaxed and shone with affection. He patted Sharavva's cheeks gently and exclaimed: 'Shivalinga, how beautiful this child is! Daughter you look like the great saint Akka Mahadevi. What's your name?'

Immediately, Chambasa came forward and said, 'She is Sharada. Please bless both of us.' He held Shari's arm, made her bow along with him and touch Namahshivaya's feet. Namahshivaya remembered everything he'd heard about them. Tears of joy welled up in his eyes and his lips trembled as he gave the benediction, 'Children, Shivalinga has blessed you.'

He raised them up and embraced them. All these unexpected events overwhelmed Yamunakka so much that she too fell at Namahshivaya's feet, unable to understand if she should be happy or sad.

No doubt, the next morning there was a clear sunrise. But because of the overnight rains, huge trees were uprooted. They had fallen across the road. It took a long time for Baramegowda to get them all chopped and moved off the roads. By the time he reached Shivapura it was already noon. The car wheels were bathed in slush. In one of the two cars, Tara and Baramegowda travelled. In the other were Kuntirapa and the Boss of the Company. They went directly to the vaade, had the lunch Bagirti had made and then drove to the House of Pleasure. Leaving Tara and Baramegowda to rest there, Kuntirapa and the Boss went to inspect the place.

Kuntirapa took the Boss to the Nirvanappa hill and showed him the spot where the waterfall used to cascade down into Mallimadu. Because of the previous day's rains, there was a lot of water in Mallimadu. It looked like a lake whose depth couldn't be fathomed. After seeing the sight from an elevated place, the Boss's face blossomed with happiness. He clapped and applauded. He shook hands with Kuntirapa. Suddenly, the wind blew. The two nilgiri trees swayed, embraced and whispered something into each other's ears! They moved away for a bit, whistled and laughed. They seemed to dash into each other and clap their hands too!

This is an unforgettable day in the life of Shivapura. Because this is the day Shivapura's history changed its course!

That night Bagirti cooked a grand meal. Kuntirapa made excellent arrangements for the drinks. The whiskey fumes which rose to Baramegowda's head slowly seeped into every vein in his body. He was full of Tara's intoxicating beauty. The guests drank nicely and ate the meat dishes, enjoying their fine flavour. Tara walked daintily to Bagirti, praised the food, shook hands with her and even presented her with a suitcase filled with lovely and fashionable underwear, snow, powder, lipstick and a wristwatch, saying that the Boss had given them to her.

The next day, after breakfast, the Boss went with Kuntirapa to inspect the place again. By the time they returned, it was noon and the sun was simply scorching. Now the commissioner who had come from Belagavi also joined them. Because of the DC's arrival, Kuntirapa's confidence doubled. The father-in-law too revelled in this blissful experience of having the DC in their village.

Before evening, Tara came to the porch of the House of

Pleasure and began to make arrangements for the party. She looked more attractive in her everyday clothes. She had worn a blue georgette sari in a way that showed off the curves of her body. Her light blue blouse was transparent enough to show the white bra underneath. The one who looked overdressed was Baramegowda. He'd worn a nicely pressed and crisp-looking dhotra, a jibba of a lighter shade of red, and a chain around his neck that was about the thickness of your little finger. He had tried to comb his sparse hair in such a way as to cover his baldness as much as possible. It was only Tara who moved all over the porch. The place was full of her. Her creamy complexion, shining eyes, the pointy breasts which stabbed your eyes, a delightful waist and full buttocks—everything shocked the Gowda. The DC and the Boss who came there, led by Kuntirapa, settled on their chairs and began discussing things. The Gowda sat smiling at Tara and went on to offer her a rose he had in his hand. She came to him, gave a white smile, took the rose, thanked him, put it under her delicate nose and smelled it. It was evident that she liked the fragrance. For a moment, she closed her eyes, and showed her appreciation by inhaling it deeply. Then she winked at Gowda. There was a dazzling light in her eyes. On her lips, danced a happy smile. He recognized the hidden motive behind her self-conscious and suggestive movements.

Although he didn't want to exhibit his joy, it was quite obvious. It seemed like he was even willing to fall at her feet to get her love.

As an introduction, the DC talked of sundry things, 'As we discussed in Bangalore, Gowda should begin his election work soon. We don't have a lot of time,' he said.

'We have no objection even if he starts tomorrow.' When the Boss said this, Baramegowda replied hesitantly, 'If you are all so vehement about it, what can I say? I am ready too.'

Everybody, including Tara, clapped and celebrated this moment.

The Big Boss gave a copy of the following set of documents to all the three to read—the map which he had made showing Mallimadu and the land adjoining it, details of the understanding between the Gowda and the Company, and the copy of the agreement. Kuntirapa was reading every word. The DC and the Boss discussed other details. Baramegowda put the file aside and sat ogling at Tara. Tara poured whiskey for everyone and also served some fried meat to munch. She pouted and gave an arch smile to Baramegowda who was staring at her non-stop and undressing her mentally. She clinked her glass with the Gowda's, toasting, 'For Gowda's victory', and drank the whiskey.

Kuntirapa was alarmed. When or how did the Boss, who didn't even know the name of this place, get such an accurate map done of Nirvanappa's hill, Mallimadu and the fields and the land on its edges? The directions on the map—Chalimele, river, stream—all these details were accurate. Even the year in which the rainfall had decreased and Mallimadu didn't have much water was correctly documented. It was also stipulated that Mallimadu should be assigned to someone's ownership, and the owner should come to an understanding with the Company. Then the Company would fill the said Mallimadu and start their programmes for the total development of Shivapura. Both maps mentioned establishing an elementary English school, a high school and a college. They merged the fields beyond Lasuma's and Balavanta's fields, which were adjacent to the lake, with the land occupied by the lake. They extended this area right up to the village. They called this plan, 'Shivapura Total Development Plan'. There was also the idea of establishing an office in Balavanta's field for this program. And there was an application from Baramegowda requesting the Big Boss's Company to do this. Reading the eight-page plan once, failing to understand some of these details, reading them again and again, and still not being able to make sense of it, Kuntirapa, who never drank in front of his father-in-law, began to drink too. Feeling happy that this gave him an opportunity to exhibit his cleverness, he pointed to Balavanta's fields on the map, and told the Big Boss, 'Sir, this field is in Balavanta's name. You have merged it with the Mallimadu region by mistake.'

'I know that Mr Erapa. You should take possession of it. The whole of Mallimadu must be in your name or Gowda's name. Our respected DC saheb will help you do that,' he said pointing to the DC saheb. Gowda didn't want to continue this cheap argument. 'Okay, we will do that. This isn't a big thing,' he intervened and glared at Kuntirapa as if to make him shut up. Now Tara came and filled the empty glasses again. With the auspicious fifth peg, all the four files were duly signed. They got up for dinner. From here on, a new chapter in the life of Shivapura continued. It didn't begin here! Because although they had all signed the papers only now, without Gowda's knowledge, the DC saheb had already started this process long ago! And what can we say about Gowda's inebriated state now? In essence, Gowda looked at Tara, prayed to Tara, dreamt of Tara, and finally, slept lost in the dreams of Tara.

After the Big Boss, Tara and the DC left for Belagavi, Kuntirapa and Gowda's faces turned rosy with joy. They got excited and began to act as if they'd already got millions of rupees from the plan. Tara gave Kuntirapa a plastic bag with ten lakh rupees as advance for the election arrangements. The Big Boss had given the money. Kuntirapa touched it and caressed it again and again. He kept two lakhs for himself and gave the rest to Gowda. Tara, who watched him like a hawk, gave another bundle of currency notes to him and said, 'This is for you.' Kuntirapa's body thrilled visibly. He imagined Tara with the proverbial twin water-pots and grazed in the pleasure pastures of his fantasy.

And Baramegowda was like a bull that had grazed on tender grass and was chewing the cud slowly and enjoying it now. He kept remembering the moments with Tara. He had now begun to feel that the whole world, including air, water, light, sky and fire, were filled with Tara. Her scent wouldn't leave his nose, her form wouldn't vanish from his eyes, and her touch remained on his skin.

Gowda didn't read the file Big Boss gave him. He didn't, anyway, know how to read English. Kuntirapa was the only one who knew how to read it. After he read it, the Boss had asked Tara to get it signed. She had got him to sign the document. Baramegowda signed wherever she asked him to sign. If he signed just one more paper, it would be so useful for filing another court case—Tara kept saying this to Gowda, and she got him to sign another four or five papers in this manner. After this, she poured whiskey and soda into his glass and made him sign some more papers. She made him drink more whiskey and winked at Kuntirapa, suggesting that he take the Gowda into the room. In that same mood of excitement, and with the DC's invitation, the team went to Belagavi and got all the papers registered there. As both Tara and the Boss had guessed, Baramegowda had signed everything. For this, Kuntirapa got another lakh from Tara. He lay with his eyes open the whole night, dreaming of the happy days to come.

The next morning, Baramegowda got up and went to the vaade. When his daughter brought the tea, Baramegowda's face was swollen as if he'd remembered something from yesterday and cried. Bagirti didn't see this. She put the tea there and went away. Kuntirapa was still lounging on the bed after getting up rather late in the morning. Bagirti came with the tea. He pretended to be asleep. His eyes were closed. He had kept the copy of yesterday's agreement on his chest. He looked like he was dreaming of a golden crown now. Bagirti took the document stealthily and turned the pages. She didn't understand anything. Only, on the last page, he had drawn a lot of bones. He had sketched the leg and arm bones, and over it the skull seemed to be laughing. Bagirti exclaimed, 'Issi!' She was about to leave. All of a sudden, Kuntirapa held the edge of her seragu and pulled. Bagirti felt as if the skull was pulling her seragu. She screamed. Kuntirapa got up guffawing.

Poor Man's Anger

The fate of a place isn't determined by one or two people, or even by the endeavours of a couple of creative minds. It is the collective will of people which influences even something that is of minor consequence. Although I had seen this incident happen in my childhood, at that time, I didn't think it was significant. I couldn't imagine then that this incident was pregnant with such terrible consequences. I can only fathom its nature now, when I can analyze things better.

Broadly, we can say that this is where it all began. The British came and imposed a whole variety of administrative institutions on us to make us feel scared and inferior, right? This led to many upheavals in our tradition. The value placed on the farmer's labour changed drastically. The value of the labour of a farmer with ten people in his family became equal to only one day's salary of an officer! From then on, the farmer community was pushed into endless struggles, despair and a final resignation to their fate. In addition, people learned to deal with thousands of castes and tribes. They had millions of gods to worship, numberless faiths and religions to follow, and many calendars to look at. They found something new that they hadn't imagined was possible until then. Meekly, and in a business-like manner, they accepted this change. Our immature politicians, even after Independence, didn't have the balance of mind to estimate the profits and losses of what we inherited from the British. There was Gandhiji, of course. But we safely turned him into a symbol, made him the eleventh avatar among the other ten. Now we must proceed slowly by experiencing things, learning a little from them and experimenting with the new. Be that as it may, let's return to the present context of Shivapura now.

Baramegowda lusted after land and women. This man could never be satiated with possessing land. He made full use of his village headmanship for this purpose. It went like this, suppose he saw some farmer's good land, he'd remember it. He'd wait until the farmer who had rights to the land died. The moment he died, Gowda would overlook the heir and add it to the account of saleable land. Later, at the right time, he'd get it written in the name of one of his relatives. There was also the greedy Talati to dance to Gowda's tunes and assist him in these shady deals. After a while, he'd get that relative to transfer the said land to his name. In this manner, Gowda had snatched away a lot of land. People gossiped that Gowda didn't wash the floor of his house with water, but with the tears of the poor.

As a reward for finishing off the heirs of that stolen land, he had distributed land to six poor farmers. These farmers paid the annual land tax. But the land papers were not made in their name. Whenever they asked about it, he kept putting it off and scaring them about the murders. He'd tell them that this would be like a proof of murder and would land them in jail. In all the documents, these farmers were only shown as his workers. But because of an error on Gowda's and Talati's part, some of the tax receipts remained with the farmers. Now they had strong evidence to claim their rights to the land. Meanwhile, Baramegowda established a sugar factory along with some of his friends, and the demand for sugarcane went up. Because of the shortage of money, Shivapura farmers began to grow a cash crop like sugarcane.

Sugarcane needs water all year round. When rains failed, and there wasn't enough stream water, the farmers took loans which were easily available. They dug wells, got pipelines made, used government fertilizer, sprayed pesticides, and for the next four years, got a very good crop. The life of Shivapura farmers grew colourful. The government also intervened and announced other facilities that became popular with the farmers. However, all this only cheapened the value of their labour. Their labour was only worth the cost of the beedis they smoked. The one who opened his eyes to things now was Baramegowda. He freed the land of these farmers and said he'd cultivate it himself. Thus he took possession of many farmers' land. The farmers who had been cultivating his land, especially the four Dalits, became destitute.

The government brought in the new law, 'Tiller is the Owner of the Land'. It appointed regional committees to implement this. But Baramegowda himself was on such committees, and he misled the members. The only recourse was to go to court. But nobody had money to do that. Even if they went to court, there was no guarantee that they'd get justice. Gowda had political clout. The farmers had spent everything they had on the land and also taken lots of loans. It was difficult for them to survive. The loans they had taken to lay the pipelines were still unpaid. But since both land and pipelines were now the rich Gowda's property, these unfortunate people were cheated out of the facilities, but still held responsible for the debts. They clutched the Gowda's feet and begged, 'The pipelines are on your land. You should at least bear the burden of these loans.' He tried to slip away with, 'I didn't ask you to lay the pipelines.' They requested him, 'Okay, we have planted and manured the fields. At least give us the crop of this harvest.' He said okay. But that year, there were no rains. Because of the overuse of chemical manure and pesticides, all the crop dried up. As the proverb goes, what seemed to be in their hands, didn't reach their mouths! Finally, what the farmers had left was about seventy to eighty thousand rupees of loans each! They were in a hopeless state—without work and without food.

Among them, Balavanta's condition was very critical. He had about twenty guntas (121 square yards) of land adjoining Mallimadu. If he had nothing else, he could at least plant horse-gram and take care of the expenses of his children's food and clothes with the money he earned from selling it. The rest he could get by doing some job or the other. His was the most crucial land that Kuntirapa wanted. The other one was Lasuma's field. Kuntirapa was secretly scared of talking to Lasuma. Lasuma was a rough man with a direct manner. If you say something, it should be cut and dried—that was Lasuma's philosophy. Moreover, Shari is the daughter of Lasuma's uncle. He had taunted her and got his teeth broken. That pain was still raw. It was dangerous for him to venture into this. When this wisdom dawned on him, he put Baramogowda on the job. He decided to deal only with Balavanta. He sent for the bank manager through his brother Ganapa.

When the manager arrived with an obsequious smile, Kuntirapa made him sit next to him. Asked after his well-being, 'How are things?' Also about the bank's well-being. Then he asked about the loan everybody owed to the bank. 'It would be good for you to get Balavanta's loan back as soon as possible, otherwise it will be harmful for the bank,' he warned the manager. He confided that the DC, who had been to Shivapura recently, told him that the government wanted Balavanta's twenty guntas of land. By saying this, Kuntirapa virtually pushed Balavanta into Mallimadu. When Balavanta heard that the government was eyeing his twenty guntas, he trembled with fear. His mouth went dry. When he felt weak in the legs and was about to collapse, his older daughter, Neelagangu, came running, held his hand and made him sit down.

In the whole of the Dalit neighbourhood, only Balavanta and three other farmers were the recipients of Gowda's benevolence. They ate and dressed in the style of those who had money. They were arrogant—felt contempt for, and maintained distance from, their poor neighbours. There were also Chambasa's farmers. But the Dalit neighbourhood feared only Baramegowda's farmers. Baramegowda had even looted his own farmers.

Besides, Balavanta's two daughters were grown up. He had the responsibility of getting them married. All this was weighing on his mind. He had no way of getting out of his debts. He stopped thinking, held his head in despair, and cried, 'Shivalinga.' He sat down feeling lost.

Now all the four farmers regretted being Baramegowda's hit men. They all sat together and thought about it; found no way of crossing these troubled waters. They decided that their sins had found them out. When the bank people threatened to confiscate their houses and whatever little property they had, without any other option, they decided to go to the Dalit Association in Belagavi for help. Balavanta wasn't prepared to go to Belagavi. His wife was sick and bedridden. He had no money for her medicine. His grown-up daughters didn't have decent clothes to wear. His son, who was working as a porter in the Gokak Bus Stand, didn't have enough money to send his father some. He had even borrowed a lot from the other three farmers. His peers, who were aware of all this, pooled in the money and took him with them. When these people went to Belagavi, Rameshi and Kuntirapa's brother, Ganapathi, raped Neelagangu.

Midnoon, the sun was scorching. Cattle were chewing cud and sleeping wherever there was some shade. Neelagangu sat in the hut, watching over the horse-gram crop in the field next to Mallimadu, trying to make sure that nobody let their cattle graze there. It was deserted outside. Nobody wanted to move around in that horrible sun. As if waiting for this opportunity, and in a totally unnatural manner, Rameshi and Ganapa came and stood in front of the hut. The girl was startled. She came out shouting, 'Who?' She screamed, 'My father isn't here. He is out of town,' hoping that if there was someone in the vicinity, or if Lasuma was in the next field, they'd hear her and come to help.

Rameshi said, 'Don't be scared. Do you think we are tigers or bears?' He came nearer. 'Look, see what he has in his hand...' Rameshi tried to turn her attention to Ganapa. Ganapa had a twenty-rupee note in his hand. Showing it to her, he said, 'I'll give you this. Will you come with me?' he said, gesturing obscenely. He leered baring all his teeth. Neelagangu shouted, 'Lasumanna, Lasumanna.' She made as if to run to Lasuma's hut. Rameshi blocked her. Ganapa held her, and lifting her up like a lamb, took her into the hut. The girl screamed four or five times. Later the helpless girl's voice went mute. Not even a crow or sparrow made a sound. When she lay unconscious, they threw the note on her and ran away.

Since the girl hadn't returned home even after dark, Kallavva sent her other daughter to look for Neelagangu. When she went there, she saw Neelagangu half-naked, with blood all over her waist and lying half-dead. The little girl saw this and started wailing loudly and beating on her mouth with her hand. A couple of farmers in the neighbouring fields went to see. They brought Neelagangu to their hut. Before you could say 'ha' the news spread all over the village. They even found out the names of the rapists from Neelagangu. People sympathized with her and cursed the two. Since all the four farmers had gone to Belagavi, the village might remain calm but only until they returned. Baramegowda was also anxious. Both Rameshi and Ganapa had absconded. Gowda sent his servant to Balavanta's house to see what was going on. He found out that all the four farmers had gone to Belagavi. He sent the servant to the House of Pleasure to bring Kuntirapa. Kuntirapa too had vanished the same day. Though he tried to think about how to confront this situation, he couldn't figure out what turn this would take.

There was a funereal atmosphere in the village. All men knew. But none talked openly about it. The neighbourhood women came to talk to Kallavva from time to time. They cursed the criminals, invoking dogs and pigs in their scolding. Neelagangu had drunk a little tea, but later she threw that up too. Kallavva was crying, and at the same time, trying to console her daughter: 'That women's cum-like God has no eyes, daughter! He troubles the poor, and watches the fun! Let him go blind and his wife become a widow. Let white ants infest his eyes. Let ants swarm over his mouth.' Thus she cursed God. She changed the girl's blood-soaked clothes and let her sleep. She was ruing their poverty and cursing God. She sat next to her daughter until the oil in the lamp got burnt.

Before sunrise next morning, there was sudden wailing and sounds of women beating on their mouths with their hands. The neighbours went to see what had happened. Neelagangu's life had left her long ago. Sick Kallavva and little girl Kamali were the only two in the house. Their sorrow was beyond words. Kallavva had wept so much that she had lost her voice now. She couldn't cry even if she wanted to. She struck her chest, her mouth, felt the ground around her as if she was searching for something and went on cursing. The neighbourhood mothers and sisters tried to console her. Then they joined in the communal mourning, cursed and wept with her. One of these neighbourhood mothers had put little Kamali on her lap. Kamali leant against her bosom and cried. These mothers came to know that both hadn't eaten anything since the previous day, and they made some tea and brought it to the house. Though Kamali had a couple of sips because they insisted, Kallavva didn't touch it. They insisted again, 'Don't you need some strength even to cry?' But it didn't work. These mothers and sisters became concerned for Kallavva's life.

Later the farmers returned from Belagavi. When Balavanta fainted in despair, the other two farmers went to Hukkeri to lodge a complaint. In the evening, the police arrested Rameshi and Ganapa and took them away. Kuntirapa, who was supposed to have instigated them, had vanished.

People came back after burying the girl. There was still mud on their hands. The next day, Balavanta drank some pesticide and died! Now even Baramegowda trembled with fear. Belagavi Dalits came, accused Baramegowda of being responsible for all this and said he should be punished. They made a lot of noise in the village. In the end, the police arrested Baramegowda and took him away.

Kuntirapa didn't return the whole month. Baramegowda was tired of facing both the police and the irate people alone. He spent two days in jail, then gave some bribe and silenced the law. He got bail from the Belagavi DC and got out of jail. He returned to the village. The Dalit Association paid lawyers to argue the case of all four Shivapura farmers.

Shivapura, which rang with imaginative stories when corpses floated in the river, now became creative with stories of Baramegowda.

Wounds

The festival of lights, Deepavali, came with a cool breeze into the village. But it didn't bring any festive atmosphere. The entire village was gloomy like it was in mourning. Varieties of stories were born, they spread and died away. Stories, which started on the lips of Shivapura farmers, circulated in Belagavi and Bangalore and then came back to Shivapura. But the element of curiosity they had in them when they went from Shivapura changed into something more sinister when they returned to Shivapura. These stories developed horns and sharp canines and were brimming with desire for revenge. Mallimadu now shone with a steely surface in the scorching sun and hurt the eyes of the onlookers. The poets of Shivapura felt themselves inadequate to describe the fun and games of the nilgiri trees. Sometimes, they stood sombrely with bent heads. Other times, they clapped their hands and danced. As usual, they whispered into each other's ears and told tales. Then again, they became like kids bending, jumping and playing. It was all horrible to watch!

Baramegowda had tried everything possible to avert his fate and failed. The cops who came the first day had arrested Rameshi and Ganapa, charging them with being responsible for Neelagangu's death. But since Balavanta had also committed suicide the next day, despite his begging, pleading and trying to bribe them, the police arrested

Baramegowda too and took him with them. Although they released him after two days because the DC interfered and gave him bail, earlier they had led him away handcuffed in front of all the people. He felt as if someone had spat on his face. His pride and arrogance had taken a beating. This incident became the subject of a whole month's gossip, discussion and analysis, and a source of new rumours in the entire district. Unable to show his face to people, and not even visiting the House of Pleasure, Gowda ate the food his daughter gave him, sat in his room and smoked all the time.

They didn't celebrate Deepavali or worship the Pandavas on this occasion. Bagirti too had sustained a shock and felt deeply ashamed. Except for worshipping the threshold of the house according to the custom, they didn't perform any other rituals. Even that was done by a servant. Bagirti, who was heavily pregnant, had only drunk some tea with her father. She hadn't cooked. Hadn't eaten anything. Akku Taayi, who had guessed this would happen, made holige, and some rice and saaru and brought it to Bagirti. She came with Chambasa. They force-fed her. It was Akku Taayi who presented Bagirti with a sari, saying that it was her brother's gift for the festival. Bagirti went to Chambasa who stood at a distance, hugged him and sobbed inconsolably. Nobody spoke. After she cried to her heart's content and grew quiet, Akku Taayi and Chambasa went home. Until they left, Baramegowda didn't come out of his room.

After the sun turned mellow and the season changed, Kuntirapa came back like a thieving cat. The moment he entered the house, he saw Bagirti's eyes burning with anger. He was scared, but didn't show it. Sat on the chair with the arrogance of a husband. Everything was silent. Bagirti, who went into the room after seeing him back, didn't come out at all. He thought her intention was to make him go into the room. He got up and inched towards the room. By then Baramegowda came out of another room. The strength in Kuntirapa's legs seemed to ebb away. With difficulty, he went to the Gowda and touched his feet. Gowda went to the front door, saw a car standing there, came in and sat down. Kuntirapa kept standing. Gowda looked at him, smoking, 'Where did you go to eat shit all these days, son of a bitch?' He asked. Although Bagirti was in her room, she was listening to the conversation outside.

'I'll tell you the truth, Mava. On the day they took you away, I went directly to Bangalore. I took the Boss with me and saw the chief minister. We made him call the DC. That's when they released you. If you want, please call the DC and ask him,' replied Kuntirapa.

The Gowda didn't believe him. Bagirti didn't believe him either. Without speaking, Gowda sat staring and studying Kuntirapa's face. Kuntirapa was not so naïve, so he understood. But he continued, 'I have arranged everything in the House of Pleasure. Come, let's discuss everything there.'

Gowda, who had shut himself away from all pleasures, got up without saying anything. The moment he got off the car and stepped into the House of Pleasure, he saw the fair beauty, Tara, standing there! The white smile that she flashed at him opened up the whole Milky Way!

On that day, both father-in-law and son-in-law put fair Tara between them and talked a lot. Each heard the other's words only partly. With the other half of their minds, they tried to figure out the motive behind the other's speech. Baramegowda was burning with anger. He got excited and kept saying to himself that he'd take revenge on Kuntirapa for pushing him into this state and absconding. It seemed more like he was taking revenge on himself.

Kuntirapa was now sure that absconding from the village without informing his father-in-law and wife was a mistake. He didn't know how to make them forget it and regain their confidence. His face was bloodless and pale. His eyes looked empty. There was neither light nor life in them. His acting talent and capacity to change his facial expression at will were useless now. He knew that the Gowda, and especially Tara and the Big Boss, knew his secret. He looked ugly. But slowly he tried to bring a meditative expression on his face. Because of the intoxicating whiskey and the proximity of the more intoxicating Tara, Baramegowda pretended to believe Kuntirapa. But the memory of the humiliation he had suffered in front of the village made him remain quiet. It was necessary to make him talk. Kuntirapa began, 'Mava, you don't know whose machinations led to all this. If you do…' he tried to bluff his way through.

'Chambasa, right?'

'Yes, Sir!

'What did he do?'

'He plans to stand as your opponent in the elections.'

At this point, Gowda began to burn all over. He had already asked Bagirti to check with Chambasa about his views on the elections. She had asked him that. He had replied that he wasn't interested in politics, and if necessary, would work for Gowda's victory along with his friends. Bagirti informed Gowda about this. Kuntirapa didn't know this. Gowda said with some warmth, 'You whoreson, don't eat Chambasa's shit for everything. Did you think I'd believe all that you say because I am drunk?'

In a minute, Kuntirapa's intoxication was gone. He perspired from every pore in his body. He was now sure that a lot of things had happened in the village in his absence. The two who could tell him about it all were in jail. Now Tara was his only support. He looked at her like a hungry beggar, as if saying, 'Come to my help.' Tara knew of his double game. But Shivapura is the centre of their project. And the centre of Shivapura is Baramegowda. The greedy customer whom you can depend on to get hold of Baramegowda is, of course, Kuntirapa. Our cripple is the husband of Baramegowda's only daughter. Therefore Tara decided to manage the situation in such a way that she didn't let down Kuntirapa either.

'Sir, that boy Chambasa? Our Boss knows him. He was educated in Belagavi and graduated from there. Don't worry about him. Your real enemies are your own Dalit farmers! The Boss wanted to make sure that you don't get into a rage about them. Erapanagowda was trying to convey this to you. But he didn't articulate it properly, and thus ended up upsetting you. According to the Boss, there are two things we need to do urgently: one, there was this farmer of yours called Balavanta, right? We must begin an office in his small field. Two, we should go to each little village in your constituency and find out what they lack. Do they need roads? School? Drinking water? Well? Make a list of all these details separately for each village. Later, when you give the election speech, you should bring up these issues, and promise them that you will fulfil their needs—how's that for an idea?'

The Gowda was now sure. There was some specific motive behind her talk. Kuntirapa, who thought that Tara was only a sex machine appointed by the Boss, now grew curious and was all ears: 'I didn't tell you about the first task that the Boss mentioned. Listen. Elections are not a small matter. It is a lot of work. You need to cater to the needs of many. The first necessity for all this is an office. Starting from the day you stand for the elections, the party workers will begin to come to you. You need a proper office to manage them. The Boss thinks that Balavanta's small field is the ideal place for it and that we need to take possession of it. It still hasn't happened. Was Balavanta obstinate in his refusal to give up that land? If you freed his land, the only financial support he'd have been left with was the twenty guntas of field. If you took that away too, his wife and children would have been on the streets. So he didn't agree to give it up. Is that wrong?

'Okay, you tell me. That is government land. Could he claim it as his?' demanded the Gowda.

'Even if he'd taken illegal possession of it, you gave him permission to do so earlier.'

'But I didn't.' Gowda argued.

Tara shut him up saying, 'Well, if the village Gowda remains silent when Balavanta takes illegal possession of it, doesn't it imply that you have given your permission, Mr Gowda? Why didn't you do your duty as Gowda then?'

Gowda shut up. Balavanta had taken possession of this land when he was using Balavanta to get his enemy farmers murdered. Balavanta had enjoyed it all those years he was alive.

'So what's the way out?' he asked.

'You have to give Balavanta [or his family] some other land of equal dimension and take his land. That's all!'

Both father-in-law and son-in-law sat there looking foolish. Tara continued, 'If you don't know this, how should Erapanagowda know it? He went and overdid the thing. He thought that if his men molested Balavanta's daughter, Balavanta would give in out of fear. So he instructed his assistant and brother to do this. You know what followed. Do you know why Erapanagowda disappeared all this time, Mr Gowda?' she said, looking at Kuntirapa mischievously.

Kuntirapa trembled. Gowda said, 'No.' Tara continued, 'Both boys grew nervous when they saw the cops. They said yes to everything the cops asked them. They admitted to the crime. Then they also said that Erapa Gowda had made them do all this. So the police began to hunt for Erapanagowda. He ran away to Belagavi. Later he came to Bangalore. He told the Boss and got you released. The Boss also made sure that the case on your men was annulled.'

Kuntirapa nodded like an old bull, put on the posture of a wronged saint and wiped his tears. Gowda forgot his whiskey and kept staring at Tara, while she continued, 'If you ask what all this was for? The answer is, "for you." You must get elected and become a minister. Don't forget that. The Dalit Association people are already asking for an inquiry about your property!'

Gowda asked, 'Why?' and sat gaping at her. Meanwhile, a servant came there and informed them that Bagirti was in labour. Kuntirapa went to the vaade. Tara put her hand on Gowda's arm and gestured to him to sit back. Like a drunk who only looks forward to his next sip, Gowda sat there staring at her.

When Kuntirapa came home, Bagirti was sleeping like in a faded photograph. There were deep dark circles around her eyes. Doubting if she was alive at all, he checked her pulse. Thank God, it was warm. Slowly, she opened her eyes and looked at the cradle next to her. Her eyes filled with tears, she choked and turned away.

The baby hadn't cried. Its arms and legs were thin. But the body was big. It was burning with fever. As Kuntirapa turned, the baby began to cry. The nurse tended to the baby, saying cheerfully, 'In this area, such strange births have happened even among the cattle.' She said the doctor had told her of this. Kuntirapa screwed up his face in disgust.

Chariot Procession

Evil prevailed in Shivapura because Gowda and Kuntirapa came together. If Kuntirapa added to Gowda's natural wickedness, Gowda was instrumental in making Kuntirapa's wickedness go beyond all limits. Nothing could stand against their combined destructive force. Namahshivaya's goodness, Tungavva's pro-life attitude, Chambasa's ideals—nothing could win against it. The material out of which Kuntirapa was made was not of Shivapura. It was definitely from outside Shivapura. He was an abomination of humanity and all its values—a monster filled with lust and violence. Like a wound that refuses to heal and oozes more and more pus, his harmful nature only got worse as days passed.

Baramegowda's victory procession before the elections was a grand affair. Not only did they hang a massive garland in front of his car, but also propped up party flags with the symbol of a burning lamp on either side of it. They changed the faded garland every afternoon and hung a fresh one. They had placed a photo of Baramegowda with folded hands. Under this were the words, 'Victory to Baramegowda'. That night they worshipped goddess Karevva of the banyan tree in grand style and sacrificed two sheep. They gave the tasty meat as holy prasada not only to the priest, but to all the devotees. In addition, they gave the Dalit farmers some happy promises. English school and college for the whole village. Plus, a maternity hospital and a police station—assured Baramegowda as he lit the lamp. When all this was happening outside, Bagirti, unable to look at her baby, or to look away from it, made the nurse tend to it. She suffered from the same mental disease her mother suffered in her last days. A victim of her father's indifference (the elections were only a pretext to keep away from home) and Kuntirapa's natural lack of concern, she was alive only because of Chambasa and Akku Taayi's care.

That day, Tara did the accounts of the election campaign. She gave Kuntirapa the responsibility of locating trustworthy party workers in different villages to garland and welcome Baramegowda when their victory chariot got there. She expressed complete satisfaction about the work done until then, brought out two more files, poured whiskey into two glasses, took a sip from one of them, gave it to Kuntirapa, wished him, 'Good luck', and winked. She gave a file each to Kuntirapa and Baramegowda, threw a seductive look and gave the Boss's phone call to Gowda. Then she called Kuntirapa inside and secretly presented him with a small bone. Later the two men signed the files, and dreaming of their victory procession the next morning, left the place.

They got up in the morning, got the blessing, 'Return victorious, Warrior' at the Hanumanta temple and started. In the very first village they went to, Nandagavi, they faced this question, 'When were the elections announced?'

'Today or tomorrow, they'll announce the elections.'

'What is your party?'

'Lamp of the People.'

'Did you get a ticket to contest the elections?'

'Why will we come here otherwise?'

'Gowda, you have our full support, all right?'

The one who asked the questions shook hands with the

Gowda. In the end, Gowda felt happy that the taunting questions had lost their edge.

Because Baramegowda was also the owner of the sugar factory in this place, wherever he went, the Victory Chariot was welcomed, and they moved without any hindrance.

Here, in Shivapura, the day after the Chariot Procession, early in the morning, something strange happened. Tungavva began scolding her brother Nagappa and son Lasuma as if she was chanting the morning prayer. She really isn't the sort to scold. Without replying to her, Nagappa quietly fed the cattle and left for the fields. Since that was a Monday, Namahshivaya came there to distribute the patri leaf. He was surprised. Why is Tungavva, who never does something like this, scolding her brother so much? He thought there was something unusual going on, and instead of going to other houses, he stood there in front of her house. As time passed, Tungavva's talk turned from Naganna to all the farmers, 'Shouldn't you advise them, Appa? These brainless monsters? They have become money-mad. Instead of growing their food, they grow sugarcane because it's a cash crop. They think that their land is too small for growing this! Rainwater and stream water aren't enough! Not enough chemical fertilizer! They keep getting loans and pouring them on the land! They can't pay back the loans. The other day, they took cart-loads of tomatoes and threw them on the streets because they didn't get the prices they wanted! And they still haven't grown wiser! We don't even have the water of our village stream to drink now! The crop we grow isn't ours! Somebody fixes the price of your crops, somebody else buys them! You take what you get, and get back home with a beaten look on your face. What kind of farmers are these, Appa? Shouldn't you make them sit in your temple and advise them a bit? And God knows why Mallimadu stinks. When I ask them to check, they tell me: "Some animal must have died." How does the corpse of an animal stink? How does poison stink? Can't they see the difference? You please advise these fools…'

Namahshivaya too was aware of the stinking smell. He had also brought this to Chambasa's attention. But Chambasa had forgotten it, being busy with his household affairs. There was another truth in Tungavva's words. The farmers, who had taken to sugarcane, had neglected the crops that were necessary for them. The wealthy farmers never ate the grain or vegetables they grew. Since there was the smell of chemical fertilizers in the grain, they'd get the grain and vegetables from other poor villages where they didn't use such fertilizers. The reason they had thrown away cart-loads of tomatoes wasn't only because they didn't get the prices they wanted, but because they couldn't eat them. That is, they didn't even have the vestiges of good sense left in them to know that they shouldn't sell to others what they couldn't eat themselves. Why should we bother about others? This was their argument. Everything, the motive behind everything, means and ends—was money and more money. Tungavva was concerned that the village was reduced to this state.

As if all this wasn't enough, goddess Gaali Durgavva came to the Gowda's vaade in the middle of the night and stood there. Some soul, who saw her in the morning, woke up the Gowda hastily, made preparations for her worship, took her idol beyond the village border, turned her face towards another village and came back. But Tungavva doubted that the goddess had really gone away. On the same day, Tungavva's buffalo lost its baby. In the morning, when she was still in bed, the pregnant buffalo began to make strange and horrible noises. Lasuma got up thinking that the buffalo might have seen a snake or something. Even as he looked around, a dead calf fell out of its womb. A bloody shapeless form with deformed limbs, this stunted calf had a head in the front and another near its tail! The front head looked like it had already grazed, and there was white foam at its mouth. Its hind legs were crooked. Fear of the bad omen and her disappointment about the buffalo's pregnancy made Tungavva cry. She cursed anyone who might have cast an evil eye and been responsible for this. She also cursed goddess Ellamma who couldn't protect them. After all this bitter cursing, she consoled her daughter-in-law who had begun to cry.

This wasn't an auspicious sign. To make sure that none of her relations came to harm, she took a vow invoking the same Ellamma. The news had already spread like a chill morning wind to all the mothers and sisters of the village. All the neighbours felt dejected because this had happened in Tungavva's house. Even as they stood watching, Naganna came, stuffed the calf into a gunny bag and took it away. The mother buffalo was making horrible sounds, and the cattle in the neighbours' houses stood with their ears perked up and heads bent, as if expressing their sympathy too. Lasuma poured nice warm water on the agitated mother buffalo's body, bathed and dried her with a cloth, took away all the dirty stuff of the womb, threw it outside the village and came back home. Everybody was restless thinking of what might befall the outcaste neighbourhood.

A week after this, Chambasa told Yamunakka about going to Belagavi. She said, 'Let's postpone it for a couple of weeks because Tungavva's buffalo delivered that dead calf.' He said, 'We are opposing all the superstitions with this marriage. Come Shari, let's go.' Sharavva said, 'Let's go.' Yamunakka too joined them saying, 'If both of

you say this, what's my problem?' The three also took
Lasuma and Namahshivaya to Belagavi. On the day and
time fixed for the wedding, Chambasa and Shari got their
marriage registered, had a photograph taken and returned
to Shivapura. Even after everything, they made sure that
Tungavva didn't know of it.

On the day they returned, Chambasa took Shari to the
Shivalinga outside the village and saluted the idol. Since
Namahshivaya hadn't come there yet, he took her to the
jambul tree where he'd first met her. He climbed the tree,
shook some fruit to the ground and also plucked a bunch
of fresh ones off the tree for her. But when he looked
at this bunch, he found that all the fruit was overripe
and shrivelled! Shari saw the fruit that had fallen on the
ground and was also surprised. She looked at Chambasa.
Chambasa, who was checking the other bunches on the tree,
finally came down with a bunch in his hand. He tasted the
fruit. It was tasteless. No juice in it either. It felt like biting
into leather. When they looked at the other trees, they
found the same overripe, shrivelled and small-sized fruit.
He thought they must be struck by some disease and felt
disappointed. The first time he saw her, he was on the tree,
and she was on the ground. When she asked for the fruit,
he had looked at her—a surge of warm feeling came over
him! At this first whiplash of youth, the boy had trembled.
On that day, when he shook a few large and juicy fruits for
her—like the spring that gives blossoms and green sprouts,
youth had bloomed on her face, and her eyes had shone.
When you look at this fruit now, it's all dried and shrivelled!

When he stood thinking about what disease might have
struck the fruit, Shari's mind was elsewhere. When there's
none around, and they are in the state of solitude ideal for
lovers, she'd expected a happy attack from him. But she

felt disappointed to see him standing there in that cold manner. Like the ripples that rise and spread in water when you throw a stone into it, her disappointment also spread and finally touched Chambasa. He put his hand on her shoulder, drew her to his side gently and told her, 'Shari you are my new festival gift. My new border-crossing.' And kissing her softly like rubbing flower against flower, said, 'Come let's go to the temple.'

Namahshivaya Swami had come. They kept the fruit, shirt, dhotra and footwear they brought for him, and also a handful of money as a respectful gift.

'Swami, are the fruit struck by some disease?'

'Yes, Brother. Last year, I saw such fruit on a couple of trees. This time all trees have the same kind of fruit.'

'What disease is this?'

'Don't know, Appa! This is the first time I too am seeing something like this. Tasteless, not edible. Looks overripe. Not even big like before. God knows what disease this is!'

Chambasa brought Shari to his house. They both saluted Akku Taayi.

She blessed them: 'Okay, you married the one you wanted. I wish you both good luck. But don't bring Shari into our house.'

Then they went to Tungavva's house. Tungavva saw them and was about to go in. They touched her feet silently. Tungavva pulled her feet away, went into the house and shut the door. Chambasa, who expected something like this to happen, wasn't surprised. Sharavva was hurt. As she wiped her tears away with her seragu, he took her to Bagirti's house.

Bagirti, who sat in despair all the time, felt almost ecstatic to see these people who were dear to her. The moment Sharavva touched her feet, she realized the situation.

'Come Shari, look where my luck has led me.' She leant on Shari's shoulder and began to sob. 'I cannot celebrate the birth of a child. I can't throw away the child either. Shiva seems to be making fun of me. Where can I go away, Shari?' She cried.

'The one I call father is my enemy. My husband is another enemy. My father didn't even talk to me about the child. My husband is salivating for, and running after, some Bangalore bitch. After seeing the child's face, he has stopped even looking at me! Tell me how he was before he married me? He entered this house wearing a torn shirt and shorts and holding a bone! If my mother calls this sort of a beggar and gets me married to him, imagine what my fate would be like! Look at this women's cum-like fellow's arrogance now!'

Chambasa stood silently until Bagirti cried to her heart's content. Sharavva kept patting Bagirti on the back, wiping her tears and consoling her, 'Calm yourself, Sister.'

Later Bagirti consoled herself, 'You came here after getting married to my brother who is like the truthful Harishchandra of the epics. What shall I give you, my sister?'

She went in wiping her tears. Meanwhile, Sharavva whispered into Chambasa's ear, 'Give me five rupees.' He took a ten rupee note out of his pocket. Bagirti came out, put a new sari on Shari's shoulder, gave her a blouse and a pair of her earrings and embraced her. Sharavva saluted her again. Then Bagirti asked, 'Brother, I am alone in the house. Can you leave Shari here for a while?'

'Sister, not Shari. Your husband is a difficult man. I will send my aunt. By the way, why don't you come to our house for a couple of days? Change of place might help you forget old things.'

'Then who'll be here in this house?'

'Will anyone steal your house?'

'That lame pimp has made my father crazy about the elections! The moment Father comes back, I'll leave him to take care of the house and come there. Now send your aunt.'

'Okay.'

Chambasa was about to leave. Shari asked, 'Sister, show us the child.'

Bagirti's face fell. Mechanically, she took off the cover on the cradle nearby. Shari was alarmed when she saw the baby. Chambasa's face went pale with pity and disgust. Shari didn't show her disturbance. She put the ten rupee note in the child's hand. The child held the note with the little finger of its left hand, shook it and chortled. Surprisingly, Bagirti too smiled.

Overall Chambasa was happy about his marriage. His aunt Akku Taayi and sister Bagirti had accepted Shari as their kin, not seen her as an untouchable! But what gave him great relief, joy and encouragement, was Gowda coming forward and blessing the couple!

Although nobody told the Gowda about it, the news of Chambasa's marriage had come to him through the grapevine. He was thrilled! He celebrated this news mentally and told himself, 'Ah, my son! You have outshone me.' He praised Chambasa again and again, 'Is it enough to keep chanting Gandhi's name? You should show your admiration in practice! Look, this lad has actually shown it in practice!' He felt proud of his nephew's act. He decided to see the children right away and called Bagirti. Bagirti came. He asked her, 'I am going to Chambasa's house. Will you come too?'

'The baby is restless. You go, Father,' she answered.

He put the gifts he wanted to give them in his pocket and left for Chambasa's house. On the way, he met Lasuma and told him, 'Bring Sharavva and her mother to the banyan tree.' He went there.

When she heard the news that the Gowda was coming, Tungavva got up in haste. Not even bothering about her appearance, she pulled the seragu respectfully over her head and ran to the tree. When she saw him, she darted a coy and sidelong glance. Then she said in an intimate tone mixed with mock anger, 'If you'd just sent for us, we would have come to you, right?' Gowda smiled at her archness and called, 'Tungi, come here,' and pointed to the place next to him. She blushed and saying, 'Thoo', stood turning her face away from him. Gowda held her hand, pulled her to him and was trying to make her sit next to him. By this time, many women gathered. They laughed loudly, held Tungavva tight and made her sit next to the Gowda looking like a shy bride sitting next to her bridegroom.

Tungavva was blushing. Blood rushed to her face. She smiled, and the flash of her white teeth lit up the whole yard. Her bright eyes shone on Gowda. People became festive as if they were getting the couple married. Tungavva looked like a very pleased village goddess. The Gowda asked, 'Where is Chambasa?'

Chambasa, who was among the crowd, rushed to him, fell at his feet and saluted him. The Gowda said, 'Splendid!' He made him get up and asked, 'Why didn't you invite me for the marriage, son?' Chambasa was crying with joy. He apologized, 'I am sorry, Father.' He saluted his uncle again. Gowda asked again, 'Where's your wife Sharavva?' Sharavva came up to him. When she was about to touch his feet, he stopped her. He made the couple stand before him, put the ring—which was on his finger—on Chambasa's finger and gave him a waist thread made of two strands of gold. He put a three-strand chain made of gold coins into Tungavva's hands and told her, 'Put it around the child's neck.' Tungavva, who sat feeling shy, brightened up, put the chain around Sharavva's neck, pinched her chin lovingly and cracked her knuckles to ward off the evil. When both touched the feet of the Gowda and Tungavva and saluted them, the happy crowd cheered and applauded. It became like a small wedding. Chambasa and Shari felt relieved since this was like getting social sanction for their marriage. Yamunakka too touched the Gowda's feet and wept tears of joy. However, there are always people who don't like you in any village, right? They talked, 'When the father himself entered the outcaste neighbourhood, will the son fall behind?' Let them talk.

Gowda, who was lost in the election frenzy, didn't hear a thing.

Election Frenzy

As time went by, the Victory Procession was getting infused with more and more election frenzy. Wherever he went, wherever people gathered, Kuntirapa made a small speech, and with folded hands, requested the public to choose the Gowda. Then Gowda would stand up with folded hands too. This was only in the beginning. In some village, they demanded that the Gowda speak a few words. Kuntirapa tried to evade this, 'Not this time. At the next opportunity, he will.' But people wouldn't listen to him. They protested that the Gowda should speak at least a couple of words and started shouting, 'We want Gowda's words.' Baramegowda took courage into his hands, came up to the mike and stood there.

Everybody was looking at him with wide-open eyes. Some faces were happy, some frowning. Those with happy faces came and sat in the front. Gowda's eyes began to shine. Well-built body. He looked reliable, strong. Gowda, in fact, had learnt a small speech by heart anticipating something like this. But he didn't remember it now. He began his speech with, 'Brothers and sisters of Sultanpura…' Then he said, 'I am a farmer like you…' and narrated all the problems he was facing as a farmer. What's more, he described the sad state of the poor farmers vividly. Then he looked around. The audience was listening silently. He continued, 'I am your man. If you large-heartedly give me an opportunity to serve you, I am ready for that. I have come here to find out how I can serve you. You too have many wants like my village has. Though it is years since we got independence, why is it that even the trifling needs of these villages haven't been met with? You need a well to drink water from. Because of the poisonous water in the stream, the health of children, older people and cattle is being affected.

'If it can't fulfil even this small need, what's the use of the present government? Why should we vote them to power? Have you ever asked those whom you voted to power about all this? No? Why? Now it's time to ask. If you vote for me and send me there, I will raise my hand and ask: "Why didn't you get this work done for the village?"' The moment he said this, deafening whistles, cheers and clapping followed. People got excited. They shouted slogans. Gowda himself was amazed at his success and became further encouraged by all this. Kuntirapa, who believed that there was none to beat him at public speaking, paled in front of Gowda's oratorical magic.

The day the Victory Procession ended, they announced the elections. The elections would take place on the 2nd of May, and on the 14th, they'd announce the results. The fact that they announced the elections on the very day the Victory Procession ended made the Gowda feel that it was an auspicious sign. He celebrated the day with Kuntirapa, and called Tara and praised her smartness.

A week passed. The party manifestos and candidate names were released. The moment Baramegowda heard on the radio that from Shivapura constituency, and from 'Jai Jana Jyoti' (Hail the Light of People) party, Erapanagowda had got the ticket to contest, he collapsed.

He thought this couldn't be possible. Kuntirapa, who

was with Bagirti, had heard the news. But he didn't tell anybody, not even Bagirti. He came out quietly and was trying to slink away outside. Baramegowda, who came there right at that moment, saw him and asked with a frown, 'What Sir, Erapanagowda? There was some news on the radio.'

'What, Father?' He asked innocently.

'It seems you got the ticket to contest from Shivapura?' Kuntirapa tried to act natural, and said, 'Che, che, you are making fun of me, Mava!'

'I told you what they said on the radio.'

'Impossible! Shall I go and get the paper?'

'Go, get it quickly.'

Gowda was agitated like a flea-bitten bull. He couldn't sit or stand even for a minute. He kept looking at Kuntirapa, who wore his shirt and pants, and left. Kuntirapa thought that God himself had given him this opportunity to escape. He ran quickly.

Gowda called Tara directly. Nobody picked up the phone even though he kept calling. Then he got a call. Some friend called and asked,

'What's this Gowda? We thought you were going to stand for the elections. But you have made your son-in-law stand for it.'

'There must be some mix up. Wait.'

He put the phone down. When he called Tara again, she didn't pick up the phone. He went into his room and started thinking.

'His mother's...! Can this be the machinations of that cripple? The bastard's face had gone dark. He came after me. Said, "Jai, jai." He told people, "Vote for the Gowda." But he is a rogue. Her mother's...if I want to ask that fair whore, that bitch too doesn't pick up the phone. What should I do now...'

Bagirti knocked on the door and informed him, 'Father, Bangalore phone.' He came hurriedly and received it. He heard Tara's voice from the other side, 'Who? Gowda?'

'Yes. By the way, what's this? I sent the application for contesting the elections. Now they announce on the radio that Erapanagowda has got the ticket! They announced it wrong, didn't they?'

'The information you got is correct. Erapanagowda is the one who got the ticket.'

'But he hadn't sent his application.'

'No, no. The Big Boss had sent the applications of both, just in case!'

'None of you told me this. Erapanagowda too didn't tell me.'

'You are father-in-law and son-in-law. It is a domestic thing. We thought he'd have told you. Didn't he?'

'He didn't tell me. If you too had Erapanagowda in mind, why did you let this election bug get into me?'

He asked, trying to control his anger and displeasure.

'Gowda, friendship is important. If you agree, then you should know two things. One, haven't you profited by our friendship? Aren't we spending our money on you and the progress of your village? If this work should get done, your background should be clean. Look now, because of your fight with the Dalits, one of the Dalit papers wrote about you: "Apart from the land of his family, how many people's land has the Gowda taken possession of? How did he do all this? We must have an inquiry into this." Have you seen it? Two, if the government considers this and sets up an inquiry, you'll have to resign your minister's post. Then won't the plan of developing your village come to a halt? Then won't all the money we have spent go waste? You think about it. So isn't it good that someone from among us, someone who can safeguard our interests, is in the government? The Vidhanasoudha? Think about it.'

When words fell fast from her mouth like leaves from a tree in winter, Gowda became mute. His frowning face blanched. His lower jaw and chin trembled. When his cheeks wobble like this, it means that he is horribly angry. He said with some warmth, 'What are you saying now? You're saying—shut your mouth and arse and stay home. The cripple will stand for the elections, right?'

'Not only this, Gowda. The responsibility of making Erapanagowda win is also yours. If the plans of building the school, the college and the hospital, and so on in your village should work, then you have to do at least this.'

'If I don't…'

'You mean…'

'If I don't, what will you do? Tell me, woman.'

'What can I do, Gowda? If it comes to that, the Big Boss and I will go away to our countries. Your bad luck will remain with you.'

'What do you mean by bad luck?'

'You should at least return the money you got from the Boss…'

'You gave it to the cripple. He'll return it. Why should I be connected with it?'

'What do you mean by saying you are not connected to it? You have written all your property to Erapanagowda. Erapanagowda has written it to the Boss. The ritual of signing was over long ago! Thoo, what kind of people are these!' She banged the phone with disgust. Tara! Gowda remembered her serpent eyes. Something in them seemed to leap up and bite him sharply now, like a serpent that spreads its hood and suddenly stings. He collapsed.

By this time, Slimy Ramesha, Kuntirapa's personal

assistant (he had ascended to this position when the Victory Procession began), came there holding the daily paper. He gave it to Gowda and was about to go. Gowda asked, 'Who? Did Erapanagowda send it?'

'Yes.'

'Where is he now?'

'I don't know.'

Soliloquy

Kuntirapa is evading me now. But earlier, he too played a part in making me submit the application for candidature. However, he hid all this about his own application from me. He held his breath and participated in the Victory Procession. He is the source of all this mischief—Gowda realized this, and his whole body burnt with anger. In the papers, they had introduced him as 'Baramegowda's son-in-law, Erapanagowda.' They had described him as the 'Paragon of Social Service', 'Light of the Poor' and also 'The Friend of the Dalits'. Before all this began, when I hadn't even thought of the elections, the one who whispered the word 'elections' in my ear, and the one who took me to Bangalore unexpectedly and introduced me to Tara and the Boss, was Kuntirapa! Finally, Gowda began to get the whole picture of such advance preparations. He got up, threw the paper aside, paced restlessly up and down the room and kicked the floor with heavy feet. God knows what came over him, he rushed to Kuntirapa's room.

It was locked. What does this bastard have in this room that even Bagirti shouldn't know of? Gowda wondered, and with the help of a crowbar, broke the lock and entered. The cabinet was also locked. He broke that too and looked inside—in one corner, there were bundles of currency notes, about seven or eight! In the other corner, there was a briefcase. He broke the lock on it. In his haste, he picked up the papers in it and strew them all around. He saw a photo where Kuntirapa stood with his hand around Tara's shoulder! It is this Cripple who pushed me to the state I am in. When this feeling of vengeance raged within, he screamed till his voice went hoarse, 'Lousy bastard!' He tore the photo with trembling hands. After tearing it to shreds, he looked up gasping. Bagirti, blanched with fear, stood there watching! He stretched both his hands and cried, 'Daughter, daughter...' and almost collapsed. Bagirti ran to him shouting, 'Father, Father...' and held him. She didn't want to make him sit in the cripple's room. She brought him outside, made him sit on a chair and consoled, 'Calm down, Father.'

It was night. Kuntirapa hadn't returned yet. Neither Gowda nor Bagirti were surprised because they both knew that he'd vanish when he couldn't face a situation. But Gowda was bent on punishing him. 'You ate my food. You flourished under my shelter. You even married my daughter. Now you have deceived me, you low-caste lout! God knows how he has deceived others too!'

Bagirti was thinking: From now on, I can't let the cripple come to me. Mother used to say that when love ends, hate begins. I bowed down to my mother's will and accepted him. He too. He pretended love to get my father's property. It was forced love on both sides. We both acted like husband and wife and tormented ourselves. It's enough now. She thought of how she should neglect and reject him. His wickedness, deception, lechery, selfishness—she thought of all the ways in which she must scold him. Then she hid all the agreement papers.

There was a very ugly change on her face. She lost control and started acting like a trapped bird. But she served her father food, hiding the fear and anxiety within her. She put on a false smile. She pressured him into eating a couple of morsels. He got up after this ritual. Of the two servants he sent to find Kuntirapa's whereabouts, one said he couldn't find him anywhere. The other said he could be in Rameshi's house. But Rameshi wouldn't give away the secret. His loyalty was towards Kuntirapa.

Silence crystallized in the house. The male servants slept in one room, and the female servants in the other. When all of them slept, only three were awake in the house: Bagirti, Gowda and the baby who chortled and kicked her feet.

Gowda was struggling. Tara, who was in the background of his mind, came to the foreground, 'She is a female who is trained to fleece men. Ah, what acting! She'd open her eyes wide whenever I said something. She'd pretend to listen to every word of mine diligently and devotedly. Didn't she act like it was her greatest joy that this rich, brave and masterful man had liked her? At night, she gave me what I wanted even before I asked for it. Whatever she got, she was grateful and gratified. She didn't ask for anything. What I gave, she took it as if she was doing so only because I'd feel bad otherwise. If I got food where we were, she fed me the first morsel with her hand. What's surprising, she gave me the happiness that my wife didn't give. In the brief time she was with me, what of Paroti, she made me forget the whole of womankind in Shivapura. The moment I saw her, an electric charge ran through my body. Like you could easily single out the rose from many different bouquets, I could tell her apart. I took her as mine, Shivalinga!' Gowda tormented himself with this. But now she looked like a rainbow-coloured butterfly that flits any moment from one flower creeper to another. 'Thoo,' he spat out and went and stood before the mirror.

Faraway, he heard the sound of drums indicating that

someone was being borne to the grave. He thought he'd die too. The fear of death, which he hadn't felt until now, came to him. He thought he was already dead and touched his arm to make sure that he was alive. How would it affect other people's lives if I die? He thought for a while. He couldn't figure it out. I have never looked at my life from such a height, he decided. Mallimadu, village, neighbourhood, village belles, Paroti, Tungavva—none of these images came to his mind. When he remembered Bagirti and Kuntirapa, he sighed, 'Haa, Kuntirapa!'

Yes, until now, I had only seen him through a tinted glass. Now he has appeared in broad daylight. Cripple, but not weak. He was polite with me. Like they say, 'Too much politeness is a sure sign of a villain!' Now he is laughing at me, laughing a cunning laugh. But earlier, the images I saw of him—of making me anxious, making me trust him, pretending love for me. Not only what I could hand him, but all that I had in my name—here's my property, here's my daughter, here's the village, here's trust, here's life, here my honour, here my fame—he made me give him everything that meant something to me. Now he has pushed me out of my own house and made me stand in the scorching sun! Okay.' He came back to his bed, turned up the light and lay down. He couldn't sleep. There was no hope of it.

Yesterday, I went to the garden. I met Chambasa unexpectedly. He saluted me. I returned the greeting. There were four or five red pieces of jackfruit in his hands. He was eating one after the other. He came to me and said, 'Jackfruit. From your garden. Taste it, Uncle.' He stretched out his left hand with the fruit. I didn't take it. The pride of village headmanship came in my way.

'But this is not a common variety, Uncle. Its taste is

unusual in all these parts,' he said. He tried to convince me. There was a unique expression of ready happiness and excitement on his face. 'Ayyo, what a pity that he isn't eating such fruit,' he seemed to say. On his face, there was the divine contentment of having eaten the fruit!

I should have eaten the piece he tried to give me, Baramegowda thought, stretched both his hands for it, pretended as if he had taken it, and with both empty hands, he repeatedly beat on his mouth and finally lay down. Meanwhile, he felt a range of emotions—the feeling that he was dying when he'd given his daughter to a low-caste criminal, not wanting to die, the realization that he was responsible for all this misery. His daughter was crying outside, or perhaps he himself wanted to cry like a child— whatever the reason, he too cried in the end!

Manifestation

When the situation grew out of control, Kuntirapa realized that he had gone wrong somewhere. All his efforts to bring things under control had failed. He felt like showing his face to Gowda once and getting scolded by him. He got scared that things might take unexpected turns, go swirling and lead to unforeseen consequences. So, instead of deferring the visit home and bringing more dangers upon himself, he decided, 'Whatever happens, I'll go there.' He put on a tired face, as if he was tired from travel, and came home.

There was the refreshing early morning light outside. There was dew too. The sun, which had just come out, was shining. The sunrays filtered through the clouds, fell on house-roofs, windows and sleeping dogs. It bathed them all in a calm glow. As these rays fell slanting on the earth, they beamed a slightly reddish-golden light and created long shadows. The green and yellow forest at the edge of the hill looked lovely, bright and joyful.

In the place where the flood water collects, Chalimele, and the marshy region of Mallimadu, the pleasant sunlight fell through the smoky clouds and painted the landscape in magical hues. When the mist moved from one place to another, it looked as if the whole scenery was moving.

But the vaade looked like it was yawning. The servants were flitting in and out, working. Though the women servants were milking cows, sweeping the dust or busy doing other jobs, they all looked like they were just fumbling around. Gowda placed his chair in the front yard and sat looking at the gate. On the stool next to him lay yesterday's newspaper.

Kuntirapa entered stealthily. Suddenly, he saw the Gowda sitting in the yard, took a step backward, acted scared, calmed himself, and as if out of politeness, bent down and walked noiselessly towards Gowda. Gowda kept staring at the gate with unseeing eyes.

Kuntirapa took off his sandals, touched Gowda's feet, and wearing his sandals again, disappeared into the house. Bagirti was watching everything.

The Gowda was boiling with rage inside.

Bagirti, who was waiting for Kuntirapa to come in, didn't know what to do. She went back to her old habit of pulling out all the clothes in the wardrobe, strewing them on the floor, folding and arranging them. She waited for him. Meanwhile, he pushed the door open and came in. She was very scared. Not knowing what to do, she stood up. Her face had blanched.

The baby in the cradle moved. Kuntirapa went near it and stretched his finger for the baby to hold. When the baby opened its legs and pissed, he frowned as if he had touched the piss. He wiped his face with his kerchief and asked his wife with the arrogance of a husband, 'Who locked my room?'

'Father.'

'Where is the key?'

'With him.'

'Sure?'

Bagirti didn't reply. He asked again, 'Will you get it?'

'I can't. You go get it.'

He was frustrated. But since he needed it, he tiptoed to

the chair. Acting as if he was scared rather than only being polite, he went to the Gowda and stood there with his head bent. 'Mava,' he called.

Gowda didn't speak to him. Nor did he turn his head towards him. Kuntirapa called again. Finally Gowda responded, 'All right, tell me.'

Kuntirapa waited to get his breath back. He said, 'I sent you the paper the other day, right?'

'Nobody gave me the paper.'

'Rameshi didn't give it?'

'You were in his house all these days. Didn't he tell you?' Now he realized his mistake. Gowda knew that he hadn't gone away anywhere but was at Rameshi's house all the time. Kuntirapa's lies were exposed. He almost thought that it was time to make another escape. But the present need? He came to the point.

'Taradevi had called me. She told me to get the original papers immediately.'

'Take them. Who's holding back your hand?'

'But the agreement is in your possession?'

'Is that right? Then they should call me, shouldn't they? If they ask you to get it, how can you do it, poor man!'

'Yes, that's true. The copy is with them. If we only keep the original, it is not of any use.'

'If they don't need our paper, why are you worried about it? If they do need it, they'll come here. Don't worry.'

'It isn't like that, Mava. The one who stood for the election is me. I am the son-in-law of this house. I have to run around as the mediator. If you had stood for elections, that would have been a different thing. Now they asked me to get it.'

'Okay. But they should at least tell me that they have sent their agent and that I should give you those papers.

If they didn't tell me, what does it mean? That they don't trust you. Then how can I give you the paper? You are a big lawyer. You should know all these legal matters.'

It was clear that this oldie was disgruntled about missing the election candidature and had turned against him. There's only one way to confront him now. Tell him about things as they are and bring him to his senses, 'Mava, we are from the same house—if father-in-law and son-in-law stand against each other in the elections, won't people laugh at us? Tara and the Boss work the strings that pull us. They can do anything they want with us. Think about it.'

'What are these strings that you're talking about? Hey cripple, are you trying to blackmail me?'

'Not blackmail. This is true. Better know it. Standing for the election wasn't my dream, it was yours. I brought the Boss because of that. Their retinue came too. Until now, they have spent millions of rupees. You had plans of starting the school and the college. They came forward to do that. Meanwhile, your problem came up. So they said not you, but I should stand. They got me the ticket to contest the election. What is my fault here? If that was the case, would I come to your Victory Procession? You tell me?'

'Yes, but why shouldn't you have done all this drama to stand for the elections? Why did they write Mallimadu in your name? When a man is drunk, he loses senses. So you thrust that woman on me and got the property written in your name. Do you even have a soul?

'Father, if not today, tomorrow you would have written the property to me.'

'No, I would have written it in Bagirti's name.'

'Are Bagirti and I different?'

'She is my daughter. I don't know who fathered you.'

Kuntirapa's body burnt from head to toe with anger.

He thought, I'll have to tell him this one day or the other. Let me do it now. 'Mava, whether drunk or not, lust for money, or Tara-lust, whatever the reason, you have written the property in my name. From now on, people who're so proud of their Gowda-ship shouldn't remain in this house.' He said this and shot out like an arrow.

Bagirti had come out of her room and heard all this talk. This is natural for Kuntirapa. One day or the other, he would have shown his true self. He'd done that today. Will a palm tree produce a mango? But she was disgusted with her father who seemed to fall for women even when there was danger. After hearing Kuntirapa's words, Gowda was shocked. He seemed to be struck by lightning. He reeled, tried to hold on to the arm of the chair for balance, couldn't get up, and looked at his daughter with plaintive eyes. Bagirti smirked in contempt and rushed back to her room. The baby chortled and laughed.

On occasions when he ran away like this, Kuntirapa used to go to Rameshi's house. He had his loyal follower Rameshi and his wife to fulfil all his needs. Gowda decided that he'd talk to Kuntirapa when he came back.

The elections came.

The elections happened according to the schedule. As they expected, Erapanagowda won by a margin and became a minister too. Gowda had been indifferent to the elections, and he stayed out of it. He didn't go canvassing. He didn't even vote. By the grace of the Big Boss, Kuntirapa became a minor irrigation minister. Tara had pressed him to bring his wife to the city and cautioned him that the Boss had ordered him to do so. Bagirti said she wouldn't leave the child and go with him. Kuntirapa didn't keep quiet, 'You are a village idiot. Can you get such an opportunity again? That's a cursed baby. The arms, legs, head—nothing is in proper proportion. It kicks with one leg and the other doesn't work. Is that a baby? Monster foetus. Okay. Give it to Tungavva, or your friend Shari. We'll pay them. You can take care of it after we get back. Get ready tomorrow morning,' he ordered, and went into his room.

Anyway, they had weaned the baby from the mother and started feeding it with cow's milk. Finally, Sharavva agreed to take care of the baby. They gave her the baby and five hundred rupees, and left for Bangalore in the morning. The same day Chambasa and Namahshivaya went to see Baramegowda.

Prelude to the Protest

That day, when Chambasa and Namahshivaya came to Baramegowda, he was walking with a heavy tread. Even the servants working at a distance were talking in whispers. Some unseen and unknown part of him was hurting. His face was swollen. He kept knitting his brows from time to time. His shoulders were bent. His charming personality that attracted women years ago was gone now. It was evident that he was suffering some unbearable pain. His body had lost its vigour. His eyes had no light in them. Desire and disappointment had crushed him completely. He looked like a sinking ship with its flags flying haywire!

Chambasa and Namahshivaya felt that they hadn't come at a proper time. But turning back wasn't respectful either. So they stood there and saluted him. Gowda asked them to sit. They sat. Thinking that it wouldn't be nice to sit silent for long, Namahshivaya began, 'We are protesting against you. We came to inform you of it. Read this,' he said, and opening the page of some newspaper, gave it to Gowda. There was the headline—'A Gandhian Who Killed His Own Dream'—he began reading it.

It was an article about Shivapura—the foul smell that was spreading in Shivapura, everybody's initial guess that it had to do with some dead animal, people later giving up that idea but remaining mute about things, tasteless jambul, cattle giving birth to hideously formed calves, birth of monstrous human babies—it had all these matters. Gowda read this and was astonished. 'Our Bagu's baby...,' he looked at Chambasa inquiringly. Immediately, Chambasa said, 'Yes, Uncle. The doctors and scientists are saying yes! They say that four such babies were found in villages where our river flows!'

He pushed another paper in front of Gowda and asked him to read.

It was titled, 'Total Development of Shivapura'. In the first part of the article, there was a lot about the fine work of the Belagavi DC. When Baramegowda sent an application to the Belagavi DC to start the English school and the college, and a hospital in Shivapura, the DC promised to get money from an American charity institution. The DC agreed, and the charity institution inspected all the places in Shivapura. Then they decided that Mallimadu was the right place. They wanted to fill the ditches, ponds and hollows, and level the land. They assured the people that the said plan of development would be implemented in this location. Accordingly, there was an agreement between Mr Erapanagowda and the American Jackson Company. Then we know that they started levelling Mallimadu. But what they are filling there is not stone and mud. It is the foreign factory's chemical fertilizer waste! Literally poison! All this happened under the leadership of the Gandhian Baramegowda who dreamt of getting an English school and college, and a hospital for Shivapura. This is not something that brings progress to the village. It is a systematic enterprise to turn the village into a cemetery—daylight robbery!

Gowda mused, 'So the DC has a hand in this!'

Chambasa bent forward, 'Not just a hand in it, it's all his doing, Uncle! In fact, even before you signed that agreement, the waste began to arrive in Mallimadu. To be precise, the waste was being thrown here through the last year!'

'What? Whole of last year?'

'But how did they throw it without us getting to know of it, Brother?'

'Uncle, we have seen the tracks of vans and trucks there! In the beginning, they came only two days a week. Later, it got more and more frequent. Then they needed this agreement!'

'It looks like you know the whole thing from top to bottom. Look, Swami! They say that since they have made a contract, they'll build the school and the college once Mallimadu is levelled…'

Chambasa intervened, 'College and school cannot be started here, Uncle! By the time Mallimadu is levelled, the whole village will have turned into a graveyard! They only tempted you with those grand words…'

'Is it true, Swami?' Gowda asked, looking innocently at Swami's face.

'Since they wanted you to shut up until the village was destroyed, they even gave money for your election campaign. They'll give more! Gowda, already the jambul is spoiled by this poisonous waste. We can't even eat what we grow. The scientists have declared again and again that "in another five years, entire Shivapura will be a grave." What else can I say?'

Gowda became really anxious. Swami continued, 'That Shivapura will turn into a graveyard is hundred per cent true. All the credit will go to you. See what you want to do about it.'

Gowda responded immediately, 'How's that possible? Kuntirapa made the contract! I am only a witness!'

'Who will listen to this? Kuntirapa is not of the village. He is your son-in-law. It was you who wrote Mallimadu in his name. You signed, and you were also a witness! Ask the cowherds in the village. They'll say that Mallimadu belongs to the Gowda. However much you try to push it away, the blame will settle only on you.'

'Okay, granted what you say is true. How do we stop Shivapura from turning into a graveyard? Or isn't there any way out? Tell me this.'

Now there was light in the Swami's eyes.

'That's why we came to you, Gowda. The intention with which you and Erapanagowda made a contract with Jackson Company will never be fulfilled. You tell them that you will show them another place. Let them build the school and college there. Then the agreement will fall through. At least then you will know their real motive.'

Baramegowda said calmly, 'Then let's do this. Kuntirapa has gone to Bangalore. Let him come back. We'll talk about the agreement. Then you and I will take a decision together.'

'Our protest?' asked Chambasa.

'You go on with your protest. Don't stop it. Do we need somebody else's permission to take care of our interests?'

Protest

That evening, Namahshivaya and Chambasa got together for a meeting under the tree. Chambasa's farmers had invited everybody to be there. Lasuma brought the Dalit farmers and those who had gone to court against the Gowda. Chambasa read out the long articles in the newspapers, and where necessary, paused and explained matters. Then Namahshivaya called it 'the destructive goddess Mari', and went on to talk about the agreement that Erapanagowda made with the American Jackson Company—the stipulations in it and the dangers it poses—he described everything vividly. He narrated the history of the monstrous happenings in the village and warned about future dangers. Many frowned, asking, 'Who is he to pledge our Mallimadu?' Namahshivaya told them about the protest and also underlined the need for unity.

When they got some indication that people were gathering together to protest near Mallimadu the next Sunday, Belagavi reporters perked up their ears. Someone among them asked, 'Instead of Sunday, why not do it the next day? Monday? That is the day Erapanagowda will be sworn in as the minister. Why not the same day?' Everybody agreed with him, the farmers especially, because Monday was the day when they rested the bullocks. On his part, Kuntirapa wasn't sitting idle either. He was getting all the news about what was happening in Shivapura every day. Moreover, he was in contact with the Belagavi DC all the time.

On Sunday evening, God knows where they were hiding! Like cattle running helter-skelter, clouds began to move all over the sky. The wind blew in every direction. By the time people ate their dinner and slept, it was pitch dark, and an unseasonal rain started. The whole night this heavy rain poured, simply rending the skies.

Chambasa got up when he heard the birds chirping and came out. The rain had stopped. The cloudless sky looked like a newly washed floor. The sun shone like it was squeaky clean after a nice bath. A gossamer curtain of fog enveloped the hill. A gentle breeze blew. The whole vista presented a lovely and luxurious green crop, tall and almost reaching up to the height of your chest. Raindrops had fallen like shiny pearls on trees, plants, creepers and leaves.

Chambasa sat on the platform around the tree and remembered everything that happened the day before. The farmers' response to Namahshivaya and his talk had been very encouraging. We think that villagers are ignorant. He had often fought, sometimes intentionally, with farmers about matters like wages, idleness and labour. But the day before, there were none of those things on his mind. Those trivial annoyances were washed away by larger community interests. Chambasa decided to shun the alienation that higher education creates in you. He felt great trust in the purity, simplicity and justness of this life. He became sure that he'd find contentment, serenity and tranquillity of mind only here. The experience of interacting with farmers the day before had given him confidence. After the meeting, they had continued their chit-chatting, singing, laughing and shouting.

Chambasa bathed in the river, had his breakfast and

walked to the tree. The moment he reached, people started crowding in. Some farmers played the drums in advance. They began to feel the spirit of the protest. Men who came to participate in the protest stood on one side, and women who came to see them stood on the other. Both groups grew. Later Namahshivaya also came and joined the group.

Now the group set off towards Mallimadu with their drums and other musical instruments. As they walked, more and more people joined in. Then Belagavi farmers and reporters also joined in. They distributed the handbills they brought with them and prepared the petition they planned to give the DC. They mentioned the reports of the specialists that had appeared in the newspapers and some personal experiences of people. 'It is true that we need schools and colleges, but if it means filling Mallimadu and building schools and colleges in its place, we don't want it. Build this school and college in some other place that we show you. But you should stop the work of filling Mallimadu right away,' they appealed to him. After everybody who had gathered there signed it, the group moved towards Mallimadu to the accompaniment of drums and trumpets. Belagavi party workers cheered the Dalit Association, Namahshivaya and Chambasa. By the time they reached Mallimadu, it was noon. When Namahshivaya was addressing the people from the high rock under the niligiri trees and telling them of the aims of this protest, a posse of policemen from Belagavi came and surrounded them.

Chambasa came to the front, saluted the inspector and told him, 'Sir, this is not a protest against any individual person. There's nobody here whom we want to protest against. We have a petition for the Belagavi DC. We will read it to these people and get their acceptance. Two among us will meet the DC saheb and present the petition to him. But if you say no, give the petition to us, we will do so. Please tell us what we should do.' The inspector, who was in the jeep, looked sharply once at Chambasa and once at the people. Filled with contempt and bitterness, he swallowed his own spit. His nostrils flared. He hit his left hand with the stick in his right hand a couple of times. His sharp moustache, which looked like the sting of a scorpion, looked sharper as he paced up and down, thinking.

'What's your name?'

'Chambasava.'

'Oh, so you are Chambasa?'

The inspector got off the jeep, and with eyes that shone with mockery, asked, 'Why aren't they talking?'

'They have asked me to talk.'

'Oh, so you are the leader? It seems he is the leader. Kick this bastard.'

He slapped Chambasa sharply on the cheek.

Immediately, another cop also slapped Chambasa. Without as much as telling him why or what, and without even letting him move, they beat him badly. When Namahshivaya saw that Chambasa was bleeding in the mouth, he came forward. The police hit him too, not even bothering about which part of his body they hit. Then they threw him into the jeep. By then, it was impossible to control the crowd. People who saw the brutish behaviour of the cops took whatever they could lay hands on and beat up one of the cops, pulled off his clothes and made him stand in his underpants. They also got the inspector, who was simply brimming with self-confidence, and started pulling at his scorpion moustache. He screamed loudly and ran for his life. In the fiasco that ensued, Lasuma was hurt in the leg. He fell screaming: 'Ayyo...' Meanwhile, somebody set fire to the Gowda's cattle shed. The cattle shed, which was full of dry hay, began to burn quickly and the cattle shrieked. Horrible smoke came out of the shed, already half the shed was filled with smoke, nobody could figure out what was happening inside. By this time, some good Samaritan untethered the cows. The cattle, scared of fire, came out leaping and jumping, and ran amok. They drove the police crazy. Now even the police began to run to find a safe place away from the cattle charging at them. They ran, got into the jeep and escaped. Balavanta's son escaped from the cattle charging at him, and while running to find a safe place, bumped against a rock. He screamed desperately when some scrawny fellow hit him. Another cop ran to escape from the crowd and succeeded.

Hitting someone, getting hit by someone else, being wounded, scared and screaming like crazy, people pushed, ran and escaped. There were all kinds of noises around, shouts of 'hit', 'beat', 'pull', 'break', and the sound of policemen's sticks lashing at people.

After the cops ran away, people came to their senses. When they looked around, they saw Lasuma who had fallen unconscious. His thigh was badly bruised. Similarly Balavanta's son, Shivarama, was also badly hit, and he lay there screaming. Immediately, Chambasa got the cart ready and took them to Konnur station. From there, he took them to Belagavi hospital. The whole village was scared. They guessed that it was all Kuntirapa's work and cursed him. They scolded him, 'After becoming the minister, this is the first service he has rendered his constituency.' There was no admirer of his in the village that day. People talked that all this was pre-planned.

In the evening, when people were sighing with relief that this cop menace was gone, the same police jeep arrived again! The farmers had dug pits and blocked the by-lane that was being used to bring waste into Shivapura from the highway. Two trucks, which brought the waste, had toppled into the pit. Surprisingly enough, Slimy Rameshi appeared now to take care of the police. Where was he? Where had he hidden himself since morning without even giving anybody a clue?

That day the atmosphere in the village was stifling. In the evening, the moment the cattle came home, they closed the doors. They didn't have the lights on either in the yard or in the porch. They managed to keep the lamp burning only in the kitchen. Never in the past had the cops patrolled the streets of Shivapura like this. This was a bad omen for the village.

Slimy Rameshi, who hadn't appeared in the morning, surfaced when the cops came the second time, right? Although his friendship with Kuntirapa wasn't any secret, the village women wondered about how canny he was. Only his wife accompanied Kuntirapa to Bangalore. This was something to talk about. Discussing his daily activities was the prime preoccupation of the neighbourhood ladies. His duties, which earlier consisted of collecting money from the farmers, had changed after Kuntirapa came. If Kuntirapa went out, he ran and placed a pair of sandals at the latter's feet. He took all the scolding that Kuntirapa gave him. He assented to everything that Kuntirapa said.

That evening, Rameshi stood in front of the Inspector to perform the duties assigned to him by Kuntirapa. The inspector shouted, 'Whoreson! You didn't show me your face through the day. Where had you gone, bastard?'

'When I came there, I saw a lot of commotion around you. By the time I escaped from there and reached home, I was exhausted.'

'Crook, don't give me lies. Go and ask what the attender wants to say.'

The attender came and told Rameshi, 'Saheb is very tired. He wants a meal. First a bottle. Erapanagowda has told you all, hasn't he?'

'I have already brought it and put it inside.'

'Along with that, get some masala and three egg-laying fowl—get them ready and bring them here. Also four or five seers of rice, two kilograms of butter. Get all these quickly now…'

The inspector lost his patience, 'You cunt, why are you still here?'

Rameshi ran.

After about an hour, the meal was ready, and its fragrance spread all over the place and outside too. The inspector's sting-like moustache stood out, his nostrils flared, he savoured the flavour and sat down to eat. He, and after him, two more constables, ate until their tummies burst, belched loudly and came out chewing betel leaf and areca nut. Slimy Ramesha sat feeling gratified and waiting for words of praise. The scorpion-mush inspector asked again, 'Has Erapanagowda told you about the arrangements for the night?'

Slimy answered, 'It's ready.'

'Tell me the plan.'

'Nothing, really. You three will go there. You get in. The other two will keep watch outside. Finish your job and come out.'

'Let's go then. Show me the house.'

Darkness enveloped the village. You couldn't see anything, couldn't distinguish between a house and a matha. They turned down the light of the lantern and followed Rameshi's steps, deciding that where he went must be the right way. Rameshi finally stopped in front of Yamunavva's house, gave the lantern to one of the

constables and disappeared. They put a constable in front
and another at the back of the house. Then the constable at
the front knocked on the door. No response. He kicked the
door violently. When it broke and fell, both Sharavva and
Yamunakka screamed loudly. Rameshi had sent Naganna
away on the pretext of some job or the other. Immediately,
along with the inspector, two others barged in, held both
women and made it easy for the inspector to beat them. He
slapped them hard on the cheeks. Sharavva fell unconscious.
When Yamunavva was still screaming, one of them tied her
hands behind her back, and the inspector gagged her. One
of them took her out, kicked her on the stomach, threw her
in the yard and stood watch. The other went to the back of
the house.

When the inspector lifted Sharavva up, she tried to
scream again. But her voice didn't seem to work. By then,
the baby in the cradle woke up and shouted, 'Gaa, gaaa.'
The inspector rushed to the cradle and pressed his hand
against its mouth.

'I beg of you. Please let go of the child. Appa, please let
go of the child,' she begged and hugged his legs. Suddenly,
an idea flashed through the scorpion-like mind of the
inspector, 'Oh, yeah! Then you shut up first. If you don't,
I'll finish this baby first and then take care of you.'

When the inspector pressed his hand against the left side
of the child's neck, it went mute. Sharavva rushed to the
cradle. Before she could reach out to the child, he pulled her
sari off, threw her violently on the floor and fell on her. In
a short while, he was contented and left belching. Then the
cop at the back of the house went in. After he came out, the
other one went in. By the time he too came out, the lantern
light had dimmed. It was terribly dark outside. Sharavva
became conscious again, and she tried to get up and run

before another man could come in. There was no strength left in her body. Her thighs were trembling. She heard the faint noises the child was making. She gathered all her strength together and stood up. She collapsed. Again, she got up somehow, draped the sari around her body, went to the cradle, picked up the child, took the bag hanging on a peg there and disappeared into the night. The lantern was extinguished.

It wasn't the chirping of the birds. But Gowda got up when someone shouted. The Gowda hadn't had a wink of sleep that night. A variety of nightmares. Bad dreams flew all around and tormented the old man. He was about to fall asleep when the cool morning breeze blew. He heard a horrible scream and got up. He recognized the voice and came out to check. The watchman knelt in front of the house, 'Appa, five corpses have flown into the stream.'

He was beating on his mouth with his hand and crying. Baramegowda said, 'Why're you doing this early in the morning, you whoreson?'

He scolded and asked again, 'What's it? What? Tell me, bastard.'

'Appa, five corpses have flown into the stream! That police party which came yesterday? The fresh corpses of all three of them are there! And two more corpses. Slimy Rameshi and Erapanagowda's brother—they are lying there too. Totally, five corpses have fallen there.'

He showed five fingers. Fear and wonder were mixed in this gesture. He screamed in a voice that scared even the Gowda.

'Go, get the panchayat members, run,' Gowda instructed, and went in to get dressed to go out. The same day, the watchman went to Hukkeri and informed the mamaledara.

The Special Issue Editorial of Shivapura's *Thondi* Newspaper

'Shivapura Is Horrified'

Not one, not two? Five corpses! Imagine all of them turning up in the river the same day!

Shivapura was horrified. Who killed? Why did they kill? When did they kill? The whole village, in fact the whole region, even the whole state, was stunned with fear and total incomprehension!

That night, didn't Gaali Durgavva come and stand in front of the Gowda's house? People said that Mother was angry and that Shivalinga had forsaken them. Some bright Shivapura lads, who had applied for police jobs and hadn't got the jobs, turned into sleuths and guessed that Kuntirapa had a hand in it. Kuntirapa tried to molest Sharavva once and had his teeth broken. Since he often runs his tongue over the empty slots where those teeth were, his revenge remains fresh. If the cops had the nerve to assault Sharavva, it must be because of Kuntirapa's incitement. But if they wanted to ask Sharavva, she had disappeared with Bagirti's baby! They still couldn't trace her.

Chambasa, who returned from Belagavi, and his farmers searched the whole forest. She wasn't found. Some of those who went to search say that she must have fallen into Mallimadu along with the baby. If they wanted to ask Yamunakka, that wasn't possible either. They had buried her corpse. Unable to see her daughter's torment when she was being assaulted, Yamunakka had fainted. But when the police kicked her on the stomach, she couldn't get up at all. Finally, she died. People buried her.

According to some others, Chambasa must have committed the five murders. The evil cops assaulted his wife Sharavva! But there is no evidence at all. Do you ask why? On the day of the disturbance, Chambasa had actually taken brother Lasuma and Balavanta's son, who had been wounded, to the Belagavi hospital. The same man, on the same night…he can't be seen in two different places, forget it…some people said.

Second Page
A farmer from the cowherd's street, who saw the inspector with the sting-mush floating as a corpse only in his underwear, laughed so much that he pissed in his dhotra. Seeing this, his wife laughed so much that her hair got terribly dishevelled. The women in that lane thought she had been possessed by the goddess and smeared bhandara on her forehead to calm her down—so said one of the reports.

But the women of the shepherd neighbourhood thought—God is great. The pot of Baramegowda's sins is full now. Therefore a demon-cripple married his daughter. In addition, a monstrous child was born. Now look, all those who are not wanted in Shivapura are dead, except one. Let him die too, and very soon, they prayed for it to happen. All those good wives of Shivapura struck the floor with their hands together and cursed him!

Third Page
In the KB School (Kannada Boys School) of Shivapura, they mourned for all the five dead. The headmaster spoke

saying, 'In the village of Gandhi-like Baramegowda, it's unfortunate that Vallabhai Patel-like Slimy Ramesha, and Subhas Chandra Bose-like Criminal Ganapa died.' He expressed his deep sorrow. He also described the sterling qualities of the other three policemen. 'Their deaths have left a void in the nation. This kind of a thing hasn't happened in history,' he said. He gave two minutes each to the dead men and observed silence for ten minutes. Then he declared the day off. Because he declared the day off, the headmaster became very popular with the children that day.

Fourth Page
Shivapura gained nationwide fame overnight. Reporters, who came in droves, got hold of anyone at all, interviewed them and left. As Shivapura became a tourist spot, people who came there, even if it meant holding their noses, went to Mallimadu, found out as much as they could to satisfy their curiosity and went back. The events that they saw there— based on what they saw and what they guessed—they wrote about all of it in the papers. Some plucky reporters even wrote about an unnamed minister's stories and 'mini-stories' of his misadventures, especially after seasoning them with the masala of their choice. Several rumours and stories about the five murders began circulating. People of Shivapura read these or heard about them and could now feel proud of their village. A couple of folk singers composed ballads about the said minister and the higher official (DC), turning them into villains. These stories became popular.

Bagirti, Baramegowda, Tungavva, Chambasa and Namahshivaya were the only ones who didn't meet anyone or participate in any of this.

Bagirti in Bangalore

The Monday after the swearing in, the Big Boss threw a party at the Tara Residence to celebrate Kuntirapa becoming a Minister. Kuntirapa's many new friends and colleagues drank, ate, danced, jumped up and down, wished him good luck and a great future and left. It was late in the night. Only a few remained there. A couple of them were still dancing to the music. Bagirti was watching with innocent appreciation and a smile of wonder, and she kept clapping. Meanwhile, Kuntirapa took Tara outside for some confidential talk. A natural beauty, Bagirti was simply shining in her new colourful clothes and jewellery. The Big Boss came and congratulated her. When he came up to her, Bagirti got up respectfully and folded her hands. She wore a Chandrakali sari. He saw her slender arms with many bangles around them. When she got up, he noticed the way in which her breasts stuck out and her buttocks rose. The manner in which her body swayed was extremely attractive. The long braid that came down on her back was swaying on her buttocks. A body bursting with youth, the glow in her eyes and her smile—seeing all these, the Boss thought that he hadn't seen another woman like this one!

He went closer and said, 'Hello Mrs Gowda, come, we will celebrate your husband's success.' He tried to shake her right hand. Bagirti flinched. Tara, who came in, called her too, 'Come, Ma'am.' Even as Bagirti kept saying no,

Tara coaxed, 'Hold his hand and shake your legs a couple of times. That's all.' She put Bagirti's hand in the Boss's. Bagirti pulled her hand back.

Seeing this scene, Kuntirapa was thrilled. The Boss himself is asking her for it! How wonderful! Can I get another opportunity like this? He came running, 'Bagirti, darling. Boss is asking. Just do a couple of steps. That'll do. Please.'

Kuntirapa put Bagirti's hand again in the Boss's left hand, placed the latter's outstretched hand on her buttock and winked at him. The Boss was greatly aroused now. He pulled her to him hard, pressed her to his chest and gave a gratified smile. Seeing Kuntirapa wink, Bagirti's eyes reddened like that of an enraged bull. She shrugged her hand off in fury and turned around. Saying, 'You beggar-bastard,' she slapped Kuntirapa hard on his cheek. Then she took her sandal off and held it in her hand ready for an attack! The whole party stood still in utter shock. Tara became alert. She pushed forward, held Bagirti's hand, and consoled, 'Madam, please, calm down.' Still consoling her, Tara took her outside.

Bagirti freed her hands and shouted, 'Now, right now, I must go back to my village. If you arrange it, you are saved. If not, I'll go into the street and shout! Did you hear me, bitch?' Consoling Bagirti again, 'Madam, please…' Tara took her into the room, phoned an assistant and made arrangements to send her to the village with a couple of maidservants and two security guards. They decided not to send her by train or by bus because wherever she went the news would spread. They arranged a special car and sent her. It's only after this that they all breathed in relief.

The next day, along with the photo of the minor irrigation minister Erapanagowda's swearing in ceremony, the newspapers also published the news of the protest in Shivapura with a photo. That day, the Big Boss dreamt of the chief minister's post, nothing short of it! He luxuriated in his imagination.

But the next day, reading the horrible news, Kuntirapa literally trembled. The Boss was also worried. Tara's face grew dark. The inspector, two policemen, Slimy Ramesh and Criminal Ganapa were all murdered. Along with the photos of all five men, the news was at the top of the front page! Seeing this, the entire state was horrified and stunned! The same day, abandoning Kuntirapa's dream of making Shivapura a piece of America, the Big Boss went back to his country.

Back to Maternal Home

When Bagirti reached Shivapura, it was scorching afternoon. The whole village looked empty as if it was in mourning. On the streets, forget people, there weren't even dogs. Though Chambasa had tried many times to call and inform him that Gowda had suffered a stroke, Kuntirapa hadn't responded.

As she reached the house, she saw the fire in the front yard and her heart beat madly. Her legs lost their strength. Chambasa opened the car door and called, 'Come, Sister.' She got off the car with difficulty. 'Be brave, Sister, be brave...' he kept saying this and led her slowly into the house. Tungavva, who sat at the door crying, cried louder when she saw Bagirti, 'Daughter!' Chambasa scolded Tungavva, 'Be brave, Mother. If you cry like this, won't Sister be more alarmed?' He led her in. She saw the Gowda's face. He was sleeping on a mattress on the floor. Not the same face she saw every day. Not the face that bloomed with love whenever he saw her of late. She saw the face of a corpse—a face all wrinkled and shrunken. She felt cold and shivered. She felt as if she too had died. No, this isn't my father, she told herself. But it was her father! When she was sure of it, she screamed, 'Appa...' She fell on the corpse and wept.

Tungavva joined her. Chambasa left them to cry to their heart's content. He went off to make some arrangements. Akku Taayi came. The mothers and sisters of the village, and Bagirti's peers, also came to express their condolences.

They all joined in Bagirti's weeping. Chambasa came out and asked the security men in the car, 'The honourable minister's father-in-law is dead. When I call, I can't get through. Will you call him and give him the news?'

'We already called and informed him.'

'Will he be here for the funeral?'

'No. He asked you to do the funeral and said he'd come later.'

They said this, and the car left immediately! By then it was getting to be evening. Until they buried the body, nobody in the village could even eat a morsel of food. The Elders, who had been waiting since morning for Bagirti and her husband, talked to Namahshivaya. They decided that if the daughter said yes, they would go ahead and perform the funeral. Chambasa checked with Bagirti. She said yes. They took the corpse away. By the time people who had gone to the cemetery returned, there were already stars in the sky.

Luckily, Akku Taayi had come back home and made some food. So everybody got to eat a morsel of rice. In the last two days, Tungavva had lost both her sister-in-law and her niece. Now Baramegowda was also gone. Her eyes had gone dry with all the crying. The moment some rice went into her tummy, she leant against the wall in the corner where she sat and began snoring.

After the meal, Akku Taayi stayed with Bagirti. Chambasa came and told her, 'I will sleep in the living room, Sister. You sleep inside. Sleep well.' He slept in the living room. Even after Akku Taayi went into deep sleep, Bagirti lay awake with her eyes open, burning the lamp. Outside, it was pitch dark. You could hear the sound of the patrolling policemen's sticks. But you couldn't hear the farmers' voices. Sharavva had disappeared. She has my child with her. But she herself has vanished; how do I ask about my child? What do I ask? And Father's predicament in his last days, his agony of being deceived, but inability to talk about it? Unable to do anything, he cried silently. His self-pity. All the memories of her father's last days went past her mind's eye. The most astonishing thing was how her father had passed away with his head on Tungavva's lap! True, they were lovers once. Stories about how her mother had come between Gowda and Tungavva, and how that led to their break up, had fallen on Bagirti's ears. As she remembered these things, she felt that she would again break into tears any moment. She tried to think of other things in order to distract her mind from her father's death.

She began thinking of the farmers. What I can't understand, and don't want to remember, is about the farmers. Father too failed to understand them all his life. Although these are the same farmers I have seen from my childhood, I have never before heard them speak in such a rough manner. She heard Tungavva snoring. Poor thing. She had lost her sister-in-law, her niece, and now, the Gowda. But she hadn't shared her pain with anyone. She slept with all that sorrow in her heart. Returning from Belagavi in the morning, her brother had buried Yamunakka. Then he buried her father. Now he slept after all the fatigue of the day. She didn't want to wake him up and talk to him either. What's wrong with these dogs? On other days, they even start barking at the stars if nothing else. Now they lie there silently, not even barking at the patrolling policemen! Again, she thought of the farmers.

This issue became extremely important because there were a lot of violent emotions circulating around her father's dead body. She'd wanted to thresh out everything even when he was alive. It wasn't possible to trust either the farmers around her or that Kuntirapa (certainly not him!). There's Chambasa. But her father's people hadn't taken him into confidence in any business matter. Same with the others—Tungavva and Lasuma. They were dependent on Chambasa. Kuntirapa was someone who pimped for his own father-in-law. One who wanted to gain by lending his wife to the Boss. These days, whenever she remembered him, she'd shake with fear and anger. On the day I went to Bangalore, Father was particularly upset. He was furious with his son-in-law. Although you couldn't hear him from a distance, his hand gestures and lip movements were enough to convey his agony. It seems he had smiled at Lasuma who came there before he died. He'd also caressed Lasuma's head, patted him on the back, and told him, 'Go, bring Chambasa.' When he came to know that Chambasa had gone out of the village, he had been quiet for a bit, and then he had screamed loudly, 'Call Chambasa, you fellow!'

Bagirti believed that Chambasa knew something. Of late, the relationship between Tungavva and Father hadn't remained a secret. Father openly and fearlessly accepted my brother's marriage with a jogti. He had given them gifts! He made Tungavva sit next to him publicly. Because Father was the Gowda, people were scared of him and gave him respect. But Tungavva is a caring, upright and honest woman. She has so much sympathy for others. This caring nature has won everybody's heart. She has been like the Gowda's wife, a Gowdthi, in her own right! Bagirti felt that Tungavva knew what happened to her father in the end. But Tungavva was snoring for the whole house to hear. Bagirti waited for the morning.

When Bagirti woke up in the morning, it was already eight. Tungavva wasn't there. Lasuma came and whispered something in her ear, and Tungavva flounced off in anger—

so said the servants. Bagirti waited, hoping she'd come back soon.

The house looked so empty. At least if the baby was there, it would have cried, called out, or made some noises. She remembered the baby, and her eyes became wet. Immediately, to forget it, she called a servant and tried to get some information out of her. She started asking questions. Meanwhile, she began to realize how terrible death was. Her aching mind was full of the thoughts of death. Suddenly, someone was calling her from the backyard. She came out, and there was Tungavva! Even now Tungavva hadn't taken the liberty of entering the house directly. When Bagirti went out, held Tungavva's hand and tried to bring her in, Tungavva wouldn't forget that she was a Dalit, and she stopped at the door. Bagirti pressed her a lot, but Tungavva didn't budge. In the end, when Bagirti wanted to bring a chair from inside and make her sit on it, she didn't even agree to that. Instead, she made Bagirti sit on the chair, caressed her head and consoled her with tears in her eyes, 'Take heart, my daughter!' Although her own mind was like a disturbed lake, she didn't show it too much now.

'Both Mother and Father are gone! I am an orphan, Aayi,' cried Bagirti, hugging Tungavva.

'Take heart, daughter! Those who are born must also die one day.'

'Did they find out where Shari is?'

'No, daughter! No news of either her or the baby.' Tungavva answered, and lowering her voice, asked slowly, 'Didn't Erapanagowda come, child?'

'He has gone to dogs, Aayi. How can I say if a man who has gone to dogs will come or not?'

Tungavva melted. However confident she was, she was still a little apprehensive about the irate farmers. She feared that they might try to take out their anger with Kuntirapa on Bagirti. In the morning, when Lasuma came and called her, she'd rushed out.

When she came there, she saw that the Dalits had assembled under the tree. There had been no indication earlier that they'd be doing this. Of late, Balavanta's family had suffered a series of disasters. The tears of the village community hadn't dried yet. She found that they had already yoked two bullock carts! Balavanta's son Shivarama and his peers are loading the household things onto the carts! His little sister is standing, sheltered by the caring old woman of the neighbourhood. She is crying. A couple of other farmers with worn out faces are standing there with their arms crossed and watching all this with a vacant look in their eyes. Although people who'd gathered there saw Tungavva come, nobody greeted her. They thought of her as another helpless Dalit woman like them. Tungavva slowly made her way in the crowd and stood in front of the yoked cart. She asked Shivarama, 'What is this, Brother?'

A Dalit farmer, who stood close by, came up to her and explained, 'Mother, he is going to Belagavi with his sister!'

Shivarama turned to Tungavva, bent down and touched her feet. He asked, 'Yavva, Mother, bless me.'

'What has happened now that you decide to leave your home and go to Belagavi?'

A farmer standing at the back came to the front and replied, 'Whatever happened, happened before your eyes. What more should happen now?'

Tungavva grew suspicious.

'Looks like you too are ready to leave, Appa!'

'What great possessions do I have here to hold me back, Mother? No house in the village, no land in the forest, it seems there's some porter job at the Belagavi Bus Stop. I too am going with Shivarama.'

Tungavva grasped the root of the matter. When the village farmers are quitting the place, at least Gowda or Chambasa ought to have been there to stop them. The Gowda is in his grave. Chambasa isn't here. I thought at least Bagirti would be able to handle this situation. But she is all set to leave the village first! She decided that she had the responsibility of quickly saying something on behalf of the Gowda family. She made her way to the yoked cart again and stood there. She tried to hold the yoke and stop the cart. Lasuma came to her help. He freed the bullocks, pushed them away and lowered the front part of the cart. Tungavva touched the forelegs of the bullocks with reverence. She sat on the ground, beating the ground with both her hands and making the dust rise. Then she folded her hands to all, and raised the folded hands over her head. She said, 'Children, I have some last words to say. Please listen to me.'

People, who watched it all excitedly, grew quiet. Tungavva continued, 'When Gowda died, I was with him. Chambasa was there too. Before he died, he gave a letter he wrote to Chambasa and asked him to read it. Chambasa read it and told me, "Gowda has written that we must return the land given to the Dalit farmers." He signed the document legally. Chambasa will bring it here and read it to you all. Now what is the need for you four men to run away to Belagavi?'

Everybody was amazed. Can you believe this or not? Those who believed it felt happy, those who didn't were confused…they kept looking at each other's faces and stood there silently. A little while later, a farmer who was older than the others came to the front, folded his hands, stood before Tungavva, and said, 'Don't be angry. Don't think we suspect your words, Avva. You too are an outcaste like us.

What if the Gowda has made someone read something to hoodwink you?'

He stood before her, his head bent. Tungavva became furious. Her eyes were like balls of sulphur. Her whole body shook as if she was possessed. With her trembling right hand, she tore the pearl chain which she had always worn around her neck in the name of the goddess, Mother Renuka-Yellamma. With the same passion, she showed it to all and declared, 'I swear by the chain of the Mother. If my words are false, I'll kill myself, son!' She struck her chest twice or thrice with the hand holding the chain. Everybody grew alarmed. They trembled in fear thinking that the goddess was going to visit them with some disaster. Immediately, Shivarama became alert and held Tungavva tight, so that she didn't do any harm to herself. The anxious village women came and wiped the sweat off her face. They snatched the pearl chain from her hand with great difficulty and put it around her neck again. They fanned her with their sari seragus. Another woman made her drink some water. The elder Dalits came to her and held her feet, asking for forgiveness. All this solicitude made Tungavva calm down a little. Her excitement abated, she wiped the sweat still streaming down her face and called Shivarama, 'Brother, let your sister be in my house. Gowda has given five acres of land to each of you. You live here cultivating that. Forget sugarcane and rubbish like that. Grow your food and live the right way. I know that none of you here have corn. Until the harvest, Lasuma will give all four of you a bag of corn each. Take that.' By the time she finished, she choked, and her voice came out hoarse like she was roaring, 'Beyond this, if you still want to cross the Shivapura border, do it over my dead body.' She shot up like a burning torch and went to the vaade.

Bagirti didn't know all of this. But she had come to know that the farmers had gathered under the tree. The reason for this was not known in the vaade. She had read in the papers about farmers torching their cattle sheds on the day of the protest. She lost her courage and trembled in fear. She thought, since Father isn't here now, I'll be the target of the farmers' anger. She sat there planning that if she somehow survived that day she'd escape from there.

After eating the breakfast Akku Taayi had made, Bagirti and Tungavva both sat in the backyard talking of this and that. Bagirti asked, 'Look Aayi, I went to Bangalore. You were here. Right? Brother was here too. There that pimp of a husband humiliated me nicely, and I came back. But what happened here meanwhile? I don't know anything. You tell me. Yamunakka, who was here when I left, is not here now! Shari isn't here! My daughter is not here! Father isn't here! Brother Chambu doesn't speak to me face to face! Whatever I ask, he says I'll tell you later. I am in a kind of limbo now. What's my fate now? At least tell me that.' She spoke plaintively.

'What can I say, daughter? What's left to tell? I lost my daughter and granddaughter. Your father was like the banyan tree. He too is gone. What's left for me now? You tell me.'

Tungavva wept until her tears and snot got mixed. She started wiping them off and ended up crying some more.

'It seems Father died with his head on your lap? Tell me about that at least. I swear, if you don't tell me, I'll begin crying too,' threatened Bagirti, sobbing. Then Tungavva narrated in detail everything that happened on her father's last day: 'Gowda too was happy within when he heard about Chambasa's protest.'

Bagirti intervened, 'Happy? Was Father happy about a protest against him?'

'Ay Shiva! You think Gowda didn't know that Mallimadu was rotting and stinking? Did he want the village to rot? No, daughter. On the same day you went to Bangalore, both Swami and Chambasa came here, met the Gowda, told him "Uncle, we will protest against you," and left. Gowda said, "Go ahead."'

'Ay Shiva!'

'Yes, Avva! The next day, Shivapura folk—men, women, old and young—all gathered under the tree, and shouting, "Chambanna Jai, Swami Jai", they went on a huge procession! Gowda stood in the house and watched! I too saw, right? He watched until the procession reached Mallimadu. Except for that overfed bull, that pimp Ramesa and your brother-in-law, everybody else was there, daughter! Meanwhile God knows who informed those police pimps, they came in a black motor vehicle—both Swami and Chambasa stood in front of them and tried to talk. Then the Gowda, who was standing on the terrace, also came down. A farmer came running and said, "Yappa, Gowda, your cattle shed is on fire!" We saw a man run out of the shed! Gowda shouted, "Get him, that bastard." Four men ran towards the shed.

'By then, the fire was already raging! Cattle shed full of smoke! Smoke outside! Smoke inside! Cattle started shrieking! A farmer came running and begged, "Yappa! Dumb animals are shrieking. I'll free them." Gowda said, "Yes." More farmers joined and ran to free the cows. The mute animals escaped, daughter! They got hold of the pimp who set fire to the cattle shed. Gowda asked, "Tell me, bastard! Why did you set fire?" You know, the Gowda took his gun and pointed it at him! That women's cum-like man got scared. He clutched the Gowda's feet and answered, "Yappa, brother Slimy Rameshi gave me hundred rupees and asked me to set fire." An amazed Gowda went into the house!

'When the cattle saw the people outside, they started charging at them. The women's cum-like cops beat anyone and anyhow! People ran here, there, screamed, cursed, yelled and sighed. Men and women shouted like crazy. The bruised ones sat and cried. They begged. It could make your heart melt…Avva, Avva, how can I say this? What do I say? People didn't take it passively. They chased the cops and beat them! Finally, unable to stand up against the people, the police drove away in their motor vehicle. Meanwhile, a servant of Gowda's vaade came and whispered something in Chambasa's ear, he ran there. People went back to their houses.

'God knows what happened that day! Gowda, who came back to the house, started drinking. It seems he sat down and wrote something. He sent the servant to bring Chambasa. After sending the servant, he raised his hand to drink. He had a stroke. I ran there when I heard the news. Chambasa too came to know and brought the doctor there. Not a bit of hope. The doctor gave an injection and some pills. I supported one arm and Chambasa supported the other. We took the Gowda to the bed and made him lie down.

'He regained his consciousness in an hour or two. Chambasa and I were sitting there. He held Chambasa and tried to say something. His tongue moved, but no sound came out. After a while, he got back his voice. But he couldn't speak. He couldn't close the lips. Left arm, left leg and left side of his mouth went awry! He pushed his tongue out and struggled to say something. He pointed to some paper with difficulty. They brought some paper and showed it to him. He nodded his head sideways indicating, not this, not this. He pointed to another paper. He began to get upset as if they were deliberately not getting the right paper. Finally, when they showed him some paper, he opened his eyes wide and became brighter. He signed with his good hand, "Open this and read." God knows what information it had! Chambasa's face filled with joy. Again and again, he tried to say something like "Vagoo, oogi, lasama." He signalled to me to keep the paper safe and got ready to sleep. Chambasa said, "Fine." And asked me to give him another pill after an hour. God knows what karma, or what old debt it is! My luck, my King put his head on my lap and slept. He didn't get up later, child…'

Tungavva began crying. Slowly, she recollected in vivid detail all those incidents in Gowda's life that related to both of them and wept inconsolably. Bagirti found it impossible to talk further and fell silent.

Later, under Namahshivaya's supervision, Chambasa performed the eleventh-day rites. Thereafter, he made Lasuma perform the rest of the rituals. He fed the whole village and made them feel good.

Baramegowda had challenged Shivapura society with his lustful life and his new reforms. In his good times, he had attracted a lot of women. He had received curses from the husbands of the village beauties. He drank well. Ate well. He was a connoisseur of arts, he had encouraged them. He felt a lot for Shivapura. He loved the people of Shivapura. He got people used to his lifestyle with his don't-care attitude. People looked upon Gowda's love-games like those of Lord Krishna's. They never left him out of anything good or bad that happened in the village.

At one time, he pointed to a new direction, a new future, for Shivapura. He brought many cash crops like sugarcane and brinjal into the village and helped the villagers make some money. But his obsession with higher education had resulted in disaster. It led to Mallimadu being filled with foreign waste, spread of dangerous diseases and the land turning sterile. He hadn't expected these consequences.

Since Gowda was born into a family of hereditary headmanship, he was naturally at the centre of all the changes happening in Shivapura. His obsequious son-in-law had always snaked his hand into the pockets of Gowda's weakness. Finally, Gowda realized his mistake. But by then Shivapura had already lost its creative and life-giving centre. He couldn't accept the fact that there were boys of the later generation in his village, in fact of his own family, who had seen more of the world than he had. By the time he got to accept this, time had passed. When he died, his near and dear ones felt great sorrow. What is more, even his enemies felt a sort of emptiness within them. Although she was a devadasi, he had respected and loved Tungavva like a wife towards the later part of his life. He had accepted Lasuma as his son.

The next day, Chambasa left the village without telling anyone. People said that he was wandering in the forest searching for Sharavva and would be back in a day or two. Only Tungavva said that in the morning, when the cool breeze blew, even as she slept, she had this impression that Chambasa had come, touched her feet and left. But since she wasn't sure if it was reality or dream, she didn't say it out loud. Bagirti too thought what the others did and sat waiting for him.

The next day, when they heard the radio news, let alone Bagirti, the whole village was reeling under the shock. Chambasa had gone to the judge, admitted to all the five murders that happened in Shivapura and shocked the media as well as the people of the state. Tungavva, Bagirti, Lasuma and Akku Taayi struggled with this trauma like worms caught in fire. For half the day, nobody spoke to each other. Only Tungavva wept, beating her chest with her hands, 'You stole a son, who was like Parashurama of the epics, you Crazy Woman!' She kept cursing goddess Renukadevi and beating the floor with her hands. The others kept wondering sadly, silently and anxiously, 'How did this happen?' They asked themselves and looked at each other's faces. Finally, in the evening, Bagirti took some courage into her hands and said, 'What Aayi, how can such a thing happen? My brother is not the type to do murders. Come on.'

But Tungavva gave her strong opinion on the matter, 'Daughter, I have no doubt about it. In this village, the only real man who can murder five people on the same day is my son! You tell me if there's any other! Daughter, the anger of good people is like this. It is these sort of people who, when they are angry, can fell, what only five even ten corpses on the ground! Parashurama is not someone else. My son is Parashurama,' she cried, and beating her chest once more, added, 'Look, he killed five. Did any pimp of a policeman catch him? He went and stood before the judge himself! He admitted to his crime and told the judge, "I am the one who killed, Judge Saheb." Did you find this manliness even in Gandhi or Nehru? You tell me?' She said this with great pride and began weeping again.

After a week, they took many villagers, old and young, to give witness. Not a single man of the village said anything against Chambasa. Everyone deposed, 'He's not the kind who'd do that,' and returned to the village. When Bagirti gave this news to Tungavva, she declared, 'Sister, even if you ask God to be witness, He'll say the same thing! My son is a Parashurama.' Even Kuntirapa, who came to Belagavi with all his ministerial retinue, couldn't create any witnesses. In the end, he accepted defeat. It was like someone throwing scalding water over the roots of all his dreams. Unable to show his face in the village, he went back to Bangalore. The same week, they also passed the judgment and gave Chambasa five years in jail. Bagirti was scared because Kuntirapa, who had come to Belagavi, hadn't come to the village. She burned with anger. However, Kuntirapa coming to the village was also a dangerous thing. When the whole village stood as one by Chambasa, Kuntirapa had tried to create false witnesses. If he'd come to the village, people probably would not have left him alive. People were disgusted with him because he was a man who hadn't even made a phone call when his father-in-law, Rameshi, or his own brother Ganapa had died.

Bagirti got worried. Now Chambasa isn't here. I have no idea what is in the farmers' mind. I am not acquainted with a single one of them. I know many women of the farmer community. But I don't know what is in their mind either. Of course, there are Tungavva, Akku Taayi, Lasuma and my four servants. But all their trust and love won't count if I have to face the opposition of so many enemy farmers.

Meanwhile, she heard someone in the porch calling, 'Sister...Avva.' She came out and saw someone standing there. He folded his hands, bent down and saluted her. Bagirti asked him, 'Who are you?'

'Avva, I am the manager of your sugar factory.'

'What have you come for?'

'You didn't recognize me, Avva! Some time back, you came to your factory guest house and stayed there twice. My daughter grew very fond of you.'

'Shakuntala is your wife, right?'

'Yes, Avva! Why don't you please come and stay in the guest house for a couple of days again? All the women there ask after you, Avva. They all felt sad about what happened to you. They have sent me saying, "Bring our sister here."'

Bagirti's eyes shone and her face turned rosy with this unexpected joy. A very soft-hearted manager, he too was happy when he saw Bagirti's joy. There was a lot of pity and sympathy underlining his happiness. He continued, 'That is also your factory, Avva! If you come there, we are prepared to guard you like the pupil of our eye. Please come. They all sent me to bring you to the factory.' He folded his hands again. Bagirti melted. She thought God himself had sent the man.

Thinking of it from any angle, this is a rare opportunity. She grew certain of it. These people want the factory to run without Kuntirapa's intervention. Chambasa isn't here. Tungavva is only a woman. So it is not safe for me to remain here. After my father's death, the factory ownership has also passed on to me. So if I go and live there, I too will have some work to do. I can forget the daily worries and live in peace. Moreover, it is not as if Shivapura is far away from where the factory is. I can come whenever I want to and take care of things here. What else? Should take care that Kuntirapa doesn't come anywhere near the factory. Bagirti felt she'd found a safe place to live. She was happy. She informed him, 'I'll come. Let the car be here. It'll be easier to load my luggage into it tomorrow,' she told him, and prepared herself mentally to leave.

Later she told Tungavva, 'Look Aayi, it seems the sugar factory is in bad shape and is about to shut down. You and Lasuma are here to take care of the fields and the house. What about the factory? So I'll go there. They told me, "If you don't come, we'll have to close the factory down. That cripple took the Bangalore route. Chambasa went to jail. We need someone there, right?"' She didn't bring up the matter of the farmers.

'Look, daughter! You take care of the factory and also

the village headmanship. This is the village you were born in. This is the village you rule. You keep this and also rule the whole country if you want to. I won't object. But I'll not let you leave the village,' Tungavva told her in a cut-and-dried manner.

'I'll be there, and I'll also be here,' Bagirti said vaguely, and began to pack. Tungavva left feeling weary.

Lasuma came when the car arrived.

'Sister, if you decide to stay back, we will be very pleased. But even if you want to go to the factory, we'll make arrangements for it,' Lasuma told her. Bagirti hurriedly answered.

'I'll go to the factory, Appa!'

'Have your meal and leave.'

'I am not hungry, Lasuma. I'll go to the factory.'

After this, in about an hour, the upper-caste farmer boys sent by Lasuma came there and loaded the luggage that Bagirti pointed to in the car boot. Lasuma stood supervising. It was time for her to leave. Tungavva hadn't come. 'You tell her, brother Lasuma,' she requested, and before he responded added, 'Thank you so much, brother Lasuma!' She folded her hands, expressed her gratitude and got into the car.

'What is this you say, Sister? You are Chambasa's sister...'

'That is what I am saying, Brother. I am Chambasa's sister and your sister too. Don't call me akka. Call me tangi, like Chambasa does.' She wept as she said this. Lasuma too cried and folded his hands. Before the car left, Tungavva came. Bagirti got off the car, saying, 'I will be back soon, Aayi,' and embraced her. She restrained her flowing tears, touched Tungavva's feet, steeled her heart and got into the car. Sobbing, she asked the driver to go. The car must have hardly travelled about an arm's length. Her eyes had gone misty. When she wiped her tears and looked—all the farmers of the village are moving towards the car in a group! At the forefront of this procession were the rebel farmers. Bagirti's heart sank. Her voice failed, she was shivering. She asked the driver to stop the car. The moment the car stopped, Lasuma came running and opened the car door. Tungavva too came there and stood between the car and the crowd like a boundary stone. By the time she got off the car, all the three rebel farmers passed Tungavva and came to Bagirti, 'Please forgive our error, Avva! You don't give us any land or anything. We will labour in your fields. You are our mother. Don't leave the village,' they appealed to her. They folded their hands and bent down where they stood. Immediately, all the other farmers folded their hands too and prostrated themselves on the ground. They told her, 'Avva, believe us. We will take care of you like you are our very life. Don't go.' They wept. Their voices echoed everywhere, 'Don't go, Avva, don't go!' They showed their devotion to her by saluting and touching the ground where they stood. Bagirti didn't know what to do. She choked, hugged Tungavva, sobbed, and slowly folding her hands to everyone there, went back into the house. Even before she stepped in, the farmer boys went past her with her luggage and deposited it in the house as she stood watching.

PART THREE

An Offering to Ghataprabha

One morning, two policemen brought Chambasa in a jeep. They completed all the procedures of handing him over to the jail officials and exchanged signatures in each other's registers. Then, equally mechanically, the jail authorities left him in a cell with sturdy stone walls and without any proper facilities. It had a window, two stone benches for beds and one door. Chambasa looked around wide-eyed. The whole cell, including the window and the door, looked like a cave made of a single rock. The cool stone walls. There was also the morning chill. He looked out of the window. In the vast yard in front, there was yellow sunlight. Here and there the Bermuda grass grew, the blades shook when the breeze blew. That was the only sign of life. He looked sharply around to see if there was any life moving in the adjacent cells. From the cell opposite his, someone thrust a hand through the window-bars and made obscene gestures at him. That man made the sign of a kiss and leered. Chambasa came back and sat on the bench.

Later a couple of sturdy men came, made him take off his clothes and wear the jail clothes. They gave him a sheet, pillow, blanket, one plate and a small water pot! They left after locking the door. The same stone cave and the same yard. Scared that if he looked out he would see the same leering man, he sat back again on the stone bench. There's another bench. This means there's another man expected here. Will he come at all? What kind of man would that be? He decided that he'd think about this when the man actually came and lay down on the bench. He looked up. What's there? Nothing, empty. Unable to think of anything else, he brought Shivapura back in his mind. The moment he did that, Namahshivaya peeped in there. He was laughing. He asked, 'How's the jail?'…Then the Ghataprabha river flowed there. He felt her cool waters and apologized, 'Mother who bore me, please forgive me.' Then came the banyan tree. Tungavva slept on the porch outside the house. She had cried a lot. Sleep had come to her only a little while ago. He knew she'd cry again if he woke her up. He touched her feet softly and turned his face away. Sharavva came now. His heart was on fire. He thought somebody had kicked at his chest. He sat up suddenly. 'Shivalinga, I came here thinking that this place was deserted. How many wounds, how many haunting memories have you sent chasing after me?' He touched his chest, and his face twisted with pain.

In the afternoon, he ate and slept. His eyelids wouldn't shut. He sank into memories again. In just two weeks, starting from the day of the protest to this day, how many things happened, Shiva! One morning and one night of the protest…protest, fire in uncle's cattle shed, police atrocities, five murders! Everything continued until I was jailed…if I remember it…even now…did all this really happen? What a strange series of events! All this happened because some puppet master botched his play somewhere! Kuntirapa sent the cops to stop the protest. At the same time, he also sent Slimy Ramesha to take revenge on me. The result? Yamunakka, Gowda…not five, but seven corpses! It is amazing how Shivapura withstood this. Murders are not new to Shivapura. If not in Shivapura, at least around that region, there was some murder or the other, and the dead bodies came to Shivapura. The village bore it well. But six corpses at the same time! That too because of the greed of a villain who isn't even of the village! It is this sorrow that broke Baramegowda's heart, and he became the sixth corpse! People knew this. Therefore, they gave statements in Chambasa's favour, saying that all the five murders were of their enemies.

The scenes of the protest came up in front of his eyes. Even before it started, I knew that Kuntirapa would do some mischief and upset the intention and rhythm of this protest. I was all eyes, watching those two, Slimy Ramesha and Tell-tale Ganapa, who were like beasts that Kuntirapa had nurtured. But neither I nor the farmers could counter his genius. As it is his head is a fox's cave. The perverse logic that is born there, and the deceptions he practices according to those ideas, these are beyond us, even if we go through a course of training in such things. Police came. Lasuma and Balavanta's son were wounded. Luckily, we found a truck and admitted them to the Belagavi hospital. I gave hundred rupees for expenses to Lasuma and hurried to the bus stand. There was no bus going to Shivapura. I waited on the by-pass road, got into a truck that was going to Maharashtra and got off at the Nirvanappa hill. There I got on another waste-disposal truck and came to Shivapura. I went straight to Yamunakka's house. What I had feared had happened. They had left Yamunakka half-dead. Sharavva wasn't there. Alarmed, I came out and shook Yamunakka shouting, 'Sister.' Luckily she came back to consciousness. Her face was swollen and scary with dried blood sticking to it. Becoming suspicious about her being alive at all, I shook her again. I heard a faint sound, 'Who?' The moment she knew it was me, she got up with my help. 'Those women's cum-like police fellows, there were three, Brother, one after the other, they raped Sharavva and left, Appa...' She beat her chest and breathed her last!

I went home. I took the blade used for cutting the stalks and went to the village square. I slaughtered all the five who slept there sloshed with drink. I took a cart that stood there, loaded all the five corpses onto it, drew the cart myself, went to the stream and toppled the cart over. Two dead bodies fell into water. With the other three, only half the body was in water and the other half still lay on the cart. I cleaned the blade, bathed and stood there in my wet clothes. Accidentally, I saw my face in the water! It appeared bit by bit in the little waves and disappeared. Is this my face? I was in agony. There wasn't a lot of time to keep looking at it. I took the blade back home. Unable to sleep, I took the pickaxe and went to the graveyard to dig a grave for Yamunakka. I dug the grave, thinking all the time about where Sharavva was.

When I returned home, the sun had risen. Somebody threw a stone at the tree. Crows cawed and flew over Yamunakka's body and over the bank of the stream. The yellow light of the early morning sun fell all over Shivapura, and the village looked like a consumptive patient. I woke up a couple of friends and asked them to make a bamboo stretcher for the dead body. I embraced Tungavva, who sat crying, and called out, 'Ee, Mother.' She'd cried so much that no sound came out of her mouth, only her tears flowed. Tungavva hugged me and began to cry afresh saying, 'Did you come now, son?' I sat consoling her. The news of the five corpses had already spread among those who had gathered there. By the time people who'd been there came here and vice versa, not bothering about who came or who left, even without informing Nagappa, some of us who were there took Yamunakka's body, buried it and came back. Meanwhile, Baramegowda had sent for Tungavva, and she went there. I was getting scared about Sharavva. She wasn't at Lasuma's place. Not even in my house. Then... by then, Gowda had sent for me. I went.

Chambasa bore the burden of all those thick memories. He felt tired. The moment he closed his eyes, sleep enveloped him like magic.

The next day I found that my status and honour had reached the skies. My fellow convicts are feeling scared of me as if I am a big officer or something! The convict, who gestured obscenely yesterday and the day before, acts like a guilty servant now. He holds his ears and beats his chin with his hands in an act of contrition! At meal time, everybody is making way for me and lining up behind me! I asked the jail official why. He replied that they were scared of this valiant, daring super hero, who committed five murders on the same day! God! If my ancestor Gowdas became heroes by fighting wars or hunting tigers, I had become the hero of heroes by committing five murders. I entered the jail. Is this a matter of pride or of shame! God! The credit should go to you who made me do all this! I looked up and celebrated my new position in the jail.

For a minute, I felt that I had said something very flippant. Did God make me murder people? Is it Shivalinga's job to get people to murder other people? Shiva, Shiva! Honourable Judge, I am the murderer! Me! Me! Only me! The one who made me do it is not Shivalinga, but Kuntirapa!

That night, in my dream, I found myself standing in court again. Yes, the kind judge sat looking at me. A mild man, his face shone with radiance. There was a fine glow in his eyes—eyes which were like lamps lit in a shrine.

I talked, trembling a bit, 'Revered Sirs, today I kept talking to myself and said something—that it was Shivalinga who made me commit those murders. I said all the consequences must be credited to His account. Forgive me, Sir. I am the murderer! Me! But the one who made me do it is certainly not Shivalinga! It's Kuntirapa!

Yes, Kuntirapa came and disturbed the life of Shivapura, turned it into slush and made sure that it would never be clean again. This is the reason. I offered my logical argument—me, on my own behalf! In front of myself! If only he hadn't taunted me again and again, got me beaten up…if he'd not eyed Shari…not allowed the waste to come into Shivapura. Or on my part…if I was a coward and had no sense of pride…the same kind of ifs and buts…anyway, what happened in the end? He was responsible for all this. That's it. If, every day, he hadn't grown into a challenge to my strength, ability and character, all this wouldn't have happened!

That day, when I bathed and looked at myself in the water, the face I saw was…yes, it was Kuntirapa's! He was shedding a red glare from his eyes. If a man makes up his mind to become a demon, with a little effort, he can do it. Kuntirapa was the evidence. In order not to lose the fire of this demonic nature, he had to keep in practice by tormenting others from time to time. He fed fuel to it often. Then I knew that this ghost called Kuntirapa, who yanks at my heart strings, is actually within me. Because of this ghost…

What appeared in water that day was the monstrous form of Kuntirapa. He leered, touched, got scared and then stood stretching both his hands up. The form I saw in the water had usurped my place. But it wasn't me, I thought. I asked him, 'You tormented Shari like that. Aren't you contented yet?'

Leering some more, he replied, 'No. No, I will torment her until she sleeps with me. Even after she sleeps with me, I don't think she will be in peace. So I'll still torment her. Before she invaded my heart and sat there, I too was a good man. But after she got into my heart, I lost my peace. Therefore why should she be peaceful? Before that, I...'

'Lies. You were never a good man. You were born a liar and thief.'

'Yes, what you said is true. But not such a big liar and thief as you think. A little more than that. Shall I tell you what I have become now? A ghost! I have become a ghost haunting you! A ghost doesn't dissolve until it gets what it wants. My hatred of you has turned me into a ghost. Neither I nor you who stand against me will ever find peace,' he declared! I was furious with him, and I killed him, but he came back as the image in the water. I killed him again. Respected Judge...I thought if I killed this one man, Shivapura would become clean in the future, and I killed him.

I killed him thinking that from now on there would only be truth, justice and righteousness in Shivapura. He came up again in the water. I asked, 'You came again?' And killed him again. He came back five times like this. I killed him five times. Righteous Judge, don't show me even a vestige of pity. Give me whatever punishment you want to give. Righteous Judge, this is true. All this is true. Nothing else is true. Give me whatever punishment you want to give me.' Even as I said this, I woke up.

Daughter Finds the Mother

On the other hand, Sharavva's life had taken a different turn. On that night of horror, Sharavva became an orphan. Sharavva, a victim of an inhuman police sexual assault, took a child not her own in her arms and left in the middle of the night. She came stumbling and staggering and knocked on the temple door. Namahshivaya got scared. Has there been any murder? It shouldn't happen because the police are around. Since he was the one to perform the funeral rites of any corpse that turned up there, he held the lantern up, and in its faint light, opened the door. He was shocked when he realized who stood in front of him. This form, with its hair dishevelled, carried a baby that seemed to be sticking to its shoulder and was covered by a cloth that looked like it was dipped in blood. He called her in, 'Come, daughter!' She was like a field that was devastated by the invasion of a heady wind or by the onslaught of a group of birds. He grasped the circumstances which Sharavva narrated hurriedly and in a state of great agitation. Immediately, he took whatever money he had, wore his shirt, flung a dhotra on his shoulder, took the baby from Sharavva's arms, held her hand, and went out saying, 'Come, daughter.' When they found a truck on the Maharashtra–Bangalore highway, they got into it. By the time they got off the truck, it was morning. From there, they travelled in a bus for another two hours. Then they got off under a tree with a crude platform around it and walked a bit. They came to a big house. There a kind old woman, who saw the state of the guests, took pity on them, and gave them a cup of gruel each and a cup of milk for the child. Namahshivaya told her Sharavva's story, and she melted. The child, which got into a tantrum and left off drinking the milk halfway, put her mouth to the bottle again and sucked all the milk. The baby's eyes shone like oil lamps about to be extinguished. The baby looked everywhere, perhaps because the place was new, shut her eyes again and went back to sleep. By the time Sharavva put the child down in a corner and came back, Namahshivaya was ready to leave. 'Daughter, we don't know what state Shivapura is in. You stay safe here. Manikamma was with us in the freedom movement. A very good woman. She will take care of you as if you are her daughter. Don't feel alarmed. I will visit from time to time. I'll write to you. Shall I leave now, daughter?'

Although this was another shock to Sharavva, it was unavoidable in the circumstances.

'Don't forget me, Father,' her eyes filled with tears as she saluted the Swami.

'You don't worry, daughter. Manikamma was someone who was with the Mahatma,' he told her as both of them came to the yard. Meanwhile, Manikamma, who came there, assured her, 'Don't be scared, daughter. I'm here, am I not?' She placed her hand on Sharavva's shoulder. Sharavva saluted her, moved back and stood protected by her embrace.

'I don't know the situation in Shivapura. I'll find out, and the moment things are good, I'll come here with Chambasa, all right?' said Namahshivaya. Sharavva nodded. He went on, 'Manikamma, I have put my daughter in your hands. The rest is your job, Mother.'

He saluted her and left. Preventing Sharavva from bursting into tears, Manikamma hugged her, and enclosing her in the warmth of her massive body, led her into the house.

It was an orphanage. Some of Gandhi's followers who had participated in the freedom movement were still alive. They lived their lives doing some good work. Among them we have seen two: Namahshivaya and Manikamma. Manikavva joined the movement in her teens, lost the best time of her youth to the movement, didn't get married and spent whatever was left of her life and money in running the orphanage. Many among the freedom fighters of those times had refused government pension. In the beginning, Manikamma had also refused it. But later she thought it would come in handy to run the orphanage and accepted it. And some other freedom fighters, who were moved by Manikamma's good nature, gave not only their pension money, but also grains, rice and vegetables that they grew in their fields, to her orphanage. In any case, the 'Kasturba Orphanage', which made a good name for itself without any government aid, gave shelter to orphan children in these parts.

There can be no other word on this matter—the good name of the Ashram came from Manikamma's sterling character. Manikavva is a massive woman, always full of life. She radiates an aura of goodness. In her dress, manner, movements and activities, you see simplicity, tranquillity and dignity. Not a beautiful woman. But because of her patience, compassion, sense of responsibility and concern for others, everybody looked up to her with great respect and trust. More often than not, these orphans were also physically challenged in one way or the other. Therefore, she was raising them with deep concern for each child's health and future. She was a woman who found fulfilment in this. She had a heart larger than a mother's. Her assistants were fond of her. So there was, in this ashram, an atmosphere of closeness. There were caring bonds among these people like those among trees, plants and creepers in the woods.

Alongside this beautiful atmosphere, Manikamma's warm love made Sharavva comfortable in the new place. But in the beginning, Madevi would go into tantrums and, always stick to Sharavva. There were sixteen children in all in the ashram. Of them, four were physically challenged, aged less than six. Madevi joined them as the fifth. There was a large fig tree in the backyard of the ashram. Except for a few hours at night, at all times birds chirped on that tree. All five children played under that tree, and learnt this and that from the guru. Sharavva supervised these children. Madevi opened her eyes wide strangely when she laughed. She drooled all the time. Because of this, the other kids didn't eat with her. At these times, Madevi made an ugly, animal-like sound and felt upset. Manikamma, who observed this, called a specialist to examine her. He gave some tablets, advised them to tie an apron round her neck, and asked them to teach her to wipe her mouth when she drooled. He also told them not to pay attention to her when she cried.

This proved effective. Madevi now sat independently. She crawled and moved around. She mixed with the other children and played with toys. Even the drooling decreased. Yet, sometimes, Madevi suddenly got up in the middle of the night, shrieked and cried like an animal. At those times, unable to console her, Sharavva cursed her fate silently and cried, 'God knows where the woman who gave birth to her is! She left this child with me and went to dogs. I cannot throw this child away. I cannot protect this child.

I don't have the strength to protect her. I don't have the heart to throw her away. I am unable to shed this baby that is like someone else's sin stuck to my life, sin stuck to my mind. Say I take this child to the temple, pat on my chin in reverence, and beg, "Mother, swallow my sins and forgive me," will the goddess even look at me when I take this abject baby there? Mother, this isn't my sin. I was asleep. Somebody put her on my lap! I have torn the pearl that I once tied around my neck in this Mother's name. Now why will she protect me?' Sharavva talked to herself in this disconnected manner and cried until all her tears dried up.

Sharavva always got up early in the morning. If Madevi got up and didn't find Sharavva next to her, she'd cry in a terrible voice. Afraid of this, Sharavva kept lying on the bed until Madevi too got up. At those times, she thought a lot about Chambasa and got upset. That day, there was a letter from Namahshivaya. She felt pleased and proud of Chambasa when she read that he'd killed all the three who had raped her, and another two in addition, making it five in all, and then had gone to jail himself. Love surged within her, making her eyes shine. The whole morning, she was in that mood. Then something happened. While eating her lunch, Madevi pushed her food away and shrieked, perhaps because she didn't like the food. Sharavva was angry because it upset her nice mood. You know what! She stretched her hand, screwed up her eyes and smacked the child hard. Shocked by Sharavva's unexpected behaviour, the child stopped crying and stared at her wide-eyed. Sharavva took the kid's hand and put it on the plate. That day, Madevi put the morsel of food into her mouth and ate by herself. Thus Sharavva began to learn to become a mother, and Madevi a daughter.

The next day, Sharavva's mood changed. She was

disappointed about Namahshivaya's letter. You know why? It was like throwing cold water on her hope that Chambasa would come out of jail, find her and take her back home. I cannot go to Shivapura alone. There's neither Mother nor Chambasa there. There's only aunt Tungavva. She perhaps thinks badly of me. She might blame me for her son going to jail. She would, undoubtedly, curse me at least twice every day. Then there's only Bagirti left. She is not really my kin. Why will she give me shelter? If she snatches the baby away and asks me to go, I have to do that without another word. Or should I keep serving this baby all my life, waiting for her to come and take it away? Then there's Lasuma. He is a married man. He is his mother's son. How can he give me shelter… She lost hope of ever returning to Shivapura. She struck her forehead with her hand twice and grew quiet.

Now Madevi was not throwing tantrums like earlier. Her neck didn't droop like earlier either. The saliva fell on the apron around her neck. She wiped her lips with that cloth. She'd try to walk, take a step or two, fall and sit down. When she was obstinate, Sharavva only had to screw up her eyes in anger. Madevi would hug Sharavva, put her cheek on Sharavva's cheek and try to be all sweet and nice. She would call her, 'Mother, my mother!' At such times, Sharavva's joy knew no bounds. She too would pet the child calling her, 'My child, my sweet…' When she bathed Madevi, she scrubbed the legs starting from the underside of her feet to her thigh. She held her little soft body, soaped it and washed it with water. Sometimes, the child shivered and screamed when the water was a little cold. The child's changing moods of joy, fear, violent anger, impatience, and stomping away—everything was adorable. Sharavva looked at the child's saucer-like eyes and forgot the whole world. They weren't orphans anymore. Sharavva had a daughter! Madevi had found a mother!

Chambasa's Pangs of Separation

Now Chambasa felt lonely. Earlier, Shari rushed into his dreams and his imagination every minute and tortured him. Why hadn't she come yet tonight? Perhaps because he slept thinking of her, she came into his dream in the morning. It was like fire coming close to the hay. She gave a scornful laugh, and her hair blew like flames around her head. She laughed a scornful laugh with her burning lips and moved towards the nilgiri trees near Mallimadu. The two trees were frowning horribly, and they looked like they were staring at him. Suddenly, he got up feeling like his insides were burning.

Outside, morning had broken. There was a slight drizzle. Cold too. He wrapped the blanket round him and sat on the bed. Sharavva returned to fill his thoughts. He struggled like a trapped animal. He could do nothing. He struggled more and more like a worm that has fallen into the fire. Where's she? What happened to her? Is she still alive? He moaned, 'Ayyo...' Many people said she might have fallen into Mallimadu and died. But how could he believe that someone who appeared in his dreams like this everyday was dead? In the dream too, she would laugh scornfully and move towards those nilgiri trees, right? Did she go directly to Mallimadu... Ayyo did she sacrifice herself in Mallimadu...but that wasn't known for sure either.

That afternoon, Bagirti, Lasuma and four farmers came

to see him. He didn't get an opportunity to talk much. He was miserable when he found out that Tungavva was bedridden. He requested all those who had come there, especially Bagirti and Lasuma, to take care of her. Bagirti had brought the letter that Baramegowda had written before his death. He read it to the farmers. It began with the customary blessing of a long life to Chambasa.

> Son, your uncle Baramegowda appeals to you thus— Lasuma (there was also a blessing for Lasuma's long life) is my son. He is Tungi's son. He is my son. Give my property to daughter Bagirti and Lasuma. Give back the lands of the Dalit farmers. Give them right away. All right? In the meanwhile, if Kuntirapa comes back, break his other leg. You should all do this jointly. All right? This is a government order. All right?
>
> Yours sincerely,
> Baramegowda

Chambasa read this and told them to take care of their land, as well as that of his uncle. He suggested that they open a school where the sugar factory was. Bagirti was ready to do this. He also felt happy that as a result the village farmers decided not to grow sugarcane this time. Then, unable to control his curiosity anymore, he asked if they had found out anything about Sharavva. He went into despair when they said no. He asked again, 'Did Namahshivaya Swami know that you were coming here?'

'He left the village and went away, Appa. Some say he went to the Himalayas. Others say he went to the Srishaila mountain. Who knows what is true and what's false! He, for sure, isn't in the village.'

So even the one link he had to find out about Sharavva was lost. His heart strings seemed to snap. He blacked out. The others sat silently, forgetting to speak. They kept looking at each other's faces. In the end, he controlled himself and asked Lasuma to take care of Tungavva. But the moment they left, he leant against the corner wall, hid his face in his hands, and sobbed, 'Sharoo, Sharoo…' He felt he had sobbed a little too loudly. Had anyone heard? He opened his eyes. Everyone had left, only Lasuma stood peeping in the window, crying and looking at Chambasa. When Chambasa looked up, he ran away still weeping. Chambasa sat in despair, holding his head.

God knows how long he sat like this, his thighs felt numb. He got up, slapped his bottom a couple of times, walked two steps to get the blood flowing in his legs and then sat down again. Of late, even if he got a couple of minutes alone, he'd bring Sharoo into his imagination and start talking to her. He decorated the path on which she walked up to him with the vivid colours and patterns of rangoli— all in his imagination! Both remembered the incidents of their life together, re-enacted those and repeated the same dialogues. Sometimes, when there was somebody around, he would push Shari away. But she wouldn't listen to him. She'd come and fill his mind again. He remembered her repeatedly, and her memories burnt his heart.

Once, he remembered a fight with Kuntirapa. Reason for the fight—hadn't Kuntirapa taunted Sharavva and got his teeth broken? He had admired Sharoo Taayi's boldness. But Kuntirapa's teasing had upset him. When he was agitated by the feelings of vengeance within him, Sharoo Taayi rushed into his imagination. Like every day, even on that day, she called him, 'Mavaa…' But when she saw his tense and angry face, she trembled, and there was sweat on the tip of her nose. There was in her voice the devotion of a woman asking God for a boon.

Even as he felt that it was all too much for him to bear,

she called again in a scared voice, 'Mava…' He couldn't control his anger anymore. It came like a raging flood, 'You were my wife until another man's hand touched you. The moment he touched you, the wife died, and now a whore stands before me. I don't recognize her. I don't want someone I don't even know to come and haunt me and hurt me like a broken thorn in my flesh, and all the time calling me "Mava" too.'

He uttered these words that reflected the unspoken pain within him.

'Is that so? Then, here and now, I dedicate all the happenings in my life to you. Accept them. You own them,' she said and shot out like an arrow.

That whole night, he was tormented by the same conflict. He felt it wasn't right on his part to have called her a whore. A woman, with those demons surrounding her, what could she have done to prevent the assault? Wasn't it an impossible situation? Sometimes he felt this way. Other times he thought, be that as it may, isn't she a pot that the dog has touched? The whole week, he tortured himself with such thoughts. When asleep there were those nightmares, and in the waking hours, sharp doubts assailed his mind. No spark of light yet. He grew tired. One morning, when he fell asleep because there was some cool breeze, Namahshivaya peeped into his dream and scolded him, 'What's this Chambasa? Sharoo Taayi is doing penance and wasting away somewhere all by herself. Forget someone like you judging her. Even God, God though he is, is scared of judging her. Who're you to do this, Appa? Leave her alone and look to your own soul! If you have a lot of work to do, bad thoughts won't enter your mind. You are a farmer. Five or six acres of black-soil land comes under the control of the jail. It will soon be time for harvest. You plough the land and plant something there. If nothing else, you can at least grow vegetables and eat them, right?'

Chambasa sat up suddenly. He saluted Namahshivaya with reverence and stood there saying, 'Forgive me, Appa.' In the morning, he went to the jail authorities and inquired about the black-soil land. They showed him some land which no convict had ever tried to cultivate. It was barren. But all the agricultural implements were there. They had yoked two bullocks. They had fixed a pipeline for water. What more do you need?

He started clearing the land and planting on the stony soil all by himself. Among the convicts, there were also farmers. One of them participated even in the first week. By the time of the mriga rains of the monsoon harvest, they prepared the land. At the time of the mriga rain, they planted the vegetable seeds. In only a week, green sprouted in their minds.

Sharavva's Pangs of Separation [2]

Sharavva sat under the fig tree. Madevi was playing the game of serving food with other kids. When she got even a little time for herself, Sharavva pulled Chambasa into her imagination. Now she couldn't. He didn't relax his frowning face. He gave her a cruel look that stabbed at her heart. She called Madevi as if for help. Madevi didn't hear her. He looked at Madevi with an expression stronger than hate, more contemptuous than disgust, and went away. Yes, this is his true nature. She remembered how he had felt disgusted when she took Bagirti's child into her arms once.

He lost his taste for me, I think. I cannot rouse his hunger anymore. Perhaps he only wanted me to be a cheap devadasi. The moment he comes to me, I should give an attractive smile, move my limbs seductively, turn when he pulls me to him, make cheap gestures and entertain him. He probably prides himself on being a man who can rule a beautiful woman like me. He wants to be a master. He just wants to use me. He shows off this pride because he knows I cannot love anyone but him.

Truth is, he doesn't have the same enthusiasm about me that he had earlier. What did he say? 'Chi, ugly child. This child is the fruit of your sins.' Ayyo, ayyo, why am I still alive after hearing this! Maybe he was waiting for me to move away on my own. Therefore, the moment he found some pretext to do so, he threw me away like a used leaf-plate after eating.

Yes, those police dogs tore at me and ate me up. I am unfit for Chambasa's love. An undeserving devadasi! I might have torn the pearl out. But I was born a jogti. Will that devadasi nature go away from me? What he said is true. I am a devadasi!

I am a lowly devadasi! Those police dogs also said that. I didn't know it until then. But Mava, what the police dogs tore at was only my body. My soul is yours, Mava! I gave it only to you. Even now, you are my master, husband, friend and God! Who else do I have except you, my king? This child is not my blood... But I will not give up this lump of flesh. I will not give up this Madevi. Her mother, God knows what debt she owed me, put her on my lap. I am her mother! Her father.

You chased me until you got me. You were all over me. After you got me, you moved away. But this lump of flesh is not why you moved away from me. I know. You must have found some high-caste woman. Be happy, my king—I will think of this Madevi as your flesh, and that I am her mother. I'll hug her like I would hug you and feel happy. You be happy, my king...

By the time she finished saying all this, her tears flowed without any check. They fell on her chin. Some girl whispered in Madevi's ear, 'Your mother is crying.' Madevi ran up to her, wiped her tears away and consoled, 'Why do you cry, Avva? If you cry, I feel like crying too.' She began to cry, wiping Sharavva's tears with her cloth. Sharavva saw the child's affection, and hugging it, cried again, 'I can't ever leave you.'

The next day, Sharavva's mood grew worse. She thought, this morning Chambasa came in my dream. The instant he saw me, he stood as if some new energy shot through his veins. He also hummed a song like he was in the mood for music. He felt that rare joy he had experienced when he saw me first. I felt the same. How exciting! He took a couple of steps towards me as if he was going to pull me to him and kiss me. Amazed, I kept looking at his eyes. I trembled, waiting for him to invade me, break the doors of my heart and embrace me. It was many days since I had seen this language on his lips, this light in his eyes. I opened my arms like I was opening my heart to him and stood there. But I heard, 'Avva', and turned. Madevi came walking unsteadily, dragging her leg. The moment he saw Madevi, he exploded with anger. His eyes flashed terribly under the heavy brows. Cruelty and pain were stamped on his face. He choked with anger, and his jaws were trembling. His whole manner changed, he turned into a different man!

I thought, 'You suddenly put out the lamp that you lit yourself.' My joy, which had blossomed just then, faded away…

Let me see him again in the future. I'll tell him properly. I never loved you, all right? Not only that, I feel disgusted when I see you. Whenever I think of you, my mind becomes polluted. I want to wash it. They say that if you go to the God's shrine your mind grows pure. Even God has forsaken me. I tore the pearl I wore for Chambasa's love. So the goddess threw me out of the temple. I don't even have a God now. I said he is my God. He too tore away from me.

That day, on the Nirvanappa hill, he lifted me up in his arms like he was lifting a child. He played games with me, and I'll tell you everything he said then. I will tell you that he grinned and confessed, 'I love you!' And how I too… threw away my shyness, my pride, my honour…everything and stood naked. All that…all that. Ayyo, ayyo… She shed tears again.

While my love made me want to get closer and closer

to him, he moved away more and more from me each day. He only cared for his pride, his honour and his status in society. My fate? Am I without honour? Doesn't he know whose child this is? Doesn't he know who dishonoured me? When he killed them, didn't he know that all this happened because of them?

The main thing is, he has a distorted sense of pride. Marrying a devadasi was a great rebellion. For that, he thought everybody was going to hail him as a rebel. Because of those villains, he thinks of me as a pond that pigs have rolled in and polluted! Did I do this to myself? Tell me, my king? Did I do all this to myself on purpose? She again felt like she was standing on a river bank which was collapsing. She cried, 'Ayyo.'

However much he hates me, I will always love him. He is a man, a high-caste man. He has many paths opening up for him, to cultivate himself, to grow and live. I don't. But I am not going to leave him. I don't know about other women. For me, it's only Chambasa. You can get him only if you are lucky. He is a rare, god-like man. Then and now! True, whenever I remember him, I feel like crying. Maybe I won't a little later. He may remain a sweet memory. Until then, I will keep remembering him and waiting for him.

Sharoo Taayi

Apart from growing more and more intelligent, Madevi had also gained the ability to understand and be sensitive to many new things. When Sharoo Taayi sat cleaning rice with the kitchen staff, Manikamma came there laughing, 'Look Sharoo Taayi, see how smart your daughter has grown! Yesterday, I started to tell them the story of the Pandavas in Mahabharata. Like all other kids, she too sat and listened to the story quietly. To check how much of the story they had understood, I asked them a question, "Who is Kunti?" Your daughter threw a tantrum crying, "I don't want the Kunti story," and sat turning her back to me! I was amused! I went up to her and asked, "Why Madevi? Why don't you want the Kunti story? Why, daughter?" I held her chin and asked affectionately. You know what she said? "Kunti abandoned the child on the bank of the stream. I don't want her."

Hearing this, Sharoo Taayi was also thrilled. With a beaming face, she put her finger on her mouth and exclaimed, 'Ah, my baby!' She was astonished, proud and full of admiration for her daughter. Even the other women found this surprising. From then on, they became careful when they talked in front of Madevi. Manikamma told this Kunti story to everybody who visited the ashram and shared her pride and amazement at the girl's sensitivity. When Sharoo Taayi slept that night, she asked the child, 'I

heard you didn't want the Kunti story. Is this true, sweetie?'
When the child said the same thing again, she felt pleased.
She kissed and fondled the kid's face, hugged her and went
to sleep.

It might have been a couple of months after this. One
morning, when Sharoo Taayi had gone to bathe, Madevi
woke up and sat on the bed. The day had broken already.
Instead of going back to sleep, she thought she'd roll the
mattress, sweep the floor and surprise her mother. When
she rolled the mattress and lifted it, the handbag under
the pillow fell. When a small photo that was in the bag
fell outside, she remembered, yes, her mother often kept it
inside her brassiere. She became curious and looked at it. It
was the photo of husband and wife standing together. She
realized that the woman in the photograph was her mother,
Sharoo Taayi. But who is the man? She wanted to ask her
mother Sharoo Taayi, who had finished her bath and come
out. Seeing the photograph in the child's hand, she asked,
'Where did you get this, daughter?'

She came closer, 'Avva, the man who is standing in this
photograph? Who is he? Father?' asked Madevi.

'Yes.'

Madevi felt overjoyed. Her eyes began to shine. She
remembered that just a few days ago, her friend Kusumi's
father had come and taken her away. Madevi asked
greedily, 'Avva, will Appa take you and me away?' Shari
Taayi's eyes overflowed with tears. Trying not to show it to
her daughter, she hugged her, wiped her tears secretly, and
then said, 'All right, daughter, if Father says he will take
only you, will you go?' She wanted Madevi's answer to be
on her side.

'No, Avva. I won't go anywhere without you. If Father
asks something like that, you tell him too that he shouldn't
take only me away.'

Hearing this, Sharoo Taayi cracked her knuckles and petted her daughter. Sharoo Taayi watched the blossoming body of her child everyday. There was an inborn loveliness in her. Though the clothes that people gave for the orphanage were either small or big for her, it looked like they were made to order for Madevi when she wore them. Even when Madevi wore those clothes carelessly, she looked so lovely. The radiance of her body shone even through the old clothes. This orphan girl's body had the beauty of a forest flower. At the same time, she could also look like an attractive princess. And the loveliness of her hair is wholly another story.

Madevi had long and thick hair. She liked to gather it at the back and braid it. Every day, she had her hair braided, touched it and made sure of the braid. If she looked at the mirror, there would be a small braid. But in about a half hour, the braid came undone, and her hair flew haywire. Even the traces of the braid were gone. 'Nobody can tie you or your hair up, my child,' Sharoo Taayi complained every day. Sometimes she said, 'The wind loves my sweetie's hair. He always plays with it.' Sometimes, Madevi also felt so. The breeze touches your body. You feel cold. But you can't catch it. If you try to hug it, it gives a warm kiss on your cheek and runs away. Besides, it plays so many games with your hair.

But that day, the blowing breeze had given her a nice feeling. At night she dreamt that her father came and took them away. The next morning, she got up and consoled her mother, 'You don't cry from now on, Father will come and take us away.'

Sharoo Taayi was really worried about her daughter now.

'Did you see a dream, daughter?'

'Yes, Avva. In the dream, Father came and took both of us away from here. So you don't look at the photo and cry. If you cry, I'll cry too. All right?' She ordered Sharoo Taayi.

'Let your words come true, Mother who gave me birth!' she wished, invoking the goddess. In this atmosphere of hope and happiness, she found the thoughts of her daughter crowding her mind. She couldn't ever imagine being separated from her daughter.

One morning, Madevi came out and saw the gentle sunlight that fell on the grass. She exclaimed, 'Ay, Shiva! Avva, look how lovely the morning light is!' Sharoo Taayi was not so amused by the sunlight, but by how her daughter had noticed what she hadn't. She thought of Chambasa and felt great self-pity.

Daughter, I have got caught in a marriage that hasn't begun yet and with a husband who doesn't want me! No mother's home. No husband's home. Nobody to bother about me. A husband who taunts me saying I am a devadasi. All those colourful patterns woven into my memories—the sari and blouse he gave, the pleasurable bruises he made when he squeezed my body. There are only traces of tears now. Yet all those are things that bind me to him. He would whisper in my ear in his sweet voice. He'd hug me and narrate his dreams. He was wringing my heart inch by inch. Now all the pleasures are gone, my daughter! They fly away. I am trying to hold onto them desperately. I try to pull them back, keep them tethered to me, daughter. I keep wishing.

Whenever I heard his footsteps, my heart would beat in sync with that rhythm. My heart became the ground beneath his feet. Can't I get that pleasure again?

Now he isn't in the village. But there's Bagirti. Who knows, she might blame this jogti for being responsible for everything, snatch you away from me and push me out!

Can I live without Madevi? Not possible. But can I separate her from her mother?

Okay, anyway, now there's some improvement in Madevi's body! Once she is fully okay, I'll take her to her mother. If Bagirti doesn't give me shelter, I can come back here.

No, I got shelter here only because of Madevi. If I leave and then try to get back again, why would even Manikamma take me back! Now Madevi is my refuge. I am hers!

Tungavva Aayi may not give me shelter. She never liked me. Whenever she saw me, she'd curse. At least if Chambasa was there, he would have said, let her live in the outcaste neighbourhood. If nothing else, won't Lasuma give me a rotti every day? If nothing works, there's always Mother Ghataprabha, right? I can fall into the river thinking of it as my mother's house. But Mother Ghataprabha, you don't turn into a Shari stream like that Mallimadu, okay? You erase me from everyone's memories. Already my husband seems to have forgotten me. Good if he has. Don't make him remember me again.

He isn't in my yard now. Can I chain him? God knows what difficulties he is going through in jail! How can he be in my mind's yard? I am not his beloved, I can't attract him anymore. Not a wife with rights. I don't even have beauty left to be a jogti now. He is like the wind. He came, smelled me and flew away!

Or he is the storm. He blew on my sprouting dreams and killed them. He made my youthful green leaves fade. Didn't Madevi say, 'Avva, the morning light is so lovely!' True, Madevi is the morning light of my life. She is my morning light, evening…everything!

Release

He has spent five years on the rough floor of the jail. The companionship of rough-hearted convicts. The harsh soil of the barren land that irks the eye. You cannot predict the onset of rains or winds. Everything made Chambasa's nerve-centres grow sensitive. But these circumstances also rubbed strength onto his muscles and made them robust. Now he knew the mischief that man, land and environment are capable of. Because of his lively nature, friendly manner and undoubted honesty, all the convicts, except for a bit of teasing, loved him. Moreover there was something in his face, manner of speaking and twinkling eyes that evoked friendliness and joy in others. In the beginning, only one convict came with him to work. Now many who hadn't even seen a plough earlier became his companions and tilled the barren land. When the entire city began to like the vegetables these convicts grew, even the others joined in.

The convicts used organic manure to grow the vegetables. Scientists praised their excellent quality. Even the big people of the village came here to buy these vegetables. Moreover, in the state newspapers, there were articles about all this, and they praised our 'miracle man' Chambasa. The judge, who had sentenced Chambasa, read these and felt happy. He also congratulated the jail officials. The jail officials boasted about this shamelessly to everybody.

That day, the morning bird hadn't crowed yet. Chambasa

got up, sat on his bed and was remembering the dream he had just before waking up. A very dark old man, with shaved head and chin and a mouthful of shining teeth came into my dream. Big talker. He kept chattering all through. But you couldn't figure out what he was saying! When you listened with concentration, it seemed like he was complaining about me, pointing his little finger at me and ordering me to do something. Scared, I folded my hands and said, 'Please talk in a way I can understand, Shiva.'

'Come back on track like that!' he said, and asked again, 'Where did the Patri Ayya go? Is he lost or something?' he cursed. 'Climb the hill and come there. I'll tell you all.' And the exasperated old man melted away with that!

His talk was like a riddle. If you say climb the hill and come there, what hill do you mean exactly? In our village, we have Nirvanappa's hill. I always climb that. If he says climb it and come there, where should I go? Who, by the way, is 'Patri Ayya?'—he sat scratching his head in confusion. The magical darkness melted, and it was morning already. He peeped out of the window. Outside, the golden morning light fell on the grass. In four or five places, the dew drops shone. He saw that and told himself, 'Ah, this is like a new morning!'

By this time, the jail official came and knocked on his door. Why did the official come at this hour? There must be something special. With great curiosity, a couple of his convict neighbours came and stood at the back. The official opened the cell door in a hurry. He came in beaming and gave him a letter, and said, 'You should distribute sweets to all of us, Chambasava.' He shook hands with him. Alarmed, Chambasa asked, 'Why, Sahebara?' 'Read the letter,' the officer instructed.

It was an order which said that Chambasa was given

one year off from his sentence for good conduct. Chambasa became speechless for a minute. He clutched the official's hand tight with both his hands. He touched it to his forehead and expressed his gratitude. In a split second, the news spread to the other convicts and their faces, even of those who didn't like him, darkened. He had been like an older brother to them. Now he was going to leave them. The officer said again, 'You can leave whenever you want to. We will get your clothes, money and everything ready. You leave after the big officer comes.' He left saying this. When he went to the door, he turned back and added, 'Ha, I forgot! An old man came from your village this morning. He is waiting for you.'

'What is the old man's name?'

'Something like Shivaya Appa—he said something of the sort!'

'Namahshivaya Swami?'

'Haa, yes! He said, say that Namahshivaya Swami has come.'

'Yes, he is our Swami.'

When Chambasa went with the officer to see him, Namahshivaya Swami had wrapped a dhotra around himself. He stood leaning against a corner and shivering badly. An alarmed Chambasa went to him and tried to touch his feet to salute him. He found that the feet were burning. Chambasa touched his body. It was burning like cinders too.

'Brother, I was going to the Mother's Hill. On the way, something didn't agree with me. Man, I have got a fever,' he announced.

Chambasa said, 'Well', took the permission of the officials, sent for an autorickshaw, lifted Namahshivaya like a child in his arms, sat him in the auto and took him to the hospital. On the way, the Swami fainted.

Shortly after the emergency treatment, Swami came back to consciousness. He drank a bit of gruel. Now he realized the condition he was in. He pressed Chambasa's hand and shed tears. Seeing tears in the eyes of a man of steel, Chambasa too cried and started massaging the Swami's feet slowly. Swami revived a bit. He said piteously, 'Yeh, Chambasa, please do a job of mine. Don't say no.'

'Tell me what it is, Swami.'

'I was going to the Mother's Hill. God knows what went wrong on the way. I got this fever. Because I didn't have any other option, I thought of you and came here. Those good jail officials felt sorry for me and made me sit there. Then you got the medicine for me. There is no strength in my legs, Brother. But I have vowed to the Mother of the hill. You take this water pot and go to the Mother. If some ayya comes and takes you inside the shrine, it is your and my good fortune! You go with him. The rest, he will teach you.' He held Chambasa's hands with both his and begged him.

Chambasa told him, 'Of course I'll do it. You become okay first. I will leave immediately.'

'No, Brother! You should walk barefoot. On the way, you should never put this water pot on the ground. You keep going and reach there on the morning of the New Year, Ugadi. Only thirteen days are left for Ugadi. On your way back, you can take a bus if you want. But the journey to the shrine must be made walking barefoot. You must do this for me, son! If you want to do this, you should leave tomorrow.' He folded his hands again.

In the afternoon, Namahshivaya had some lunch and went to sleep. Chambasa went to the jail, got the permission of the higher officer there, picked up his clothes and wages of labour, said goodbye to his fellow convicts and came back to the hospital. He gave hundred rupees for Namahshivaya's expenses. Namahshivaya had woken up. Chambasa instructed him to get back to Shivapura after he got well. Then he sat at Namahshivaya's feet and asked about the route to the hill and of villages on the way where he could rest. He also got detailed information about the duties to be performed at the hill and the rules to be followed to fulfil the vow. The next morning, he bathed and went to Namahshivaya, touched both his feet, pressed the latter's hands to his eyes with reverence, took the water pot and carefully placed it in the sling bag on his shoulder. He set off for the Mother's Hill.

Everything had happened as if in a dream! Everything unexpected! Release from jail was the first unexpected thing. The other surprise was seeing the dark old man in the dream before his release. The old man had not only told him to climb the hill, but also asked, 'Where is Patri Ayya?' Then he'd melted away.

Now he knew something about climbing the hill and about who Patri Ayya was. But he came to know all this only after Namahshivaya's arrival. Then is all this Namahshivaya's miracle? Have I ever thought of going to the hill in my life until now? Moreover, the hill, Patri Ayya—set these things aside for a bit—apparently that dark old man is Namahshivaya's agent! Who is he? Where's he from? Who sent him to my dream? Chambasa mused. Didn't get the answers, though. Finally, he told himself:

'At times, when I lost my mind and entertained thoughts which disgusted even me—that old man, Namahshivaya, advised me good things. He has shown the right path to our villagers. I cannot fathom God's mystery. It isn't within my reach. But Shivalinga himself has come in the form of Namahshivaya and given me this work. So it is my duty to fulfil it. Shivalinga, the Victorious One, give me success and show me compassion. Protect me, God! Give me success, and let Namashivaya know that I have succeeded. Make me worthy of all this, my Father!'

Thus he saluted Savalagi Shivalinga in his mind and set off. He felt bad about having to take leave of his fellow convicts in such a hurry. Except for a couple of criminals, the rest had seemed like characters out of Tungavva's folk stories.

When animals, birds and humans came into Tungavva's stories, they took off their clothes and other colourful trappings and came in their natural form. For example, thieves looked like poor creatures who had been caught in the act of thieving. But when they tried to justify their act, they put on those trappings again. They'd clothe their act in lies. Make it seem like they did something heroic. The honesty that was in the act wasn't there in the words. The loyalty or bravery or heroism that they imbued their act with, when they spoke of it, couldn't be trusted. They also swore upon their soul, the supreme soul, conscience, and God and tried to make you believe in them.

But there were also others who were different. Those sorts loved, fought, hurt each other and killed. In the end, they too died. Since my own interests and weaknesses were mixed up with theirs, I thought they were a part of my life. Therefore I had compassion for them. Che, after I return from the hill, I should go and meet them once, he decided and walked on.

Now he didn't have fear and anxiety about those murders he'd done. His mind was filled with tenderness, joy and serenity. He was like a poor man who'd found a treasure. A newness filled his heart and breath. He walked with a lively tread.

He was three days late compared to the Shivapura

pilgrims. He had walked on the road Namahshivaya had told him about. He took long strides. But the pilgrims had rested in some village. Then they'd walked on to the next, about twenty or twenty-five kilometres, and rested again. He, on the other hand, walked for about thirty or thirty-five kilometres and rested after that. But he hadn't met the Shivapura devotees on the way. He had cramps in his legs. His feet were bleeding. Because of the harsh winds that blew and rubbed against his face, his face was chapped badly and was burning. Still he continued with determination. He reached the Mother's Hill on the Ugadi day. He bathed in the river that is believed to have sprung from the netherworld. He had the holy darsan of the Mother's idol. He begged her, 'Give Namahshivaya the reward of his vow, Mother!' As he stood eating the sesame-and-jaggery prasada, the Shivapura pilgrims arrived!

On the Mother's Hill

The instant they saw Chambasa, all the Shivapura pilgrims shouted, 'Ho'. Their faces shone with excitement. They ran up to him, hugged him, distributed sesame and jaggery and celebrated the meeting. When did you come? When did they release you? When will you come to the village? So on and so forth. They made him answer a hundred questions. He too asked, 'Did Sharavva come back?' Everybody bent their heads in dejection and replied, 'No.' They felt sad. What is more, among the Shivapura pilgrims, there were also two of the four farmers who had earlier been cheated of their lands. They too consoled him, 'Brother, when she comes to know that you are back, she'll come back too. Don't worry.' They took his hand and led him to lunch. They shared the rolls of rotti wrapped in cloth that they had brought with them. Since they were leaving for the village the same night on the train, they went to buy the eats and prasada at the fair. Chambasa said he'd come to the village later and stood there waiting for the ayya that Namahshivaya had told him about.

At the end of the day, an ayya came. 'Brother, are you Chambasa?' he asked.

'Yes, me,' he replied and saluted him.

'Look, Brother! Do you see the banana grove there? Beyond that—look there—at the top of the hill. There is a boundary stone. Come there.'

He said this, and without waiting for Chambasa's reply, went away. Chambasa set out.

On the way, he did find a banana grove. When he went past it, he could clearly see the boundary stone at the top of the hill. But what if he goes all the way only to discover that it is not the right one? He stood there for a while thinking. He asked a bearded man, who was coming towards him, 'Sir, is that what they call the boundary stone?' The bearded man looked him up and down, and asked, 'What do you want the boundary stone for at this age?' He left looking at Chambasa with pity. The hill is in front of him. The boundary stone stands there too. Unfamiliar hill. Can I go there and get back before the sun sets? He tried to gauge the distance. Then thinking that he had to do it anyway, he set off towards the stone.

Now the only one who's in the forest is me! You can't even see a bird feather or hear a sound. No trace of any animal. He walked on sand with small pebbles in it. He could hear the jarring sound of his own footsteps. He exclaimed, 'Shivalinga!' He was astonished to hear someone else exclaim, 'Shivalinga!' Is it an echo? Or is there someone else here? He looked around. To test it again, he exclaimed, 'Shivalinga!' Instantly, he heard another exclamation, 'Shivalinga!' It began to feel like there was a stranger with him! Look, he is standing next to the thicket! He stared, but there was no one there. Although he knew there was no one, the fear that there was someone wouldn't go away from his mind. Now he was even scared of looking around...when he looked up, he could see that single boundary stone clearly, it was distinctly visible to the eye from anywhere at all. That! Yes, that one...he kept saying this to himself and infusing himself with confidence. Not taking his eyes off the boundary stone, being guided by it, he walked on.

To his misfortune, as if by some magic, clouds appeared in the sky from nowhere and shut off the sun. He thought once, should I go back? Or should I walk on getting drenched in the rain? He felt that there was some spirit of the same size and shape as himself following him! He decided to go on, whatever happened. Drawn by some force beyond himself, he walked on. The clouds were jostling in the sky already. Before you could say 'Ha!', darkness enveloped the place. The thunder was deafening. The lightning that accompanied the thunder did lift the veil of darkness for a second, making visible the trees and surroundings. In this light, which tore through the darkness, thick rain drops shone. He could also recognize the cave beyond the boundary stone. He almost ran up the hill. The rain fell as if it was rending the skies apart. He remembered all the stories he had heard in his childhood about the deluge. He came to the boundary stone, wading through flowing water and slush. In another flash of lightning, he saw the cave on the other side of the stone. He went and stood near the cave. He thought he should find the man who could permit him to enter. He shouted, 'Who's there? Come out.' Nobody came. No sound either. He was drenched in the rain. It was impossible to bear the cold. He inched into the cave just so far as to stay away from the splatter of raindrops. Darkness everywhere. He shouted again. No reply even this time. In the scary solitude, with the fear of wild animals inside him, he stood shivering and looking around, although he could see nothing. God knows how long he stood there!

A long time passed in fear, surprise and anxiety. When there was another flash of lightning, he thought he saw a big man sitting with his knees bent and his head between his knees.

'I salute you, Sharanare.'

He greeted. Didn't get any response. The man didn't even move. He went and sat in a place where the rain couldn't splatter on him. When the lightning flashed again, the man was still sitting in the same posture.

'Can I sit here, Sharanara?' He asked. No reply to this either. The rain had stopped. It was cold.

Things that have never happened in my life are happening now, he felt. The wind that blows on high mountains seemed to blow here and purify his body and mind. I thought I knew everything when I had only seen the forest and the river in my village. But when I see this here, I know that I have never had this vision of nature. I came here alone in the terrible darkness and walked in the dense forest. Did some unknown force lead me here, making sure that I didn't take a single wrong step? As he kept thinking such things, it became clear to him—there is some unknown force moving around me. The moment he thought this—in words—a strange thrill went through his body.

Now he was free of fear, his mind was lighter—whether in reality or in dream, an ayya came from the cave in a hurry, held out his hand and pulled him up. Chambasa was astonished. 'Arre, could this be the dark old man who came in my dream in the jail?' Chambasa greeted him in a tone of familiarity, 'I salute you, Swami!' As if anxious that Chambasa would try to be familiar or because of something else, the man glared at him, held his arm, took him to the entrance and then pushed him out.

'There are five corpses sticking in your memory. Throw them out and get back,' he ordered contemptuously. He even closed his nose to prevent the smell of corpses from reaching it. As if that wasn't enough, he stood watch at the entrance making sure that Chambasa didn't enter! Immediately, Chambasa knelt down, folded his hands and begged, 'I pray, Holy Sir, please listen to a couple of words I want to say. I have read the records of my life and regretted them often. I have cried many times when I read them. Please be kind enough to listen to me once.'

Ayya stood without saying anything.

'Holy Sir, I have now realized that blaming the murders of those five bodies on others was wrong. This happened only because of my distorted pride. They were murders I committed. They beat me up because I touched Shivalingaswami and polluted him, right? This is true, Holy Sir.

'That day, when I threw the bodies into the river and looked at my reflection, what appeared was the face of a boy! Young face. There were still sparks of revenge in his eyes. His face was steely and harsh. His hair was dishevelled, and his face looked like that of a wild beast out for prey. I was shocked! Shivalinga! I disturbed the water, I felt like somebody had gargled and spat the water on me. I felt ashamed. I also thought I had seen this boy somewhere. Where? When? I couldn't remember. Who is this boy? Ha, the one who threw stones at Shivalinga! Isn't he the same? I remembered now. Yes, it's him! I was sure. I got angry with the boy! I called him, "Come here." He smiled at me. Who knows, probably he thought I was pleased with him! Isn't he the one who threw stones at God? To stop myself from laughing, I frowned. Immediately, sparks flew from the boy's eyes. Look…I don't know why. I was afraid. I killed the boy and threw him in the river! He resurfaced. I killed again. Thus I killed him five times! I am the murderer, Swami. No one else. I should get the punishment, I should get it.'

When he shook off these heavy thoughts from his head, he became free. He fell at the feet of the Swami who stood watching.

Chambasa lay there. He tried to remember the mother who had given him birth. But Tungavva surfaced. She too had cried much and fallen asleep. 'This is what happened, Mother...Forgive me...' As he pressed his head to her feet and felt lighter, his tired body fell asleep.

In his dream, he felt cold and was warming his feet in front of the fire. Suddenly, his feet caught fire and his body was on fire! By then, someone who was flaming from top to toe seemed to be there too. Someone stood leaning on the door of the shrine in my house! Is this the dark ayya? Even as he thought about it, he heard the sound of many people walking...he got up. When he opened his eyes, he heard whispers, 'It's almost time for the Swami to come.' From God knows where—from the depths of the cave, from outside and from elsewhere—people started coming in and crowding around the altar! Among them, many had shining bodies. There were also those whose bodies looked ethereal because of their luminosity. Among them, he particularly noticed a five-year-old girl who stood in the middle. Before he could recognize her, the trumpet, the karadige and many other kinds of drums—all sounded in unison! The sound made you feel as if the whole cave had exploded. Nobody knew who, when, where—and what was happening. People were jostling in the crowd. Look now, like dense smoke, silence fills the cave. You see nothing. Darkness? Or Light? Chambasa was in a state where he knew, and also didn't know, what it was all about! He sat wide-eyed!

When the girl went to the altar and saluted, a black stone appeared. No, the dark ayya who called him to come to the hill when he was in jail. He sat there! He looked at the child and Chambasa with kindness, smiled a smile that was like lovely moonlight and signalled to Chambasa to come closer. Chambasa couldn't get up because he was frozen by the snowy wind. The girl came to him, took his water pot, bathed the Shivalinga with it, returned to him, gave back the water pot, pulled him up by his hand and led him slowly to the dark ayya.

Chambasa touched the ayya's feet and saluted him with devotion glowing in his eyes. The old man's smile was not of this world! This vision of beauty, which had in it the loveliness of nature, the splendour of all seasons, magic of moonlight, countless joys and many mysterious lights— flashed before his eyes in a single epiphanic moment. Chambasa was stunned into silence. He folded his hands. The old man took a small basket which was there. There were four flowers in it. He took each one out, and showing them to Chambasa, told him, 'This is for Patri Ayya, tell him his vow has reached me. This is for you, and this, for your wife. This is for your daughter!'

The musical instruments sounded again. Then there was silence. Now the dark old man raised his voice and said as if he was prophesying:

> This is the Hill of Truth, You are Truth's disciples!
> Truth's disciples shouldn't believe in anything other
> Shouldn't speak, or act in any other manner
>
> If you remember the Truth, You are near Him
> In His presence are all the ends
> Your blessed daughter stands at the door
> Build a new Shivapura where you stand
> Thus speaks the Shiva's Drum

With this, the speaking of Shiva's drum ended. All the musical instruments sounded together, rising to a crescendo. It looked like the cave was about to explode. Suddenly, everything went still! Even as he looked around him, there wasn't a single creature there!

Back to Shivapura

Chambasa was more and more surprised and excited about the matter of the old man in the boundary-stone cave, and the old man of the dream he had seen in jail. It also looks like I have seen the basket the old man gave me and that Shivalinga stone somewhere else. I have seen such things only in two places. One, in the temple outside my village. The other, here of course. Yes, it is indeed the Shivalinga in the temple outside my village! Even this basket, I have seen it there. He remembered how Namahshivaya had collected the stones he had thrown at the linga in a basket! Can this be the same basket! He was thrilled. Suddenly, he hugged the sling bag on his shoulder tight. Is this the blessing I got for throwing stones at the Shivalinga? Did Namahshivaya fill the basket with them and bring it here? Was the basket here all these years? All this looks like something out of the karma stories that Namahshivaya told me—the stories I didn't believe in! But this stone is so like the one in the temple outside my village, isn't it?

Just as it is possible for the same kind of Shivalinga to be in many places, it is also possible for the basket to be there too. Why not go in and see the Shivalinga here again? He stopped and turned back to look at the boundary-stone temple. He couldn't see it! Maybe you couldn't see it from this dense forest. Shall I climb there again? He looked up at the top of the hill again. Namahshivaya peeped in his mind and whispered, 'Why do you carry those stones uphill? You have the basket next to you, right? Look at it.' The basket was there. There were also four fresh flowers in it!

Although he walked further, he was restless. For every act, there must be some reason. That was missing here. When he thought of the boundary-stone temple, he remembered the old man giving him a basket as a form of blessing. The hair on his body stood up. This couldn't be understood by applying any kind of logic. In the end, he thought, 'I am only a common farmer. Why should I bother about the otherworld? There's Namahshivaya to take care of it.' Thinking in the same vein, he came to the bus stop. He ate at a restaurant there and got on the bus.

When the bus stopped at Belagavi Bus Station, the sun had already risen. He got off the bus and looked about… surprising! Namahshivaya is waiting for him! What a man! Chambasa touched his feet. Then he thought: did Swami talk to the dark old man? He asked Namahshivaya directly.

'Do you know the dark old man, Swami?'

'No.'

'But he blessed me and asked me to inform you that your vow reached him! He called you "Patri Ayya". He gave me a flower basket saying, one for Patri Ayya and three for you. Take this basket. What is all this? Please explain it to me.'

He looked at Namahshivaya in a confused manner and gave him the basket.

'Oh, that? We'll discuss it later. Now let's go to the Nehru stadium immediately. Come. Manikamma will be there. We'll meet her.'

Namahshivaya hurried him. Manikamma? Is this like another dark old man story? He couldn't contain his curiosity and asked, 'Now who is she?'

'Manikamma is a woman who runs the Kasturiba

Orphanage in Doddalli. A very great human being. She was with us in the freedom movement. Let's meet her and get back. Come now.'

They had their breakfast in a restaurant nearby and went to the stadium.

The stadium was full of students and people. As a part of the zonal competition, physically challenged children from four districts were going to compete in the running race. The minister-in-charge of district affairs was going to come. Three children from Manikamma's orphanage were participating in this competition. It was difficult to find Manikamma in the crowd of all those kids and people. Okay, they thought, let's wait until the competition gets over. Until then, we can watch the competition, they decided, and stood there.

The field was full of people. Among them were students, male and female. They formed the majority of the crowd. The minister, who was to give away the prizes, hadn't turned up yet. Competitors, as well as people, were waiting. The officers were looking restless, especially because the journalists were there. Finally when the minister came and decorated his chair, teachers who were with the physically challenged children came on the field. Some of the competitors came limping, some others came dragging their feet. Finally, they all came and stood in their places. In the end, Manikamma came holding the hand of a little girl who was dragging her feet like she was crawling. Manikamma led her slowly. The instant he saw her, Namahshivaya's eyes lit up like lamps. He stood on tiptoe and urged Chambasa, 'There, look, look!' Chambasa turned his eyes in the direction Namashivaya was looking. This woman or that, unable to decide whom he should look at, he stood searching. By then, some official came and announced, 'The minister is here!' He said everybody, except the competitors, must go out. The competitors were twelve young girls and boys. They all stood ready in their positions on the tracks.

Some spectators, seeing the stance of the children, might have felt that the kids weren't ready yet. But then they realized with compassion that these were children with disabilities and that's how they could stand. There were a couple of whistles. At the third whistle, the race began.

Since all of them had practised well, it was fine at the beginning. The length of the race was approximately three furlongs. The teachers and guardians were calling out the names of their kids and cheering them. But overall, everybody who had gathered there encouraged all the children. When the race proceeded slowly, the tracks where the children ran looked like chains broken here and there. As time went by, there were more and more gaps between the contestants. Manikamma was screaming until her voice grew hoarse. She screwed up her eyes, stood on her toes and cried in excitement, 'Madevi! Madevi! Just a little. Only four steps. Run faster, daughter! Another couple of steps! Run my darling,' she shouted animatedly. All the blood in her body had risen to her face. Her face was as red as a red ant, and it shone in the sun. Well, even Namahshivaya became animated! He too began to cheer the smart kid called Madevi who was dragging her feet. Everyone began to cheer Madevi, who ran at the front, but she was running with difficulty and trying to overcome it every moment. Chambasa too felt excited seeing this Madevi and Manikamma.

Suddenly, Manikamma jumped up like a child and shouted, 'Little one, only two steps, daughter!' Madevi had come closest to the goal. The way she cutely bit her teeth

and dragged her steps, the difficulty she was undergoing—
seeing all this, grown-ups and children shouted alike,
'Madevi, Madevi, buck up Madevi!' The other children,
even those whose legs were of equal size, were struggling.
But they fell back. There was no doubt that she would reach
the goal any moment. Because, forget going past her, they
weren't even able to equal her. Suddenly, the child who
was the last in the race screamed, fell down and holding
her feet, began to moan, 'Ayyo, Ayyo.' Madevi, who was
in the forefront, stopped the moment the child screamed
and looked back. The child kept screaming, and unable to
bear the pain, held her feet and began to roll on the ground.
Instantly, Madevi stopped running towards the goal and
started running towards the child!

'Ayyo, what's gotten into this child, Yavva! Eh, Madevi,
Maadi, not that way, the goal is on this side!' Manikamma
struck her forehead with her hand repeatedly. In the end,
she let the hand rest on her head and stood watching! When
the other children, amused to see Madevi go back, also
began to look back, Madevi ran like lightning to the child
who was crying, pulled her up, and massaging her aching
feet, consoled, 'Don't cry, Avva. You shouldn't cry!' She
slowly wiped the child's tears and again began to massage
the feet where it hurt. The whole crowd that was cheering
Madevi until now became still and stood dumbfounded!
Even the other competitors were stunned. Madevi massaged
the feet of the child for a bit and asked, 'Are you okay now?'
The child had stopped crying and looked a little more
composed. She patted the child, wiped her tears, got up,
pulled the child also up and slowly led her on! Unaware
of what they were doing, some people clapped. Even the
other contestants came back now, gave their hand to the
ailing child, then holding each other's hands, they walked

in a row slowly, keeping step with the bruised kid! Without realizing what they were doing, as if in a trance, all the people sighed in unison and started clapping! The row of children, which looked like a shining row of herons in a clean sky, moved slowly. All the children reached the goal at the same time and got qualified for the first prize!

Tears of joy streamed down Namahshivaya's face. He couldn't speak. He gestured with his hands and mouth, pointed once to the row of kids and once at Manikamma, held both hands up to the sky, became emotional as if he had seen God, and since he hadn't regained his voice yet, stammered, 'Gandhi...ji.' The whole gathering applauded with a deafening sound. In their excitement, they began to jump up and down. They congratulated the winning team. Chambasa was moving towards the child without even being aware of it. Namashivayi also followed him.

Before they reached there, Manikamma went up to Madevi, picked her up proudly and petted her. Madevi was still holding the hands of the other contestants. When Manikamma turned to look at Chambasa walking towards them, Madevi also saw him with great joy. She cried out, 'Appa!' She, who was in Manikamma's arms, leant towards Chambasa as if she was asking him to take her in his arms. Chambasa held out his hand, took her in his arms and looked at Manikamma with surprise and pride. Manikamma introduced her to Namahshivaya, who was also standing there, 'Your granddaughter!'

'You mean?'

'Ayya, have you forgotten already? This Madevi is the daughter of your daughter, Sharoo Taayi.' Suddenly remembering that Sharavva brought Bagirti's daughter Madevi when she was a child, Namahshivaya whispered in Chambasa's ear, 'Haa! Eh, Chambasa, this is Bagirti's daughter Madevi! When she went to Bangalore, Bagirti had left her child with Sharavva. Do you remember?' He asked, and turned to Manikamma, 'Manikamma, where is my daughter, Sharavva?'

'I left her to take care of the ashrama and came here.'

Meanwhile, there was an announcement on the mike. It said that all the children had got the first prize and asked them all to come and receive it from the honourable minister. Chambasa was lost in a whirl of happiness. When people heard that all of them had received the first prize, they gave another round of applause. To receive the prize, the ashram kids, led by Manikamma, and followed by Namahshivaya and Chambasa, went there. When they reached there, what do they see? The minister, who has come to give away the prizes, is Kuntirapa! Now Namahshivaya's words began to make some sense to Chambasa, if she was Bagirti's daughter, Sharavva too…?

They announced on the mike, 'Madevi from Doddalli Kasturi Ba ashram come here.' Immediately, the crowd in the stadium clapped and whistled. Some called out her name and everybody showed approval. Whether it was some providence, or irony of fate, Chambasa, who had taken her in his arms, put her down and sent her towards Manikamma. Namahshivaya stood smiling at the game of providence. Manikamma took Madevi, and along with other children, went to Kuntirapa. Kuntirapa too had seen and admired Madevi's performance. He had seen and heard the whole gathering of people praising and applauding her. He didn't want to fall behind. Or maybe something tugged at his heart. He called Madevi near him, gave the prize, asked the journalists crowding there to take a snap, posed for it and getting encouraged by all this, told Madevi, 'You are my daughter!' and kissed her on the cheek! Instantly,

Madevi flinched like someone who had stepped on fire. She screamed in a horrible voice, 'No!' Spat on the minister's face and came running to Chambasa shouting, 'Appa.' She hugged him, rubbed her cheek with his dhotra as if she had touched shit and started crying. Kuntirapa felt insulted. He rushed to catch Madevi, screaming, 'Eh, bitch! Wait I'll show you who I am.' Chambasa grasped the situation, picked Madevi up in his arms and stood in Kuntirapa's way! Sparks flew from their eyes. They both stood silent for a minute. Kuntirapa trembled like he was struck by unexpected lightning. Chambasa looked at him sharply and smiled. By then, since the media people came and whispered something in Kuntirapa's ear, Kuntirapa kicked the floor with his lame foot, and mashing his teeth and cursing, disappeared into his retinue without even making a speech.

Press people, who were watching this drama, decided it was all very dull now, and left the stadium. Namahshivaya, who stood watching too, asked with a smile, 'This child called Chambasa "appa", didn't she? Why?' he asked in Manikamma's ear.

'Ayya, why don't you ask her?'

She answered with a bit of anger. And with a confidence in Madevi's ability to answer. So Namahshivaya asked her, 'Madevi, how did you know that this was your father, Avva?'

'Avva has her marriage photo! She looks at it every day and cries…'

She informed with a weepy face. Chambasa's heart went out to the child. The moment he stretched his hand and picked her up in his arms, Madevi hugged him tight with her small hands. Chambasa, who now became sure that Sharavva was alive, felt a thrill running over him and exclaimed, 'Shivalinga!'

To Doddalli

The next morning, along with Manikamma and her retinue, Namahshivaya and Chambasa also went to Doddalli. All the papers that day had published the news of the physically challenged children getting the first prize as a team. There was also a rhapsodic report, full of interjections, about how Madevi, who was at the forefront of the race, boldly came back to help the child who was crying in pain and brought this child slowly back into the race. Namahshivaya bought all those papers, read them out and made Manikamma feel happy. The children were all nodding with sleep on the bus. Madevi hadn't left Chambasa even for a second. She hadn't got off the bus at all. Chambasa kept thinking about Sharavva, her state and her fate now. Her name wound round his heart like a lovely creeper.

About six hours later in the day, they all began to feel hungry again. The moment the conductor shouted 'Doddalli', they got off. A crude platform under a big strangler fig tree—this was all there was to Doddalli bus stand. From there, Kasturi Ba ashram was only two furlongs away. Already two servants of the ashram were waiting for them there. When they saw the children, they beamed. And the children opened their eyes wide and recognized the people waiting for them below. Their faces were beaming too. Manikamma got off holding onto all the papers with great pride. A servant, who was with them, secretly ran to the ashram and informed Sharoo Taayi about Chambasa coming there.

Sharoo Taayi didn't believe it at first. But why should he lie to her? After he gave the details, she began to trust his words. She cried with happiness. But there was no time even for that. She wiped her tears, pushed the hair on her ears and forehead back. Realizing that her hair was dishevelled, she tried to smoothen it with her hand. Then she tried to cover the dishevelled head. She looked at her face in the window glass there. She got scared on seeing someone else. Sunken eyes without light in them, the gaunt cheek bones that jutted out of her face, dried up chin and a mouth that seemed full of teeth! She asked herself, 'Am I Chambasa's Shari? Are these the cheeks that Chambasa caressed? Ayyo! He was already burning with hate. Now he'll make me burn, make me die. Fine, I am a mother! I will face this.' She got up hurriedly and smoothened her sari. Smoothened her hair. When she looked at the glass again, she thought her face looked a little brighter now. Today is my lucky day!

When they came to the ashram, Madevi got off Chambasa's lap, and dragged her feet in a hurry to go to Sharavva. She ran shouting, 'Avva, Avva, Father came.' Sharoo Taayi, who was waiting for her, stood in her room and looked out of the window. Seeing Chambasa, half-asleep and dull-faced, her heart leapt up like a flame. Dark, sun-tanned skin and coarse feet that had walked in jail— although they did look good on his robust body, he had become lean. The beauty of his face had vanished. There was a certain roughness in his jawline. But the long nose, and under the dark eyebrows, those wide and searching eyes. When she realized that these eyes were searching for her, a current ran through her. Blood from all over her body rushed to her heart. Her face grew red. His eyes came to meet hers! That look made her lose herself completely. On the pretext of replying to her daughter, she ran out, hugged the child and gave a sidelong glance at Chambasa. She drank him in with her eyes. Manikamma, who noticed this, said excitedly, 'Look, Sharoo Taayi! She won the race and also brought her father here.' Then she instructed, 'Everybody is hungry, daughter. Please serve them all some food.' Sharavva, who came back to her senses, saluted Namahshivaya and Manikamma. When she bent to touch Chambasa's feet, he pulled his feet away. Sharavva was disappointed. Her dark eyes under the heavy lids had been shining. A smile had played on her lovely curved lips. Now her lashes drooped sadly and she left the place.

Even while serving the meal, the same thought burrowed into her mind. Has his love cooled off? Has it staled? She also realized that she could do nothing about it. Can I live without his love? The thought made her tremble. She had believed that love was the greatest joy of life. Both of them had lost a lot—morally and physically. It seemed like their meeting after all these days lacked intensity. She felt like a flower whose petals he had shorn and thrown away.

Is there some strategy of making him love me again, Shiva? She moaned. One strategy would be leaving her daughter and living with him. Can I do this? What if Bagirti comes and snatches her daughter away? She worried. Meanwhile, she heard Madevi's footsteps as she came to have her meal. When she looked up, she saw him standing and watching her. He had arrived before he was expected! She felt bad about being lost in thought and quickly laid the plates.

During the meal, Namahshivaya was describing the details of Madevi's miracle in the race the day before. He was telling Sharoo Taayi that she should see the photos in the papers of that day. What he was saying didn't reach Chambasa. His mind and eyes were following Sharoo Taayi. His eyes drank her in as much as they could see of her. Sharoo Taayi served food, apparently listening to Namahshivaya, showing mock-anger and annoyance at her husband, and wounding him with her sharp glances.

In the evening, Manikamma came to Sharoo Taayi and told her, 'Sharoo Taayi, take your husband to the stream for a walk. Madevi, you be with me. We will go later. Both of us haven't done any spinning today, right? Come, we will do that.' Sharoo Taayi looked at Chambasa. He followed her.

Beside the flowing stream, there was an oleander tree. They sat on the huge boulder under this. Sharavva gave an honest account of how she had finally escaped from the police assault on the protest day and how Namashivaya helped her to come to this ashram. Chambasa was looking at her. She looked thin. Her cheeks were pale, and she had lost weight. Her cheekbones were jutting out, and her eyes were sunken.

After she finished her story, Chambasa in turn told her his story of the murders. For a while, there was silence between them. When two hearts beat in sympathy…

'Avva, Appa, where are you?' Madevi came shouting and dragging her feet! Manikamma, who was with her, also made a dramatic entry into the scene, clapping!

Shiva's Drum

Here, in Shivapura, the pilgrims who returned from the Mother's Hill distributed the prasada to everyone and also disseminated stories of Chambasa that were a fine mix of fact and fiction. Besides, when she got to know that he was coming to Shivapura along with Namahshivayi, Bagirti had sent the factory car to Doddalli.

Even as the sun rose in the morning, Namahshivaya woke up uttering, 'Shivalinga!' Surprisingly, Madevi, who had thrown tantrums last night and slept next to Chambasa, was up already!

'Why Madevi? You are already up. Didn't you sleep well last night, daughter?' he asked. Madevi didn't say a word. She got up and went out dragging her feet.

'Where are you going?'

'I'll wake up Mother.'

Appreciating her excitement, he too got up.

After breakfast, by the time Sharavva left for her husband's house after taking leave of Manikamma, children and colleagues, it was nearly four hours. The children were inconsolable. They hugged Sharoo Taayi and wept. Manikamma cried more than the children, 'Daughter, you came, served me with love and made me forget that I had nobody, no kith or kin! You became an older sister to everybody, filled life in the ashrama. Spending five or six years with you seemed like spending five or six days! This is your maternal home. Visit here on a festival day or any other happy day. Write to me. We'll visit you too. All the children will remember you. Don't forget to do this,' she said hugging Sharoo Taayi. She kissed Madevi and bid them farewell.

Sad about leaving the ashrama, neither Sharavva nor Madevi were in a mood to talk. Soon Madevi put her head on her father's lap, feet on her mother's, and went to sleep. Sharavva's mind was disturbed too. She too didn't want to talk. She closed her eyes and kept reminiscing about the ashrama life.

Chambasa sat remembering the Shivapura he had lost until now. His childhood. His days at school. The loud laughter that sometimes rose in the class despite the fear of the master, other little joys and pleasures, the rainbows they saw on Mallimadu with glossy eyes, the bright and golden dreams. After everyone slept, how the sky looked at its reflection in the river water…Sky brought its face so close to the water that its breath touched the little waves… then it slowly moved back…and there was the darkness of night…the cockerel crowed and it would be morning…we are singing Shivapura songs—about air, rains and light in the village, about our flowing rivers…

By the time their car reached Shivapura, the cattle were coming home. People had gathered at the village entrance. The joyful sound of drums and trumpets began the moment the villagers sighted the car. When the procession came up to the outcaste neighbourhood, Chambasa got off the car and went to Tungavva's house. Along with him went Sharavva, Namahshivaya and daughter Madevi. When they found out that Tungavva was waiting in the Gowda's vaade, the procession moved towards the vaade.

The procession reached the vaade. It was already time to

have dinner and sleep. Bagirti had made arrangements for Chambasa to stay in the vaade. Not only that, she wanted Chambasa and Sharavva, along with Madevi, to live in the vaade. Lasuma and his wife would be in Chambasa's old house. Tungavva could live in the vaade if she wanted, or if she wanted to be with Lasuma, she could do that, or she could even be in the house in the fields with her... Bagirti planned. She made Lasuma agree to it.

The moment they entered the house, the smell of warm cow dung filled their nostrils and made them feel the joy of homecoming. There were a few changes made to the house too. It seems, that day, Bagirti had invited a cow as a guest for Chambasa's return home! The cow dung was the result of this. But Chambasa actually said he felt happy, that he enjoyed this first smell of Shivapura.

Shivapura had changed now. According to Chambasa's advice, Bagirti had contested the village panchayat elections and become its president. They had given access to the well to Dalits. The greater reform was that they now had only one cemetery in the village, and everybody, including the high castes, had agreed to have funerals there. Shivapura was now a different village. There were so many changes that it seemed like it was years since they had left this place. People, cattle, poultry, same Mallimadu and same river. But so many changes. Or maybe he had changed! He felt as if many years had passed since he left this place.

Or maybe the one who has come back isn't the same Chambasa. This new Chambasa had burnt away the old Chambasa—the one who was lost in the forest of superstition, murder, robbery and revenge—like a bundle of old clothes. Chambasa of the past had animal strength. Terrible vengefulness. Now he didn't want any of those violent things. The vengefulness of the past was gone and was replaced by self-restraint and wisdom.

The moment they entered, the new couple went to Tungavva with their daughter. Time had taken away a lot of old people. Only Tungavva sat cherishing the old memories and waiting for death. You could see the marks of age on her body. She saw her son, daughter-in-law and granddaughter. Tears streamed down her face. She hugged them and cried. She cracked her knuckles to ward off evil. Unable to speak, or let Chambasa or even Sharavva and Madevi go, she held them and cried until all her tears were dry. She hugged them again and again. Remembering old sorrows and thinking of new joys, she cried!

They passed that night remembering old things. Bagirti and Sharoo Taayi were in the same room. 'Madevi doesn't look at me, Sharoo. What is my fate now?' They began talking, and God knows when, but finally did fall asleep. Madevi didn't go to either Sharoo Taayi or Bagirti. She slept next to Chambasa in another room.

Swami had sent word to Chambasa and Sharoo Taayi to come to the temple outside the village on Monday morning. Until now, they had spent all the time meeting the village people. When they got ready to go to the temple around eight in the morning, they called Madevi too. She had attached herself to Tungavva since morning. She didn't go with them. Lasuma assured them, 'I'll bring her. Both of you go first.' They left.

Swami wasn't in the temple. He hadn't returned from the Nirvanappa hill yet. They decided to walk around until he returned and came to the jambul trees.

When he came under one of the jambul trees, Chambasa became emotional. Seeing the excitement oozing out of his face, Shari, who sat leaning against the tree, asked, 'What did you remember?'

'I first met you under this tree. Do you remember?' He sat down next to her.

'How can I not remember, Mava?'

'Shari, it's been six years since we left Shivapura!'

'It's been six years since we parted.'

'Yes. When we parted, did you ever think that we would meet again someday?'

'No, Mava. So I wanted to die,' she said in despair. He patted her cheek violently, almost like slapping her, and said, 'Thoo, say that good things will happen.' Overwhelmed by emotion, he held both her hands and pressed them hard, 'When I lost you, do you know how desperate I became, woman? Thank God you are alive! I am lucky.'

The restraint of all the years melted away. Unable to suppress the surging love, she cried out, 'Mava, Mava...' and beat him violently on the chest a couple of times. She looked into his eyes, and her eyes lit up. He saw the inner light reflected in those eyes. Chambasa was wonder-struck, as if he had seen her very soul. He too shed his mask of fear and hesitation. They came together with the same spirit of innocence again. Chambasa pulled her to him, hugged her, and kissed her lips and eyes as if he was re-asserting his rights on her lips. Shari softened, 'Stand with your feet together. I will salute you. When I wanted to touch your feet in Doddalli, you pulled your feet back. Why did you do it?'

'How can we younger ones have people touching our feet when there are elders around?'

When she touched his feet and saluted him, he too bent to do the same. She said 'Thoo!' coyly and moved back.

'We are alive and have come together only because of Madevi. The credit goes neither to you nor me. It is our Madevi's! I can't live without her, all right?'

'You keep her with you. Who's objecting? But along with her, keep me with you too. That's all I ask of you! But there's something else I want to ask.'

'What?'

'You should not remember anything bad that happened. If you do…okay, I warn you!'

Sharavva nudged her husband's chest with her shoulder and looked at him with mock anger. The pain that her heart had suffered until now was gone. She felt like someone coming up for air after escaping from a dark room where she had been imprisoned for long. It was an experience like touching the sky with your hands to make sure it was there! She exclaimed, 'I feel so happy, Mava!' Some villain's machinations had left her polluted, and she'd fallen into the gutter. But now, she felt like she had cleansed herself and was born as a new human being.

A rosy hue reappeared on her pale cheeks. Her femininity, her youth, all the richness of beauty—all returned. She seemed to go back to those times. When her love rushed from the depths of her womanliness, she held his hand with both her hands, looked into his eyes, attacked his lips suddenly, kissed him hard and bit his lip. Chambasa was lost in his pleasure.

By then, they heard Madevi's voice, 'Avva, Appa.' Madevi was a treasure gained by the penance of their six-year long separation. Namahshivaya came there holding the small basket in one hand and Madevi's hand in the other. She was the light of their life, the light of their eyes! She came there shouting, 'Avva, Appa', and dragging her feet. She ran to Sharavva and hugged her. Unable to withstand the force of her love, Sharavva was about to fall. Chambasa supported her back with his palm and helped her stand up. The sun, who was hiding behind the clouds, came out. In the bright morning light, Chalimele shone.

Namahshivaya also sat down and said, 'Look Chambasa, nobody has heard the Shiva's drum speak like you did!'

He took the basket out and added, 'Look, there are four flowers here. One is mine. The message that my vow reached Shivalinga. My vow was, "You two must come together again." That's happened now, right?

'The other is for you, another for your wife.

'The third is your daughter's.

'Now, listen to the Shiva's drum:

This is the Hill of Truth, you are Truth's disciples!
For Truth's disciples, there can be no other truth

Those who come here shouldn't believe in anything other
Shouldn't speak, or act in any other manner

If you remember the Truth, you are near Him
In His presence are all the ends

Your blessed daughter stands at the door
Build a new Shivapura where you stand

Thus speaks the Shiva's Drum

'You ask anyone if you want. Nowhere else has the Shiva's drum spoken these words! Come on!'

So saying, Namahshivaya handed the flower basket to Chambasa.

'Please unravel this enigmatic speech.'

'What is there to unravel, Brother? Both of you have suffered a lot until now. You have cried and shed tears. Shivalinga says: let it end here! Forget the past. A daughter like Akka Mahadevi has come to your house. Build a Shivapura where she stands and a Shivapura that she wants. Build a Shivapura that is free from all the current corruption, murder and looting. She will live that blessed life and give you life too. If anything goes wrong, anywhere at all, invoke my name. Think that I am present there.

Shivalingaswami Himself has said this to you. Which God will tell you anything better than this?'

The tense faces of his audience, listening to what the Shiva's drum said, relaxed now and were filled with happiness. A bright and soft smile lit up everyone's face.

When all the four saluted the Swami and got ready to leave for Shivapura, Sharoo Taayi held Madevi's hand and asked, 'Sweetie, what did grandmother Tunga tell you?'

'It seems the yakhsi ran away!'

'What yakshi, child?'

'It seems she was in the lake. She saw me and ran away.'

Something flashed in Chambasa's mind. He asked, 'Did she run away because she saw you? But why?'

'Because I will defeat her in the race. That's why!'

Chambasa laughed loudly: 'Ahaha!' Love surged within him. He made her sit on his shoulder. Everybody laughed and set off to Shivapura.

Trees and plants that were shedding shadows as thick as themselves until then, now began to glow like bodies of light. Mallimadu flowed with great vigour and shone like glass. All this heightened the mystery at the heart of their happiness.

Here Shiva, Here Hara
Let the Shiva's Drum begin here

Glossary

Aaya: The annual share of grain that the hereditary workers of the village collect for the work they do for the community.

Akka: Older sister

Appa: Father

Avva or Aayi: Mother

Ayya: Sir or master. It is usually used to refer to an elder or a respected man in society. Here, it also has religious connotations.

Baagina: The gift of a series of household items related to women like grains, cloth, bangles, auspicious vermilion, and so on. Exchanged particularly on auspicious occasions. A small quantity of these household things are symbolically placed in a winnow basket and exchanged among women, or offered to the female deity.

Bhandara: A mix of turmeric powder which is offered to, or smeared on, the idol. Given to the devotees as a form of blessing.

Jogti: A jogti of Ellamma is a woman dedicated to the temple of Ellamma in Savadatti in Karnataka. Although these women, also called devadasis, were in the service of God, they were known to perform sexual services for wealthy patrons.

Karadige: A unique two-sided drum. It is considered auspicious to use it during the worship of Shiva.

Mamaledara: A taluk (district sub-division) officer.

Mava: Father-in-law or maternal uncle (who is also seen as a prospective husband for the niece since such marriages are allowed in this society).

Nagara Panchami: A festival dedicated to the Snake God. In North Karnataka, on this day, married women visit their maternal homes.

Parashurama: In North Karnataka mythology, Parashurama figures in the story of goddess Renuka Devi/Ellamma. He beheads his mother at the behest of his father, Jamadagni. Later he brings his mother back to life with a boon his father gives him. Parashurama is seen as a model of strength and valour.

Sahebara: Sir. 'Ri', 're', 'ru' or 'ra' are suffixes added to names to indicate respect (plural forms are used to denote respect even in the case of addressing, or referring to, one person).

Sangya-Balya: A popular North Karnataka folk tale. The story is about two friends, Sangya and Balya. Their legendary friendship is sorely tried when Balya, a poor man, is tempted by money to betray Sangya. The tragedy that follows is a painful tale of love, hate and treachery.

Saaru: Usually refers to lentil soup.

Seragu: The loose end of a sari draped over the shoulder.

Sharanare: A devotee of Shiva in the Lingayat or Veerashaiva faith. This twelfth-century faith rose against traditional Brahminical religion in North Karnataka. Founded by Basavanna, it is well-known for is protest against the caste system and ritualism in traditional religion.

Tangi: Younger sister

Vaade: A big house that belongs to the prominent person of a village such as the Gowda (village headman).